MORE PRAISE FOR EMILY BRYAN!

DISTRACTING THE DUCHESS

"Bryan has a great handle on the material and her characters, creating a charming, colorful story with an intricate, fast-paced story line."

—*Publishers Weekly*

"*Distracting the Duchess* is a delightfully unique tale....Great dialogue and quite a bit of humor add to this enjoyable tale. There are some sizzling hot love scenes that will have readers fanning themselves! All in all, *Distracting the Duchess* will make for a unique, totally fun read."

—Romance Reviews Today

"Writing as Bryan, Diana Groe gives readers a sexy, fast-paced romp that will appeal to fans of Cheryl Holt, Lisa Kleypas and Celeste Bradley."

—*Romantic Times BOOKreviews*

"Wickedly witty writing and wonderfully entertaining characters are the key ingredients in Bryan's sinfully sexy historical romance, which touches shrewdly on many key elements of the Victorian era, from extreme decorum to empire building to passions for the classical past, science (including anatomy), and art."

—*Booklist*

Distracting the Duchess is "fun, fresh and sexy."

—Dear Author

"I found this story to be downright engrossing and I cannot recommend it highly enough! Author Emily Bryan simply oozes talent!"

—Huntress Reviews

"*Distracting the Duchess* is a wild ride, told in the tradition of Dumas with intricate plot twists and subtle intrigue leaving the reader wanting more and wanting it now."

—Loves Romances Reviews

Winner Takes All

"Right now, you and I are partners in my search for the Roman treasure, split in half when we find it," Lucian said. "For each hand I lose, one percent more of the money we find will be yours."

"Ah! And if I lose, that one percent shifts to you," Daisy guessed.

"No." A slow smile spread across his face. "I'll take my winnings now in satin."

"How do you mean?" she asked, thankful he couldn't see her puzzled frown from behind the half mask.

He reached forward and gave the top ribbon on her camisole a tug. The knot gave and her bodice sagged open enough to bare the meeting place of her breasts above her pounding heart.

"Do we have a wager?" he asked. "Or are you afraid you'll lose?"

A true courtesan wouldn't be able to resist such a naughty game. "Ah! *Monsieur le Vicomte,* either way, I win."

Other *Leisure* books by Emily Bryan:

Emily Bryan

Vexing the Viscount

LEISURE BOOKS   NEW YORK CITY

To my dear husband,
a man who knows a woman only vexes the one she loves.

A LEISURE BOOK®

March 2009

Published by

Dorchester Publishing Co., Inc.
200 Madison Avenue
New York, NY 10016

ISBN 10: 0-8439-6134-1
ISBN 13: 978-0-8439-6134-8
E-ISBN: 1-4285-0611-X

The name "Leisure Books" and the stylized "L" with design are
trademarks of Dorchester Publishing Co., Inc.

Printed in the United States of America.

10 9 8 7 6 5 4 3 2 1

Visit us on the web at www.dorchesterpub.com.

Vexing the Viscount

*Item: One clay lamp after the fashion of an erect phallus
—from the manifest of Roman oddities, found near London,
England, 3 July, in the Year of Our Lord 1731*

Chapter One

"Hmm! I wonder if that's life-size," Miss Daisy Drake murmured. She leaned down to inspect the ancient lamp on display in the corridor outside the Society of Antiquaries lecture hall. Talking to herself was a bad habit, she knew, but since none of her friends shared her interest in antiquities, she often found herself without companions on this sort of outing.

"Of course, it would be on the most inaccessible shelf in the display case." Solely to vex her, she suspected. Daisy scrunched down to get a better look at it.

The clay lamp was only about four inches long, but in other respects, so far as Daisy knew, was perfectly lifelike. The terra-cotta scrotum served admirably for an oil cruse, but even though she knew the ancients decorated their homes with such unseemly things, she still wondered about how the lamp worked. She opened her small valise and drew out paper, quill and inkpot in order to take a few notes. "Where *does* the flame come out?"

"Right where one would expect," a masculine voice sounded near her.

Daisy's spine snapped suddenly upright. The crown of her head clipped the man's chin with a *thwack* and she bit her tongue.

"Jupiter!" One of her hands flew to her throbbing mouth, the other to the top of her head, where her cunning little hat was smashed beyond recognition. Her sheaf of papers fluttered to the polished oak floor like maple leaves. The small inkwell flew into the air and landed squarely on the white lawn of the man's shirtfront.

"Oh, I'm so dreadfully sorry." Daisy dabbed at the stain with her hankie and succeeded only in spreading it down his waistcoat. A black blob dribbled onto his fawn-colored breeches. She decided not to chase that stain with her handkerchief.

At least, thank heaven, plastering the man with ink covered her unmaidenly interest in that lewd little lamp. It was clearly a mistake to come to the museum today, but the topic under discussion at the Society of Antiquaries was the possible discovery of an ancient Roman treasure. The lure of an adventure drew her like a lemming to the sea.

"How clumsy of me!" She made the additional mistake of looking up at the man. Her mouth gaped like a cod's.

Lucian, she almost said aloud. When she saw no trace of recognition in his dark eyes, she drew her lips closed by sheer strength of will.

He'd grown into himself since she'd seen him last. His fine, straight nose was no longer out of proportion to the rest of his face. As he rubbed his square jaw, Daisy saw that the little scar on his chin was still visible, a neat triangle of pale, smooth skin. She'd recognize that anywhere.

After all, she'd given it to him.

His dark hair was hidden beneath a dandy's wig. Oh, she hoped to heaven he hadn't taken to shaving his head, as some did. Daisy's uncle Gabriel was a dogged opponent of the fashion. Said it was nothing but French foppery. Since Uncle Gabriel's opinions were only slightly less authoritative than a papal bull, his aversion to wigs had rubbed off. Besides, hiding a head of hair like Lucian's was a sacrilege. Or ought to be.

An ebony wisp escaped near his left ear.

Good. Daisy breathed a sigh of relief. His dark mane was one of Lucian's finest points, after all. Not that there weren't plenty of others.

His lips twitched in a half smile.

"An interesting piece, isn't it?" He was still the same old Lucian. Still direct, even at the expense of propriety. He wasn't going to play the gentleman and pretend he hadn't caught her ogling that Roman phallus.

"Indeed." She met his gaze, determined to make him understand that her interest was purely intellectual. "Obviously a cultic object of some sort. It is certainly a curiosity."

"It is gratifying to find a young lady who is . . . curious."

Daisy lifted her chin in what she hoped was a confident manner. "Of course I'm curious. Such an item makes one wonder what the people who used it were like."

"I suspect the ancients were more like us than we want to admit. People have been born into this world with the same wants and needs since Eden. Though I'll grant you our taste in home decoration has changed," he said with a laugh.

"Actually, I read a treatise only last week on the new fashion of tassels. The writer felt they were merely phallic symbols in subtle form."

"Hmph. I shall never look at a tassel the same way again."

His eyes narrowed in speculation. Daisy hoped he might show some sign of remembering her, but it had been more than a decade since they'd met. She'd been a flat-chested ten-year-old, and he'd been a haughty woman hater of twelve. With soulful eyes and a blinding smile.

Now he turned that charming smile on her without a hint of recognition in his intense gaze. "You must possess an unusual library."

The library Daisy frequented most often belonged to Isabella Haversham, her great-aunt. Isabella had once been a famous courtesan. But even now that she was a married lady—the wife of an earl, no less—she still entertained philosophers and artists and "freethinkers" with regularity. Lady Wexford might be painted with scandal's brush, but an evening in her company was far more diverting than squirming through the tortured clavichord recitals that took place in other parlors around the city.

Daisy wangled an invitation to Isabella's soirees as often as she could. For that reason, as well as her great-aunt's library, Daisy suspected her education was considerably broader than that of most young women her age.

"Innocence and ignorance need not forever clasp hands," Isabella was fond of saying.

Daisy looked pointedly back at the lamp. There was no denying she'd been studying it before. She might as well put a bold face on it.

"I was wondering if there is any kind of mark on that lamp," Daisy said. "One that might indicate who the maker was."

"He left no mark," Lucian said.

"He? So you believe a man fashioned it?"

"Men were the artisans in antiquity," he said with confidence.

"Hmm. That surprises me," she said with wide eyes. "I can't imagine a man wanting to set one of those alight."

Lucian coughed out a laugh. "But you can see where a woman might have reason."

"Certainly. Male domination of nearly every field of endeavor springs to mind." *As well as possession of the memory of a gnat,* she added silently. "But the lamp poses a host of questions."

"Ah, yes, and you raised an intriguing one." One of his dark brows arched, a reminder that he'd overheard her. "I'd be happy to help you discover the answer."

Was he suggesting something improper? If he was, it would serve him right if she gave him another scar.

"You owe me no further assistance. Not after I ruined your shirt. And your waistcoat. And your . . ." She shouldn't have allowed her gaze to travel the ink's path down the front of his breeches. For a moment, she imagined an appendage shaped like the lamp affixed to his groin, and felt her cheeks heat. To cover her embarrassment, she sank to the floor to retrieve her scattered notes.

"Think nothing of it." His voice was no longer the adolescent squeak she remembered. "I should be more careful where I put my jaw. I do hope you have not suffered an injury to your head."

The way his deep baritone rumbled through her, the fact that she even had a head temporarily escaped her notice.

"Please allow me." Lucian set down the valise he'd been carrying and knelt beside her. He helped her reassemble her pages. Then he offered his hand to help her up, and she took it.

Had someone loosed a jar of june bugs in her belly?

"Thank you, my lord," she murmured, for lord he was.

Lucian Ignacio de Castenello Beaumont. Son and heir of Ellery Beaumont, Earl of Montford. Daisy assumed Lucian was now styling himself Viscount Rutland, one of his father's lesser titles, since the earl was still very much alive.

But Daisy remembered Lucian as Iggy.

His ears had turned an alarming shade of red when she called him that. "Iggy" was not dignified, he'd complained. As if a skinny, dirty-kneed twelve-year-old were capable of anything remotely like dignity.

But Lucian was no longer twelve. He was a man. And the last time Daisy heard his name bandied about in polite society, the sober matron doing the talking lowered her voice, but the words *reclusive rake* and *wastrel* were unmistakably used.

Neither of which did anything to slow her racing heart, Daisy admitted with a sigh.

She accepted the stack of papers from him. "There's no salvaging your ensemble, I fear. Please permit me to have a new suit of clothing made for you."

She could afford to be generous. After all, she'd discovered the family fortune beneath the stones of Dragon Caern Castle just when other members of the nobility were losing theirs in the South Sea stock swindle.

"I wouldn't hear of it," he assured her smoothly, though she knew Lucian's father had invested heavily in the failed company. Perhaps his mother's family was still solvent. She'd been a noblewoman in her homeland. Nearly all the vestiges of Lucian's Italian accent were now gone. Daisy thought that a terrible shame.

"I've been meaning to retire this suit in any case," he informed her. "The style is *tres passé, n'est-ce pas?*"

That would be a pity, since the cut of that green frock coat does wonderful things for his shoulders, and as for those bree—Daisy caught herself before her thoughts completely ran away with her, but lost her fight with the urge to flick her gaze to where his breeches molded to his thighs.

He caught the direction of her gaze and an amused grin tilted his lips. "My! You are a keen observer, aren't you?"

"Forgive me. Ruining your suit has upset me," she said, her cheeks flaming. "I'm acting like some pudding-headed debutante." Instead she was firmly on-the-shelf spinster of one and twenty.

"If you were a debutante, I'd have remembered you," he said.

Daisy doubted it. Especially since he showed no signs of recognizing her yet. Surely she bore some resemblance to the young girl who'd followed him about like a puppy so many years ago. His family had spent only a week in residence at Dragon Caern, but it had been the most frustrating, most splendid, most memorable week of her young life.

"However, if you want my advice," he continued, "your chances of remaining unmarried will decrease if you try not to douse every man you meet with ink."

"Perhaps remaining unmarried is my choice." She frowned until she noticed the way he flashed his teeth at her, clearly teasing. Lucian was the sort of man a woman might forgive anything so long as he smiled at her.

Daisy bit her lip to keep from babbling further. She sidled away from the case where the phallic lamp was on display.

Lucian looked around the nearly deserted exhibit hall. "It seems there is no way for us to be properly introduced, but perhaps you will allow me the honor of giving you my name."

Final proof that he truly didn't recognize her. Her belly spiraled downward in disappointment.

How was it possible that she could carry his image in her head for all these years while he completely forgot that Daisy Elizabeth Drake even existed? Bristling with indignation, she took another step backward to put more distance between them.

Before she could remind him that he should already know her name (and quite well, thank you very much!), the door behind her swung open and whacked her soundly on the bottom. Then the door slammed shut as whoever opened it realized he'd hit something. Daisy stumbled forward and Lucian caught her in his arms.

She was pressed tight against him, suddenly engulfed in his masculine scent, a clean whiff of sandalwood and soap. Beneath her splayed fingers, the musculature in his chest was rock hard. Her breath caught in her throat.

"Are you injured, miss?" Lucian asked.

"Only my pride." Daisy pushed against him as a signal he should release her. She wasn't about to admit that her derriere throbbed.

"No, I fear we have another casualty," he said, not loosening his hold on her a bit.

Daisy followed his gaze to her décolletage, where some of the ink from his shirt and waistcoat had been transferred. Part of the stain marred her pale blue stomacher and part darkened the mound of her breast that rose above it.

"Pity. An alabaster bosom should never wear black." He drew a fingertip along the froth of lace at the neckline she'd always thought of as modest, but never would again. "Alas, I forgot *my* handkerchief this morning or I should return the favor and try to wipe it off."

The thought of his hand on her skin with only a thin layer of cloth between them made her belly quiver.

The door creaked behind her and eased open a tentative few inches. A monocled gentleman peeked in and waved Lucian over with urgency.

"There you are, Rutland. We've been waiting for you."

Daisy started and jumped away from Lucian. She recognized the gentleman as Sir Alistair Fitzhugh, head of the Society of Antiquaries. She'd petitioned for admission several times, only to have Sir Alistair blackball her membership on account of her gender. The man cast a quick dismissive gaze over her and turned back to Lord Rutland.

A baron's niece counted for very little when measured against a viscount, she supposed.

Fitzhugh's monocle popped out and dangled from its silver chain as he eyed the large, oddly shaped ink stain on Lucian's clothing. "Good God, man, what's happened to you?"

"It was—" Daisy began.

"My fault entirely," Lucian finished for her. "I will be in directly, Fitzhugh."

Lucian turned back to Daisy. "Perhaps once I've delivered my presentation—"

"Hold a moment," she interrupted, stunned. She'd expected an Oxford-don type would lead the discussion. "You're the speaker?"

He nodded with a wry grin. "When I'm allowed to be."

She covered her mouth with her fingertips. When had Lucian become an expert in Roman antiquities? Or, more specifically, lost Roman treasure.

"As I was saying, I hope we may continue our discussion at a later time. I'd enjoy learning what else such a charming young lady finds . . . curious in these dry halls." He retrieved his valise, made an elegant leg and shot her a wicked grin. "And for your information, the answer is no."

"No?" Her brows nearly met in a puzzled frown.

"It's not life-size."

"Miss Drake, it is my sincere hope this will be the final time I am called upon to send you notification of rejection for membership.

With respect,
Sir Alistair Fitzhugh, Esq."

Chapter Two

"What colossal cheek!" Daisy gaped at Lucian's retreating back. The man had the gall to turn her quest for knowledge into something decidedly bawdy.

Of course, he might argue that she started it when she asked if the blasted lamp was life-size. But in her defense, she'd been under the assumption that she was talking merely to herself.

Why, Lucian was a veritable eavesdropper.

And insufferably smug.

To top it off, the dark-eyed devil hadn't even invited her in to hear his blasted lecture! He was no better than the rest of the gentlemen in the Society.

And he'd committed the further unpardonable sin of not remembering her.

Sir Alistair had refused to admit Daisy to the lecture hall earlier. The study of antiquities was far too "earthy" a subject for a young lady, he'd said, looking down his long Scottish nose at her. Now that Daisy knew the speaker was only Lucian Beaumont, she was of half a mind to return to her great-aunt's town house.

But the door to the lecture hall hadn't latched behind Lucian when he took his leave, and Daisy wasn't the sort to let an opportunity slide by. With a quick glance up and down the corridor to make sure she wasn't seen, she pulled the door open and sidled through as small a crack as possible.

The entire back row of chairs was empty, so she slipped into a seat and hoped no one would notice. Once she got a look at the mosaic propped up on the dais, she was sure no one would spare her a second glance.

The myriad of tiny colored tiles were almost completely intact. Even from her distant vantage point, she could tell that the artwork was splendid. But Daisy could see why this mosaic wasn't on display to the general public. The subject matter would shock a sailor, and since she'd been raised by a prodigal pirate, that was saying something.

The work was nearly the size of a hogshead of beer in a public house. All around the outside of the circular mosaic, there were scantily clad figures depicted in odd poses, some bent over, some with limbs entwined in uncomfortable-looking positions. A few were joined in groups of three instead of two.

Daisy squinted, wishing she'd thought to borrow Great-aunt Isabella's lorgnette. She turned her attention to the much larger representation in the center of the circular design.

The figure was a man, his calm Roman eyes looking out on the world with amused interest, the slightest upturn to his mouth. He stood proudly, his short tunic displaying muscular legs.

And protruding from beneath his tunic was an organ that would put Uncle Gabriel's stallion to shame. It was as long as the man's forearm and nearly as thick.

Hmph! Bet that's not life-size either, Daisy thought, shifting uncomfortably in her seat. *It looks more likely to impale than pleasure.*

Daisy often sneaked into Isabella's library to read her collection of love poetry. Most recently, Daisy had discovered the unpublished memoirs of Mademoiselle Blanche La Tour, a French courtesan, who led an extremely adventurous life in and out of the boudoir. Mlle La Tour was not reticent in her description of either type of exploit, so Daisy's knowledge of intimate behavior far outstripped her personal experience.

She was reading through the journal slowly, asking Nanette, her great-aunt's French maid, for help when her own grasp of the language proved too schoolgirlish for the subject matter. Nanette proved a font of information, as well. Daisy never imagined so much could be accomplished with something as small and seemingly insignificant as a tongue.

She jerked herself back from her naughty musings. Lucian was speaking.

"This mosaic was unearthed on my father's estate in the ruins of what I confidently believe was once a Roman proconsul's residence," he said. "Only a regional governor would have commissioned such a work."

"Why do you say that?" one man spoke up. "It appears to me that any man with means would choose to have himself depicted as Priapus. I'd fancy something on that order on the boudoir walls myself."

Several gentlemen laughed with him.

"Phallic cult art has always been popular, Lord Brumley, but only a politically well-connected gentleman would project his power in such a display in the foyer of his home. He must have been a proconsul, a man accustomed to obedience from those around him," Lucian said. "And one who had no fear of his own wife."

Daisy covered her mouth with her gloved hand to stifle a giggle.

Lucian certainly knows how to silence a detractor.

Lady Brumley's public set-downs of Lord Brumley were legendary, as was *her* family's close connection to the Crown. Her less well-placed husband quaked behind her, walking a narrow line indeed. Lord Brumley made up for this humiliation by blustering loudly and bullying others whenever Lady Brumley was absent.

"As you can see from the artist's rendition," Lucian was saying, "the Romans led a varied and experimental life of the flesh. However, as fascinating as this mosaic is, the find I'm about to unveil is even more beguiling."

To a man, his audience leaned forward in their seats.

Lucian reached down into his small valise and pulled out an object no larger than Mlle La Tour's journal. "A wax tablet and stylus."

The assembly loosed a collective sigh of disappointment.

"Well, it seems in remarkable condition," Sir Alistair said. "But I fail to see how a tally of grain shipments or slave purchases—"

"I know that's usually what one finds on these things, but not so in this case." Lucian cradled the tablet as if it were his firstborn. He reached a finger to trace the delicate writing, then pulled back as if he'd thought better of it. "No, gentlemen, this is the treasure I promised to share with you in this lecture. Or rather, the way to find the treasure."

"Well, don't riddle us, Rutland," Lord Brumley grumbled. "We have neither the time nor the patience."

Nor the intellect, Daisy added silently.

"What is it then? Out with it," Brumley said.

Lucian held the tablet over his head like Moses descending from Mount Sinai. "This is the record of a Roman treasure that went astray and was never recovered—a year's pay for the entire Roman Legion on the British isle."

Daisy could almost hear the men calculating the sum in ancient coin as they settled back into their seats.

This time, Daisy leaned forward. The lure of a treasure tempted her as though she possessed a dragon's attraction to shiny hoards. When she was a little girl, she had discovered a pirate's cache of Spanish gold beneath the stones of her home, Dragon Caern Castle in Cornwall. The sudden wealth changed her family's life forever. Her uncle might be a mere baron and a former pirate, but the Spanish gold meant even dukes now sought him out for friendship and counsel.

Though Daisy and her sisters couldn't claim a title in their own right, a generous dowry had landed a match with a marquess for her older sister, Hyacinth. The twins, Posey and Poppy, were engaged to an earl apiece. Only Lily was still in the schoolroom.

Daisy could have married thrice over, but she had little use for dandies. The men who danced attendance on her with visions of Spanish doubloons sparkling in their eyes were irritating in the extreme.

And more than a little dull.

Besides, none of them ever made her heart race like a certain skinny, dark-haired boy with an Italian accent had.

Drat the man! How could he not even remember her?

"What I offer you today," the dratted man in question was saying, "is a chance to partner with me to find this Roman payroll."

The thrill of finding Dragon Caern's treasure had never paled in Daisy's mind. It was the finest adventure she'd ever had.

She longed to do it again.

"After all this time, it's not probable the treasure is still intact," Lord Brumley said with a sniff. "Does the tablet give the location?"

Lucian flashed a quick grin. "If it did, I'd not be likely to divulge it, would I? However, it's not quite that simple. This tablet, though convincing, doesn't contain the whole story. The narrative is unfinished, but it contains a sworn statement that the entire payload had been cached in one location. So I have to conclude that another as yet undiscovered tablet contains the rest of the information. Now we—"

"I understand you can't give specifics, but what, in general, does the tablet say?" Sir Alistair asked. As head of the Society of Antiquaries, he was a bona fide scholar. Of all the men in the room, Daisy judged him most likely to be able to read an ancient Latin text. Daisy had a passing acquaintance with many of the others in attendance—Lord Lindley, Lord Halifax, Sir Benton Wembley, to name a few—and she'd never have guessed at their interest in antiquities.

Perhaps it was the risqué nature of the ancient art that commanded their attention.

"The tablet details a crime, a theft committed by the proconsul's steward," Lucian explained. "The named felon was one Caius Meritus, a freedman in the governor's service. It seems he absconded with the pay wagon—"

A hiss of whispers circled the room. A wagonload of Roman coin, then. The mental calculations resumed.

"He hid the money and tried to flee the island, no doubt planning to return later to retrieve the treasure when the furor died down. Caius Meritus was killed in his escape attempt, but he left clues behind as to the whereabouts of the hoard."

"What clues?" Sir Alistair asked.

"That is information I reserve to be shared with my partners in this endeavor," Lucian said.

Sir Alistair waved a dismissive hand. "What assurance do you have that the Romans didn't find it themselves?"

"Their own testimony that they didn't," Lucian said. "Caius Meritus's cryptic deathbed statement left them bewildered."

"But you fancy yourself able to decipher it centuries later. This reeks of arrogance, young man!" Brumley said.

"I make no claims for my own abilities, but I daresay the scientific method and use of reason improve my chances significantly." The slightest tightening of Lucian's jaw was the only sign that Brumley's needling bothered him.

"Where did you find this tablet?" Lord Brumley demanded.

"In the same general area of our excavation as this magnificent mosaic." Lucian waved a hand toward the well-endowed proconsul. "There's no question of its provenance. I'm convinced we'll find enough clues at this site to lead us in the right direction."

"What is it you require from your partners, Lord Rutland?" Sir Alistair asked.

"An excavation is an expensive undertaking. Already I've invested a considerable amount from my own resources." Lucian named a sum that sent a ripple of murmurs around the room.

Lucian was either very confident or very desperate, Daisy decided.

"I would require a similar investment from my partner," he said. "We will share credit equally when the discovery is made, and my partner will be entitled to half the value of the items uncovered."

"In other words, you're selling blue sky just like your father," Lord Brumley said with obvious disgust. "Luckily, I pulled out of the South Sea debacle in time to keep from sinking with Lord Montford, but plenty of other good men didn't. I see you intend to follow in your father's footsteps and lead others to ruin."

Lord Brumley stood and turned to stalk out. Angry shouts and denunciations came from all corners of the room. Daisy rose and scurried toward the door before anyone could catch her trespassing on the Society's meeting, but she tossed one last glance at Lucian before she made good her escape.

The look of cold fury on his face caused all the small hairs on her arms to stand at attention.

The South Sea Bubble. She'd been a child in the fall of 1720, but she remembered the financial scandal well. Probably because it was all tangled up with the visit of Lucian and his family to Dragon Caern. Lord Montford, Lucian's father, had been trying to convince Uncle Gabriel to invest his newfound wealth in the South Sea Company. The Crown had given the investment group exclusive rights to trade with South American markets, and it was poised to make obscene profits.

Uncle Gabriel had argued that *obscene* was the right word for it. He hadn't sailed the Spanish Main under a pirate's flag for all those years for nothing. He knew the ships that plied those waters. And their cargoes.

The South Sea Company's chief import to the New World was slaves from the African coast. Some of Gabriel Drake's pirate crew had been runaway slaves. Daisy remembered her uncle Gabriel shouting that he'd be damned if he'd ever invest in a slaver. Not even so much as a halfpenny.

Lord Montford had stormed out of the keep in a huff, dragging his family with him. Daisy hadn't even been able to properly say good-bye to the boy she'd bedeviled all week and become secretly enamored with.

In less than a fortnight, the stock price of the South Sea Company nosedived, taking the entire financial market with it in a crippling plunge. A good deal of speculative investing led to the crash. Many families of ancient wealth were reduced to poverty. Even Sir Isaac Newton reportedly lost over twenty thousand pounds.

Of the loss, Daisy read that the brilliant man had said only that he could not calculate "the madness of people."

Lord Montford was ruined.

No wonder Lucian was furious when Lord Brumley compared his current scheme to his father's greatest failure.

Daisy stood off to one side in the corridor, seemingly fascinated by the amphora collection behind the wavy glass of the display case, as more gentlemen filed out of the lecture hall. "Dreamer" and "ill-advised" were the kindest comments she overheard. "Charlatan" would rankle Lucian most.

Finally, Lucian emerged. When he saw her, he inclined his head toward her.

"I regret, miss, that I am unable to continue our pleasant conversation at this time." His lips were pressed tight in suppressed irritation.

"Then let us conduct a business conversation instead, Lord Rutland," Daisy said brusquely. "Your excavation intrigues me. I have the means you require. I should like to become your partner in the endeavor."

Lucian bit back a weary smile. "Miss, you mistake me. I'm not the fraud the Society of Antiquaries would paint me. I'm in need of investors, admittedly, but I'm not yet so desperate that I will take money from a young lady to whom I've not even been properly introduced. Good day."

He turned and began to stride away.

A frustrated puff of breath escaped her lips. The man had an ego as large as that of the well-endowed proconsul in the mosaic.

"Then perhaps you could prevail upon 'Iggy' to introduce us," she called after him. "For he and I knew each other well."

He halted in midstride and turned back to face her.

"Daisy Drake."

"Indeed, milord." She bobbed a curtsy. "I'm gratified to learn that your memory is not as pocked with holes as I feared."

He raised a brow. "You can hardly fault me for not immediately connecting a charming young woman with an irritating tomboy."

Her chin lifted; she was both mollified by the compliment to her now and incensed by his characterization of her then. "And yet I knew you almost instantly. It's good to see you looking fit after all these years."

"After the way you tried to spit me with a pike at our last meeting, I find your interest in my health less than comforting." He rubbed the little scar on his chin for emphasis. "Of course, this must have made it easier for you to recognize me."

"That was an accident and you know it. If only you'd kept to the way we practiced the fight scene, I wouldn't have nearly skewered you."

Daisy and her sisters produced plays for their own amusement in the same way other families produced mediocre poetry. The theatrical merits of their dramas might have been questionable, but the Drake siblings always managed to have genuine fun.

And very infrequent bloodletting. Really, Lucian ought to have forgiven her by now.

"In fact," Daisy continued, "one might argue that your injury was as much your fault as mine."

"One might," he agreed.

"Then you'll accept my offer to become your partner?"

"With regret, no," he said stiffly. "Given our history, you'll understand my reluctance to form another alliance with the house of Drake. It was only the greatest good fortune that kept my head affixed to my shoulders last time. I'm not one to tempt fate."

"The decision to become a courtesan is not to be made lightly. A woman must be willing to make her own choices. And pay for them."

—the journal of Blanche La Tour

Chapter Three

"And then the insufferable prig walked away without so much as a backward glance." Daisy accepted the eggshell-thin china teacup from her great-aunt Isabella's beringed hand. "He obviously needs the money. Why would he not accept it from me?"

"Because it was from you." Isabella Haversham, Lady Wexford, dropped a brown lump of sugar into her own cup and stirred gently. "It's the way of the world, sweeting. Men are incapable of bending where their pride is concerned."

"And they have the gall to claim women are vain," Daisy fumed. "Just because I gave him a scar on his chin."

"Oh, no, Daisy. I'm sure it's not what you gave him. I suspect it's more what your uncle wouldn't give his father." Isabella took a sip of the aromatic tea and then settled the cup back into its saucer with a barely audible clink. "Lord Montford made no secret of the fact that he felt the South Sea Company would have rallied if your uncle had invested heavily at that juncture."

"That's ridiculous. The enterprise was doomed."

Isabella arranged her delicately boned hands on her lap. Faint blue veins laced her pale skin. She was still a striking woman, but time was chipping away at the former courtesan with a relentless vengeance. However, advancing age had made no dent whatsoever in Lady Wexford's sharp mind.

"Of course, the South Sea Company was doomed, but if money or love is concerned, when is the human race not ridiculous?" Isabella said, with a shrug that seemed curiously French. "But however misguided, if Lucian is loyal to his father, you shouldn't hold it against him. I suspect you'd do the same if you perceived a slight to your family."

Daisy sighed. "I suppose you're right. But I so had my heart set on an adventure and finding another treasure would be a grand one. Each day is so like another, sometimes I think I'll burst out of my own skin from sheer boredom." Her lips curved in calculation. "You know, I just might be able to bear this disappointment if you'd let me come to your soiree this evening."

Isabella fixed her bright-eyed gaze on Daisy, considering the matter. "I suspect Jacquelyn would have my head if I did."

Jacquelyn was Isabella's daughter. Even before Daisy's parents died, Jacquelyn Wren had been the Drake sisters' fiercely protective governess. Once Mistress Jack married Daisy's uncle Gabriel, she was no less protective as their aunt. In truth, Daisy thought of Jacquelyn and Gabriel more as her parents than as her aunt and uncle. And even though no actual blood tie bound Daisy to Isabella, Lady Wexford had fallen into the role of doting great-aunt with relish.

"I'm no longer a child. What I do or don't do is none of my aunt and uncle's affair," Daisy declared. "Besides, I'm of age. And an independent woman."

"Only thanks to your extremely enlightened aunt and uncle," Isabella reminded her gently. Even though Daisy had discovered the family fortune, her guardians were under no obligation to be so generous to her. The fact that they gave her control of her own funds was a measure of their love and trust.

"Please, Isabella," Daisy wheedled, not sounding particularly of age or independent. "I've spent time in your salon before."

"Ordinarily, I'd agree, but this is no pitched philosophy discussion or poetry reading. I'm giving a masquerade in honor of Geoffrey's birthday." Isabella rejected the notion that she should refer to her much younger husband as Wexford. Their marriage was unconventional by all standards. Her mode of addressing him might as well be, too. "When people don masks, they feel free to do things, outrageous things they'd only dream of without the cloak of anonymity. This evening is bound to become . . . complicated."

"If by that you mean there will be lovemaking in every curtained alcove, you needn't worry that you will shock me." Daisy scented victory and tried to sound worldly enough to have earned it. Isabella's masquerade would definitely be exciting, and at this point, Daisy longed so for an adventure, she wasn't about to quibble over what form it took. "Thanks to Mlle La Tour, I know what happens between a man and a woman, probably even better than Hyacinth. And she's already a mother."

"What did you just say?" Isabella was rarely shocked by anything, but she sounded stunned now.

Daisy's fingertips flew to her mouth. Her reading the courtesan's memoirs was a secret between her and Nanette. "All right, if you must know, I've been invading your library every day for a month. Haven't you always said a woman shouldn't be forced to remain in ignorance? Mlle La Tour's journal has been . . . very educational."

Isabella loosed a tinkling laugh. "It is that. Well, I see there's no point in closing the stable door. It appears the filly has bolted."

"Oh, no!" Daisy protested. "I haven't acted upon any of my knowledge."

"I'm gratified to hear it. Not because I think it wrong for

a woman to take pleasure, Lord knows, but because I think it might be wrong for you now." Isabella raised a questioning brow at her. "You know your family still hopes you'll wed. It is inconceivable for a young lady of your birth and generous portion not to be set upon by suitors. No beaux in the offing?"

"None I care to encourage." Daisy leaned her cheek on her palm. Her outspokenness discouraged the more desirable gentlemen, while her fortune enticed the worst. "Gallants and dandies, the whole lot. When they look at me, all they see is the pile of doubloons Uncle Gabriel has settled on me. They never seem to see *me*."

"And yet Lucian Beaumont refused your offer of funds," Isabella mused into her teacup. "I'm beginning to think I should like this young man."

"No, you shouldn't," Daisy said, wishing she didn't. Lucian obviously wanted as little to do with her now as he had when he was twelve. "He's stubborn as a—"

"A Drake?"

Daisy rolled her eyes. "Point taken. But you've changed the subject. Back to your masquerade. Please, Isabella. Haven't you ever wanted something . . . anything exciting to happen to you so badly you didn't care if it was right or wrong? And if something didn't happen soon, you'd be forced to take drastic measures to affect an adventure, devil take the hindmost?"

Isabella eyed her thoughtfully for a moment. "My dear, you sound quite desperate."

Daisy hadn't realized herself how very unsettled she felt until the words slipped from her mouth. Like a fledgling sensing the power of her untested wings, Daisy was dying to take flight.

"Desperate? Heavens, no." She forced a laugh. "Just bored to tears. But if I were to attend your masked ball, it might take the edge from my tedium."

"If—and mind you, I said *if*—I thought it advisable for you to come tonight, what sort of costume might you assemble on such short notice?"

Daisy cast about in her mind. "I once wore a small papier-mâché boat strapped to my hips and a hat like a sail on my head so I could be an English schooner fighting off the Spanish Armada."

"If you want men to notice you, and not your fortune, appearing as a warship is not the best idea." Isabella shook her head. "Besides its being totally impractical on the dance floor, we haven't time for the papier-mâché to set."

"Well, I once wore a suit of mail for another play, but it was deucedly heavy."

"Again, the subtext of that costume is excessive defense," Isabella said. "Perhaps, my dear, the reason men have not seen you is because you're not ready for them to."

Not ready? She was twenty-one, for pity's sake. When would she be ready?

"No, I think you'd best not attend this fete." Isabella shook her head. "This is not a childish play, Daisy. This is an adult masquerade. And the amusements will be correspondingly . . . adult."

"I am an adult," Daisy said flatly. "And it is time I was treated as one. Perhaps I could come disguised as a courtesan. Mlle La Tour herself." Daisy was pleased by the hard blink of surprise Isabella cast her. "Nanette has shown me your old wardrobe from your days as 'La Belle Wren,' and the gowns are still stunning."

"My, my, hasn't Nanette been a busy little bee?"

"Don't scold her. It's my fault. She hasn't done anything I haven't asked." Daisy's heart raced a bit at the thought of appearing in public as a woman of pleasure. "You might have been a bit smaller than I, but surely there's a gown in that collection I could squeeze into."

"Being a courtesan is far more complicated than squeezing into a revealing gown." Isabella drummed her fingertips on the arm of her chair.

"I know." Daisy warmed to the idea with every breath. "I'd have to charm all the men in the room while making each one feel that he alone held my interest. I'd have to be gay and witty. Be available, yet unattainable." She winked slyly. "I'd have to be you all over again, Isabella."

Her great-aunt smirked, but Daisy could tell she was flattered by the reminder of her glory days.

"Please," Daisy said.

Isabella raised her hands in mock surrender. "Very well. If we are going to do this thing, we're going to do it right." She tinkled the little bell on the serving tray, and Nanette appeared in the doorway. "Miss Daisy is attending the ball tonight, Nanette. She will wear the red tulle gown and my best wig."

"Oui, madáme."

"She is coming as Mademoiselle Blanche La Tour, woman of pleasure, so give her the full regimen of toilette a courtesan must endure," Isabella said.

Nanette's eyes went round, but she merely bobbed her understanding in a shallow curtsy. "I shall prepare the bath *tout de suite.* This way, *s'il vous plaît,* mam'selle."

Daisy stood to follow the lady's maid out, but Isabella stopped her with a hand to her forearm.

"This may be just a game to you, Daisy, but it's a dangerous one. You wanted men to see you. In this costume, I promise you, they shall," Isabella warned. "You will feel very powerful tonight. When a woman knows men desire her and she has it within her to please or thwart them with a glance, it can be heady. But there is another power at work."

Daisy raised a questioning brow.

"Desire can overtake a woman as easily as a man. A mask may hide a person's identity for only a short time," Isabella said. "In the morning, you'll wash your face the same as always, and I would have you bright eyed before your looking glass. Therefore, I must have your solemn promise that whatever may happen this night, the dawn will find you in the same state of purity you now enjoy."

"I am in perfect control of my own person," Daisy said, tight-lipped.

"I'm delighted to hear it. Just also make certain you control the men who will seek your attentions."

" 'Do this. Don't do this.' " She gently pulled away from Isabella. "Honestly, you sound like Aunt Jacquelyn."

"Then my daughter is a wise woman," Isabella said. "I'll be the first to admit there are pleasures aplenty in a lover's bed, but there are snares as well. I'd spare you, child. When you do finally go to a man's bed, I want it to be with your heart's and mind's consent, as well as your body's."

Daisy leaned down and pressed a kiss to the older woman's cheek. "It will be. Thank you, Great-auntie."

"How many times have I told you to call me Isabella?" she said with feigned severity. "How shall I maintain the illusion of eternal youth if society is constantly reminded that I'm old enough to have a grown great-niece? Off you go, now."

Isabella watched with fondness as her great-niece rounded the corner and disappeared after Nanette. Then she checked her mantel clock. Yes, if Isabella hurried, there was just enough time for her to issue one more invitation for tonight's masquerade. Her footman would have to hand-deliver it.

There was always the possibility that the gentleman had a previous engagement, but Isabella would lose nothing in the attempt. Daisy wanted an adventure. This was the best way Isabella could make sure she had one.

Lady Wexford settled at her escritoire to compose a carefully worded request. Lord Wexford's birthday masquerade would be lacking if not graced by the noble presence of Lucian Beaumont, Viscount Rutland.

"Beauty requires a certain homage, a sacrifice, if she is to be coaxed into making an appearance."
                                        —the journal of Blanche La Tour

Chapter Four

"Are you sure this is the way it's supposed to be worn?" Daisy eyed herself doubtfully in the long looking glass. The stays built into the red tulle gown cinched her waist so tightly, she could scarcely breathe.

That wasn't so bad. She'd been laced snugly before, but this gown also seemed designed to shove her breasts up, presenting them squeezed together like a baby's behind. Thanks to a hot bath and determined scrubbing, Daisy had succeeded in removing the ink stain, but now her skin was flushed. Not only that, her nipples peeped above the scooped neckline.

"Bien sûr," Nanette assured her. "Oh, la! I forgot the rouge."

The lady's maid dipped her thumb in a paint pot, then brushed Daisy's nipples with the garish color. Daisy consoled herself that at least they matched the gown now. Nanette spritzed a liberal dose of jasmine perfume over Daisy.

"There," Nanette said. "Much better, *non?*"

"If you say so." Daisy coughed at the strong scent. She'd never worn anything heavier than a dash of rose water.

Daisy slipped on the plumed mask that covered the upper half of her face. The slanted slits tilted her eyes up at the outer corner, making her seem almost feline, despite the feathers. She also wore a top-heavy powdered wig and a black heart-shaped beauty mark affixed near one corner of her mouth. Combined with the mask and the deep décolletage, Daisy stared at a stranger in the mirror.

An exotic, stunning stranger. A creature of night and passion and dangerous allure.

Daisy had never considered herself more than mildly presentable on a good day. The woman in the mirror was decadently gorgeous. "Jupiter!"

"You are lovely, *oui?*" Nanette said, obviously pleased with her final product. "The soreness, she is gone?"

"Mostly." When Isabella had ordered the full toilette of a courtesan for her, Daisy had no idea that entailed the removal of all the small hairs from her body.

Even in her most intimate places.

Nanette's hot beeswax left her skin smooth and sensitive. When Daisy tottered across the room on the tall Venetian-style platform shoes that added a full six inches to her height, the air moving beneath her voluminous skirt caressed her in unexpected places.

Strains of the string quartet wafted up to her.

"It seems the ball has started." Daisy thanked Nanette for her unflagging efforts and glided to the door, walking in the tall shoes more gracefully with each step. The slight pressure of her own thighs on her freshly denuded sex sent a shimmering tingle through her.

She recalled Isabella's warnings. Her body did possess a power of its own.

"Forewarned is forearmed," she murmured, determined to ignore the strange warmth in her groin. She drew as deep a breath as her stays allowed and pushed open the door. Thanks to the boning built into the gown, her posture was perfectly erect.

Now if she could only bolster her confidence to match.

She wanted an adventure, she reminded herself. Only her own timidity would ruin this one for her. She'd seen other women, perfectly respectable women, sporting a neckline just as low as this one, and without the benefit of being masked. Only last week, Lady Lucinda Throckmorton bared her nipples as part of her décolletage at the opera in a daring froth of Parisian lace. It was unthinkable that a courtesan would do less.

And yet Isabella's advice echoed in her head. Whatever happened this night, she would have to wash her own face in the morning. Even courtesans should be allowed modesty when they wished it. Perhaps she could be a courtesan on holiday, not seeking a patron, and therefore not displaying her wares quite so boldly.

Daisy skittered back over to the dressing table and selected a filmy red fichu to tuck around her neck and into the deep-cut bodice. Her rouged nipples still showed darkly through the delicate fabric, but the slight additional covering gave her a measure of relief.

She caught Nanette scowling at her in the mirror. "You wish to say something?"

"Only that mam'selle has ruined the line of the gown," the lady's maid said with an injured sniff.

"Perhaps," Daisy allowed. "But now the line of my conscience remains untroubled. Blanche La Tour is not trying to entice a new patron this evening. This is daring enough."

Uncle Gabriel always said she could have had a career on the stage, if only the theater weren't so tawdry an undertaking. She would look upon this evening as if it were a play, Daisy decided. The Venetian shoes lifted her to a new height. The gown was more daring than plain Daisy Drake would ever think of donning. She would speak nothing but French for the rest of the night. Her accent was excellent, and the nasal quality of that tongue should effectively disguise her voice, even if she met someone she knew.

No one would penetrate this disguise.

Daisy slipped into the role of Mademoiselle Blanche La

Tour, bird of paradise, albeit with a few of her finer feathers discreetly tucked. With a lace-gloved hand on the brass railing, she descended slowly to join Lord Wexford's party, already in progress.

Lucian accepted the flute of champagne from Lord Wexford's butler and surveyed the long ballroom. He rarely attended such events. Since the family fortunes were so depleted, Lucian didn't have the resources to be fashionable. Cultivating the image of a misanthropic rake was more palatable than letting the threadbare truth be known.

The only enticement that drew him out this time was Lady Wexford's suggestion in her invitation that he might find an investor for his newest enterprise this evening. He was surprised she'd heard of it so quickly. The gossip mill in London was obviously as ruthlessly efficient as ever. No doubt the news of his excavation and his hopes had been trumpeted and tittered at all over town.

At least Lady Wexford hadn't laughed at him as the Society of Antiquaries had.

"Bunch of gossipy old hens," he grumbled to no one in particular, and turned back to gaze over the assembly.

The theme of the masquerade seemed to be a bacchanal. Several guests sported Roman togas. One randy old fellow had bared his sunken chest, donned furred leggings and was cavorting about the dance floor. Already seriously in his cups, he chased the female dancers and interrupted the stately lines of the gavotte, proclaiming himself Pan incarnate. Finally, one of Lord Wexford's servants in the guise of a praetorian guardsman firmly escorted him off the floor.

Lord and Lady Wexford looked cool and classical in their flowing white robes and gold leaf laurels. Though the lady was reputed to be her husband's senior by some fifteen years, she still turned heads as they glided from one group to the next, greeting their guests.

Given the lateness of his invitation, Lucian decided his hostess couldn't quibble about the fact that his costume consisted solely of a silk mask and a decidedly old-fashioned frock coat and knee breeches, all in black. The original buttons on the ensemble had been ornately worked silver, but he'd been forced to sell them to fund his work. Now somber pewter was his only decoration. If anyone asked, he supposed he could claim he'd come disguised as a Puritan.

And a good stretch that'd be, he thought with a wolfish grin. His financial state might keep him from seeking gentlemanly pleasures, but his imagination was rife with them. Lucian dreamed of a well-stocked stable, membership at the most exclusive clubs and a beautiful mistress tucked away in a fashionable love bower. Of course, once he found the Roman hoard, he'd upgrade the family estates and ease the plight of his even poorer tenants. But after that was accomplished, a gentleman had a right to tend to his own needs.

However, at the moment, he was the nearly penniless Viscount Rutland. His father was kept from total ruin by a degradingly small stipend from Lucian's mother's family. When his mother had died, his Italian grandfather threatened to cut Lord Montford off, and probably would have if not for Lucian. Still, his father was deucedly tightfisted with his meager coin. Lucian couldn't have afforded to hire a Roman-themed costume for this masquerade, even if he'd received his invitation in a timelier manner.

Still, Lucian didn't feel too out of place. Despite the classical theme, many revelers had decided to dress to their own tastes. There was a smattering of medieval lords and ladies, a Turkish pasha accompanied by a shapely harem girl, and one fellow wearing an ass's head.

"He's either supposed to be Bottom from *A Midsummer Night's Dream* or he's being honest about his true character," Lucian murmured.

"*Bien sûr,*" came a musical voice at his side. The speaker

obviously understood English, but she continued in French. "Sometimes we must don a mask before we can be completely ourselves."

He turned and found a vision in red tulle at his side. The statuesque beauty met his gaze squarely, her slanting cat eyes glittering behind her mask like jewels embedded in velvet. A beguiling whiff of jasmine swirled about her.

The expensive and lavish scent announced her occupation more clearly than if she carried a placard. A top-tier courtesan, he guessed.

She looked away, as if she hadn't spoken to him. Then she raised her own glass and sipped, baring her long, pale neck. His gaze drifted lower to where her nipples were only partially obscured by a thin fichu. By rouging them, then covering them, she had achieved a neat juxtaposition of the virgin and the wanton. The cagey lady drew his eye to her pert charms more effectively than if she'd laid her silken breasts bare.

For a moment, he remembered gazing down on the ink-stained bosom of that fascinatingly curious girl outside the Society's meeting. At least, he'd thought her fascinating till he'd discovered she was Daisy Drake, all grown up.

Miss Drake was nothing but trouble. Especially since his father had conceived a hatred of all Drakes.

Lucian shoved aside the memory of the maddening girl, now grown into a maddening woman, and stole another glance at the courtesan's peekaboo décolletage. Her rouged areolae were like ripe strawberries. His mouth watered. If this was a sample of what he'd missed by not attending this sort of fete, perhaps he'd have to swallow his pride and show himself to society more often, threadbare gentility exposed or not.

"Do you talk only to yourself, monsieur?" she asked, still in French and still not deigning to look directly at him. "If so, I must apologize. It is the height of rudeness to eavesdrop on a party's conversation with themselves, don't you think?"

"No, I mean, yes, I was talking to myself," he responded in the same tongue. "But I'd much rather talk to you. I fear you caught me admiring your . . . costume. That red is a bold color, even in this dim light."

Behind her feathered mask, her eyes flicked toward him. He wished the hall were lit well enough for him to determine their color as well.

"I am a bold woman, monsieur," she said. "But you have mistaken me. This is no costume."

So she was precisely what she seemed.

"Clever," he said. Like her beguiling nipples, this courtesan hid in plain sight.

Lucian wished his financial state allowed for a dalliance with a woman such as this. His father had always said every man needed an experienced mistress at least once in his life. A woman to teach him the subtleties of fleshly love with no further expectation beyond the exchange of gifts and mutual pleasure.

Of course, his father said a great many things that were totally impractical.

Lucian made a smooth, courtly leg to her. Even though he teetered on bankruptcy, he could still afford the manners of a gentleman.

"Viscount Rutland, your servant, mademoiselle."

"So forward, sir? This is a masquerade. Our true selves may be on display, but our identities are supposed to remain the gravest of secrets." She flicked open her fan and waved it languidly before her décolletage—now hiding, now exposing herself to his gaze. "Would you speak so to any other woman to whom you have not been properly introduced?"

"But you just told me that you were . . ." His jaw gaped

slightly. "I crave your pardon if I have offended you. I simply thought—"

"You thought a member of the Cyprian corps wouldn't insist upon civility?" she said archly. "*Monsieur le Vicomte,* a woman in my line of employ must require polite discourse, for who will guard her dignity if she does not?"

"Surely your ardent admirer would," he said, fascinated by this exotic creature. She seemed a quixotic blend of worldly and naive, insisting upon a proper introduction while driving him mad with stolen glimpses of her breasts. "I certainly would."

"Then I shall forgive you," she said simply. "Ah! But here comes our hostess. Lady Wexford, if you are acquainted with this gentleman, please introduce me to this . . . *pardonez-moi,* what shall your costume be?"

"A Puritan."

"Then I stand corrected when I said that in the concealment of the masquerade our true selves were on display, for I suspect yours is far from pure," she said throatily.

"The lady is as astute as she is beautiful," Lucian countered.

"Well, you two are getting on famously without benefit of introduction. It seems a shame to disrupt what is so seemly begun." Lady Wexford arched a silver brow at the courtesan.

"Please, madame. I did not come all the way from Paris not to meet a few well-chosen people."

"Very well," their hostess said. "If my eyes have penetrated your disguise, I believe I have the honor to present Lucian Beaumont, Viscount Rutland. Milord, this charming creature is my dear . . . friend, Blanche La Tour."

The lady extended her gloved fingertips to him, and Lucian bowed over them, pressing his lips ever so lightly to her perfumed knuckles.

"Enchanté, mademoiselle," he said, surprised to feel a slight tremble in her hand. It was what he might expect of a nervous debutante rather than a woman who exchanged her favors for rich gifts. He found the tremor amazingly endearing.

"Actually, your meeting is highly fortuitous," Isabella explained. "Blanche, dear, this is the gentleman whose interest in Roman art I told you about."

"Indeed? Ancient art is my passion." Blanche's red lips curved into a wicked smile. "One of my passions."

Lucian didn't imagine the teasing sparkle in her eyes behind the plumed mask. Definitely a top-tier Cyprian. If he had it to give, he'd willingly part with whatever she demanded for the privilege of being initiated into her passions.

"Then permit me to tell you more of it. Actually, my work might be more aptly described as antiquities rather than ancient art."

"Ah, but it is the art of the ancients that is oh, so naughty, is it not?" she countered.

The salacious couples and trios ringing the mosaic he'd displayed for the Society of Antiquaries flashed in his mind.

"Naughty indeed," he agreed. "And I have unearthed some unusual pieces. Perhaps you'd care to see them."

"I should like that very much. Oh!" Her head turned as the string quartet launched into a fresh set. "Is that a minuet?"

"I believe it is." He extended his arm. "Would you dance, mademoiselle?"

"I'd adore dancing, especially the minuet, for it means you shall have to kiss me very soon, milord," she said, laying a slim hand on his.

Lucian led her onto the dance floor, silently blessing the nameless dancing master who devised a dance with kissing built into the prescribed steps. True, it would be no more than a chaste peck, but he'd feel the petal softness of her lips beneath his and dream of more.

Perhaps much more.

"Please call me Lucian," he urged.

"Lucian," she said softly, with barely a hint of an accent before she continued in her own tongue. "And if you are planning to show me naughty art later, perhaps you should call me Blanche."

"In the banquet of love, a kiss is the appetizer."
—the journal of Blanche La Tour

Chapter Five

Daisy was panting with exertion when they finished the stately set. Her stays so constricted her breathing, the courtesan's dress wouldn't have allowed for a reel. Besides, she feared she might turn an ankle on the narrow platforms strapped to her feet. Nanette had assured her the tall shoes were all the rage in Venice, but they seemed almost suicidal on the dance floor in London.

At least the gavotte allowed a dignified glide. She couldn't bear the thought of her nearly exposed breasts bouncing along in public. Each time she caught Lucian gazing at them, her nipples drew up so tight, she was tempted to cover them with her palms to ease the ache.

But Blanche La Tour would never do such a thing. A real courtesan would revel in allowing a man to look his fill, so Daisy tried not to shrink from his hot glances.

Instead she laughed. She teased. She said every outrageous thing that popped into her head. No one expected decorous behavior from a courtesan, after all.

Being Blanche was gloriously liberating.

They completed the last turn in the minuet, and it was time for the prescribed kiss. She leaned toward him, lips slightly pursed, her eyes closed.

His mouth covered hers in a warm, heart-stopping moment. The kiss was supposed to be a mere peck, of no more import than any of the other steps in the minuet, but Lucian slanted his lips on hers and lingered.

His mouth tasted of sparkling champagne. An answering fizz of effervescence bubbled inside her, spreading warmly from her bosom downward. The tingle that settled between her legs surprised her.

Lucian Beaumont was kissing her! This moment was the embodiment of her girlish dreams. Even though he'd barely tolerated her when they were children, she'd always wondered what it would be like for that little Italian boy to take her in his arms and kiss her as she'd caught her uncle Gabriel kissing Aunt Jacquelyn. When Lucian released her, an invisible fist compressed her heart.

"A very missish kiss," he said with raised brows.

"A woman in my profession must be all things to all people," Daisy replied, tamping down her disappointment at his evaluation of their kiss. She'd found it wonderful. "I assumed you would be more accustomed to kissing debutantes and governed myself accordingly. Besides, on the dance floor, we are but puppets of the dance master, and our kisses must be suitable for public viewing. If we were elsewhere, we could be our own masters."

"Then by all means, let us take ourselves elsewhere." He offered his arm.

She slipped her hand into the crook of his elbow, and Lucian led her into Lord Wexford's fragrant garden, the scent of lavender and night-blooming narcissus heavy in the air. He was about to put her bold words to the test. Her belly jittered in anticipation.

The memoirs of the real Blanche La Tour had been very detailed on the art of the kiss. Daisy ran through the particulars in her mind. Placement of the lips, time between altering positions, taking care to inhale adequately prior to beginning the kiss—*Oh, Jupiter!* There was so much to remember, Daisy only hoped she'd absorbed enough to fool him.

When they stopped by the splashing fountain, he took both her hands in his.

"Now, Blanche, we are our own masters."

An idea leaped into her mind. She grabbed at it as her only means to escape detection. "Ah, I very much fear only one of us will be master in this situation."

"How do you mean?"

"Men, you always wish to have control, do you not? You meet a woman like me and you think you may take whatever you like."

"I assure you, I shall do nothing without your consent," Lucian promised.

"Really? Then here is what I wish. Being a wanton sometimes palls. I am on holiday here in your country," she said, extemporizing as she went. "I wish you to make love to me as if I were a young lady whom you were courting."

His brows drew close in a puzzled frown.

"We make honey kisses together. Sweet kisses. Here, let me show you." She leaned forward and kissed him, molding her lips to his, careful to observe all the real Blanche's directives. If he found her kiss "missish" again, now she had a perfect excuse. Her lips softened under his, and she curled her fingers around his lapels, pulling him closer.

Reading about kissing and actually doing it were two entirely different things, she decided. Her soft palate ached with the sweetness of his mouth on hers.

His hands found her waist and brought her snugly against him. Even through the heavy boning of her bodice and the yards of fabric, she felt the warmth of his body.

Especially where her skirts pressed against her naked sex. Usually, the fact that she wore nothing beneath the broad flare of skirts but the stockings that were gartered at her knees gave her a wonderful sense of freedom. Now she was acutely aware of the cool fabric against her freshly hairless mound.

And his hard maleness on the other side of the thin shield of tulle.

Then he shifted his mouth, her lips parted and the kiss changed. Deepened. Flared with heat. Her bones melted. She should have expected his tongue when it slipped into her mouth, but she was so distracted by the sudden gush of warmth at her groin, she lost track of the kiss for a moment in the rush of sensations. She jerked in surprise and pulled away.

"I did it wrong, didn't I?" He let his hands drop from her waist.

"No, no, your kiss was very—"

"Inexperienced," he finished. "I rushed things, didn't I? Well, there's no hiding from you. No doubt you've guessed already."

"Guessed what, Lucian?"

He sank onto the stone bench, pulling her down beside him. "That kiss was the pinnacle of my experience with the fair sex."

What was he saying? That he had no more firsthand knowledge of physical love than she? Daisy was dumbfounded.

"Surely you jest, *Monsieur le Vicomte*. Young gentlemen of title and wealth are expected to have—"

"Ah! You've hit upon the problem squarely," he said. "I'm a gentleman of title, but no wealth. I've no desire to court when I have nothing to offer a wife but my name. And lack of funds means I'm unable to pay for . . . well, to form a relationship with a woman for the sake of pleasure."

"But surely there have been willing maidens in your past." Tales of dalliances between the lord of the manor and his house servants were grist for the penny novelists' mill. Daisy had read more of them than she probably should.

"Perhaps," he conceded, "but however tempting it might be, it never seemed fair to take one of the upstairs maids to my bed."

"Commendable," Daisy said, liking him better by the

moment. "Especially since those sorts of liaisons invariably end badly for the girl who hopes to raise herself through them and rarely does."

He met her gaze directly. "Is that what happened to you?"

"Me? No, of course—" She remembered that he thought her a "soiled dove" and naturally wondered how she'd come to fall from society's grace. Daisy lifted her chin and recalled Blanche's defiant record of her own life. "I became a courtesan with my eyes wide open. I ask you, milord, would you be content to go through life being treated as if you were a child or an imbecile?"

"Of course not."

"Yet such is the plight of a married woman. When a woman becomes a wife, she becomes a man's property. I might have married, but I wished to retain ownership of myself," Daisy said, understanding Blanche more as she allowed the courtesan's words to flow out her mouth and into the garden's fresh air. "So I pursued an education that I might converse wittily on all subjects and chose to take a lover in exchange for rich gifts instead of a husband. And in so doing, I retain control of my moneys and goods as well as my person."

"And do you have a lover now?"

A trace of his old Italian accent crept back into his voice. Daisy doubted anyone who hadn't known him as a boy would have even marked the slight Latin huskiness in his tone. But it made her pulse dance.

"I am without a patron at present and in need of nothing. My last protector was very generous," she purred. "I will take another lover at a time of my choosing."

"Well, then, it certainly sounds as if you've done well for yourself in your choice," he said with a laugh. "Perhaps I should take a page from your book and hire myself out. That would be one way to fund my work."

Daisy glanced up at him sharply. Sitting beside him might be a mistake, she realized quickly, for the difference in their heights was pronounced without her tall shoes. She rose and pulled him to his feet.

"Ah! But a gigolo must possess amatory skills that you confess you lack," she said.

He came willingly and looked searchingly at her for a moment.

"Blanche." His rumbling tone caressed her false name. "Please don't confuse lack of skills with lack of interest."

Then he raised a hand to mold the column of her neck. She cocked her head reflexively into his touch as he drew his fingertips along her thin collarbone. When his fingertip met the fabric of her gown where it dipped off her shoulder, he traced the neckline on her dress as he had that morning at the Society of Antiquaries before he knew she was Daisy Drake.

Only this time, her décolletage was much more daring, and he slid his fingers beneath the thin fichu to skim her bare skin instead of just brushing the froth of lace.

As Daisy Drake, she should slap him soundly.

But what would Blanche do? Daisy wondered. A courtesan without need of a patron might still allow a gentleman such liberties simply because it pleased her.

And Lucian's touch pleased her very much indeed.

When he reached her exposed nipple, he drew his fingertip around the tight little mound in a maddening circle. Daisy scarcely breathed. A dull ache throbbed between her legs.

"I confess I do not possess the wealth required to become your patron. Not yet, at any rate. But I would happily become your devoted pupil," he suggested as he continued to massage her nipple with his thumb. "You could teach me those amatory skills."

His touch was hypnotic, and she leaned into it like a cat

demanding a more thorough petting. Daisy's lips parted, and she gasped at the zing that arced through her body, streaking from her breast to her womb. She gave herself a shake and rapped his knuckles with her closed fan.

"I think you already know much more than you admit," she accused.

His eyes flared with sudden knowledge. "You liked that."

"Of course I did." Daisy dug through her memory for Blanche's treatise on the care and titillation of a woman's nipples. The shiver of sensation coursing through her effectively blocked her thoughts. She resorted to honesty. "I'm very sensitive there."

"Are you?" he asked with surprise. "I'd have thought such a slight touch would be second nature to one in your line of work. A caress on your breast would seem of no more import than a handclasp."

Daisy glared at him. "If you are intent on insulting me, *Monsieur le Vicomte,* I shall bid you adieu."

"No, stay." He grasped her wrist. "I meant no insult, truly. Blame it on my inexperience, not my manners. Believe me, Blanche, I hold you in the highest regard. Please don't go."

"You think to toy with me."

"No, never."

She turned back to him, a portion of Blanche's wisdom sounding in her head. "It is a mistake to assume one can separate one's body from the rest of oneself. Men may deceive themselves into thinking the life of the body has no bearing on their heart, but it is not so."

He captured her hand and held it to his chest. "My heart is fully engaged, as you can feel for yourself."

The great muscle in his chest pounded beneath her palm.

"You make sport of me. A physical heart will gallop so

because one is merely aroused, monsieur. Your invisible heart may or may not be involved."

"And that's important to you," he acknowledged.

"It is. I cannot enter an affair of the body without a corresponding affair of the heart. Perhaps a base harlot can manage such a feat, but only out of self-preservation. She lies with so many men, she must hold back her heart lest it shatter like a paste jewel beneath her patrons' heels." Daisy pressed her palm to his cheek. "So I do not take lovers lightly or often, for it means I must give away a portion of myself. If we become . . . involved, I cannot answer for the consequences."

He covered her hand with his, then turned and pressed a hot kiss into her palm.

Her knees trembled.

"It's a risk I'm prepared to bear." His dark eyes flashed feral in the moonlight.

"But I am not." She pulled her hand away and walked slowly along the torchlit path. He fell into step with her. "At least, not yet. Though I like what I know of you, Lucian, I know very little. Tell me of your work."

She listened with half an ear, since she'd already heard his lecture that morning. Steering the conversation to Lucian's excavation gave Daisy much-needed time to recoup. Every time Daisy glanced at Lucian from under her lashes, she felt a bone-deep tingle, as if she stood on the topmost battlements of her uncle's Cornish castle.

Inches from certain annihilation and quiveringly alive.

"An ancient Roman treasure. How exciting! So all you need to complete your work is an investment from a partner?" she said when he was finished explaining about the Roman wax tablet. "Your search is at an end. I shall be pleased to join you in this endeavor."

Lucian flashed a brilliant smile. "While I welcome your investment, the work that goes on at the site is grubby in

the extreme. I hardly think an excavation is likely to interest you."

"Bien sûr," she agreed with a sudden burst of inspiration.
"I shall send an agent to represent me at the site. Someone
who will bring the needed funds to you and possesses
knowledge of Latin. Someone who can help with your
work, no? Will that suffice?"

"Perfectly." He went on to describe the location of the
find and arrange for the time for her agent to join him on
the morrow. "But I wonder if I might still call on you?"

"I shall count on it." She allowed her voice to drift lower,
as she'd heard her great-aunt do when she was in seductress
mode. "Remember, you did promise to show me your
naughty Roman art."

"So I did." He snapped his fingers. "I have it! What
would you say to an exchange? Authentic Roman antiquities for lessons in love."

"Not a love affair?"

"No, just lessons," he said. "Teach me what I need to
know to please a woman."

Daisy's heart sank to her toes. How could she teach
something she knew precious little of herself?

"I am not in need of a lover at present," she lied, trying
to ignore the way her heart hammered against the whalebone
prison of her bodice.

"Teach me what you know of kissing then," he said.
"That seems safe enough."

He had no idea how his kiss melted her inside. Yet the
thought of spending time with him, of exploring the mysteries of kissing him, was too delicious an adventure to pass
up.

"Very well." Daisy took his arm and led him toward the
splash of light pouring from the open doors to her
great-aunt's home. "Bring me a suitably naughty Roman
object of art and I will teach you what I know of kissing.

But in the meantime, we should rejoin His Lordship's party. I believe that's a saraband I hear. And I do so enjoy the dance."

Daisy decided she'd trip through one more set, then plead exhaustion and head for bed. She was sure she'd be up half the night, rereading Blanche's entries about the artful use of the lips, teeth and tongue.

Chapter Six

The reek of smoke and unwashed humanity surged over Sir Alistair Fitzhugh with the force of a Brighton breaker. The chimney at The Unicorn was drafting poorly again, so all the smells of the pub—yeasty ale, oily mutton stew, excessive perfume from the slumming dandies in the corner and the ripe tang of the serving girl who'd just as soon spread her legs for a man as bring him his brew—coalesced into a single stale stink.

Sir Alistair sniffed in appreciation. It was the smell of life, of honest, hard work. Barring the dandies, of course, but the pub needed them to keep the pickpockets from preying on the locals. It reminded him of the smell of his home pub back in Edinburgh.

Or as near to it as he could manage in the spidery sprawl of London town.

His eyes adjusted to the hazy dimness as his gaze swept the room. There in the far corner, a man in a greatcoat with the collar upturned was nursing a pint.

So, he came after all.

Sir Alistair made his way toward the booth and slid in across from the man without a word. A blowsy girl ambled over with a brimming mug in one hand and the other fisted at her waist. Her breasts threatened to spill over her tightly laced bodice. He dropped a coin between them and gave her already hard nipple a tug through the cheap muslin. She giggled and blew him a kiss, promising to return with bread and two bowls of stew. As she turned away with a flip of her skirt, Alistair scented a whiff of her, wet and swollen, beneath the homespun.

"Expect I'll have a bit of that later," his companion said.

"I wouldn't if I were you, Brumley," Alistair said. "If she isn't riddled with the French pox already, she will be soon. Better to frequent a reputable brothel, where the madam makes certain the girls and the patrons are both clean. Surely you've the coin for it."

"Not with the pittance my wife deals out," Lord Brumley said with bitterness. "It was in the marriage contract. Winifred retains control of her considerable dowry by special decree. Always reminding me how tightly her father's lips are pressed to King Geordie's arse."

"Bleedin' German sod," Sir Alistair muttered, not meaning Lady Brumley's father.

"Quite."

Might as well cinch the matter. Alistair hefted his mug. "To the king over the water, then."

Not meaning the German usurper.

Brumley eyed him sullenly, lips drawn tight. This was the moment, and the bastard knew it. Lord Brumley drew a deep breath. Once pledged, he was in.

Alistair had cultivated the unhappy lord for months, enticing Brumley with visions of what his life would be like without the heavy-handed King George. The poor bugger wouldn't be crawling to his well-connected wife for every scrap. James Stuart placed on his rightful throne would mean rich rewards for those who helped restore him, and a free hand for Lord Brumley into his wife's deep pockets.

And not a damned thing her father could do about it then.

Brumley lifted his mug. "To the king over the water."

They clinked rims and drank. The sour bite of ale was

mother's milk to Alistair. And the sharp sting was made all the better by the enlistment of Lord Brumley to the glorious cause.

"What did you make of Lord Rutland's claims this morning?" he asked.

"Roman treasure? A fool's errand, if you ask me," Brumley said.

"And yet perhaps not so foolish." Alistair wrapped his hands around his mug and stared into the dark brew as if he were a Gypsy fortune-teller considering tea leaves. "The antiquities he's unearthed so far are convincing."

"So?"

"So, it could add up to a tidy sum if it's true," Alistair said. "I've done a bit of research this day. A particular friend of mine holds the classical studies chair at Oxford. I happened to catch him in town. He says scholars agree the *stipendium* for a Roman legionnaire's pay was a silver denarius a day. Multiplied by a three-hundred-day year, the calendar used by the ancients."

"You expect me to become enthusiastic over three hundred silver coins. What twaddle!"

"At one time, the number of Roman soldiers on our island swelled to fifty-five thousand men," Sir Alistair said. He raised a brow. "Mayhap you need quill and ink to do the cipher."

The sudden bob of Brumley's Adam's apple showed he was quick enough in his head with figures. "Holy God."

"Holy God, indeed. Think what we could accomplish with millions in Roman silver. If we'd had such a cache of coin in '15, the Rising might not have failed," Alistair explained.

The Scottish Uprising in 1715 had met with sharp resistance from the English, who inexplicably preferred George I, the dour German Protestant, as king over His Catholic Majesty James Stuart. Alistair didn't give two figs about his monarch's religion, but his Scottish blood called for a Scottish king. And now that the first George was dead and gone, this second one was no more palatable than his predecessor.

"If the Roman treasure is real, it could go a long way toward the Restoration," Alistair said. "An army has needs, ye ken."

Ordinarily, he kept his accent at bay through intense concentration, but when he felt passionately about a subject, the brogue resurfaced.

"War is a messy business. An assassin's dagger has fewer needs," Brumley suggested.

"Very forward-thinking of you." The Scot raised his mug in approval. "But that requires a hand close to the king being willing to wield the blade. Your wife's connections put ye in the royal circle, near enough to do the deed. If ye felt yourself equal to it, we might keep the lion's share of the Roman hoard *and* earn the gratitude of the true king by dispatching the usurper. But to kill a king, even a false one, is no light matter." Alistair leaned forward and skewered Brumley with a searching look. "Is it in ye, man?"

Brumley's gaze dropped to the worm-eaten table.

"Never ye mind," Alistair said. Even a weak ally was better than none. "We'll see if we can search out the truth of Rutland's Roman coins. If we can manage to slip that treasure out from under the whelp, we'll have done well enough by James Stuart. Besides, I've another idea or two yet."

And another unhappy English lord besides Brumley whom Alistair judged ripe to entice into his web.

"A man will dispute it with his dying breath, but in his secret heart, he lives to be deceived."

—the journal of Blanche La Tour

Chapter Seven

"Your pardon, milord." Avery, the estate's aging butler, leaned over the lip of the pit as far as his arthritic back would allow. "Your new . . . partner has arrived. She awaits your pleasure in the parlor."

Lucian drew his bare forearm over his sweaty brow. He and Percy, the stable lad, had managed to move a good bit of earth since breakfast. Now he'd reached a level where he must lay aside his shovel and rely on a small whisk broom lest they destroy a delicate artifact with the sharp edges of their spades.

"She's here? I thought she was sending an agent." He shrugged on his discarded shirt before turning back to the boy who was digging with him. "Keep working with the broom, Percy. If you find something, don't try to remove it. Just brush the dirt away and I'll be back directly."

Lucian climbed the ladder out of the excavation pit and strode toward his father's manor house. From this distance, the shoddy roof and neglected gardens weren't as readily apparent. Montford had suffered over the past years not from lack of care, but lack of funds. There simply wasn't enough left after meeting their basic needs to put into new roof tiles or roses.

But that would change. Lucian would see to it. Montford would be his someday, and even though he wasn't English-born, enough English blood flowed in his veins for him to feel pride of place.

He'd been born in Italy, his mother's homeland. His first memories were of sun-drenched palazzos and the fecund smell of warm Tuscan earth. He loved the gentle hills and the round little donkey his grandfather let him ride whenever he could catch the stubborn thing. When his English father came into the earldom and insisted they return to claim his lands, Lucian was excited about traveling to the distant British isle.

But his mother had hated the chunky gray stone of Montford after the warm ocher marble of his grandfather's graceful villa. She missed the golden quality of light in her homeland. And the damp English weather settled in her delicate Mediterranean chest. Within a short spate of months, Lucian and his father buried her under a leaden English sky.

About the same time his father lost his fortune.

Lucian sometimes liked to imagine that his Italian roots would save them yet. Not only was his grandfather's miserly stipend keeping them afloat at present, but the ancient Roman relics Lucian had discovered were Montford's future. The meandering stones poking through the turf at the far end of the meadow had proved to be the capitals of buried upright Doric columns. They were also proof the Italians were here long before his English forebears. His father traced his lineage back only to the Norman conquest. Lucian wondered if he might somehow be connected by a much longer bloodline on his mother's side to the Romans who settled Londinium.

And he dreamed of resurrecting the glory of Montford, raising the standard higher than it had ever flown before.

Now, thanks to Blanche, he had access to the funds that would make it all happen.

And other things might happen as well. He'd unearthed

a nearly intact statuette of Faunus, the goat-god known as Pan in Greek tradition, that morning. The tip of the figure's erect penis had broken off, probably a millennium ago, but what remained of the organ was still amusingly outsized. Lucian thought Blanche would enjoy the naughtiness of it and perhaps be willing to exchange even more than kissing lessons for it.

Just the thought of the exotic Blanche set Lucian's groin aching. For a moment, he wondered if he should take time to change his shirt, but he hated the idea of keeping such an exquisite creature waiting. Besides, she must have known he'd be hard at work and certainly wasn't expecting to see her this morning. She was supposed to send an agent, after all. Surely she'd forgive a grubby collar and a bit of honest sweat.

The truth was, he could barely restrain himself from breaking into a run at the thought that she was near.

He hurried to the parlor and found her standing, facing away from the door, gazing out the tall Palladian windows at the overgrown garden. Light-wreathed and ethereal, the golden curls spilling down her back made her seem more angel than temptress. Last night he'd wondered about the color of her hair beneath her powdered wig, just as he'd puzzled over the color of her eyes behind the plumed mask. Her scent and the satin feel of her skin were enough to torment his sleep all night. Once she turned to face him, he'd have even more to fuel his dreams.

"Blanche," he said simply, loving the liquid sound of her name as it poured over his tongue.

"No, milord. Mlle La Tour rarely rises before noon. I, however, am quite rested and ready to start work." She turned to face him.

"Daisy Drake."

"Lucian Beaumont," she returned smoothly. "Now that we have settled the issue of our identities, we can begin. As you can see, I've brought the investment you required of Mlle La Tour."

She waggled her fingers toward a small chest resting on the glass-smooth walnut of the refectory table in the corner. Lucian desperately needed the funds, but he didn't see how he could accept them by Daisy Drake's hand.

"Hold a moment." Now that he thought about it, he chided himself for imagining for an instant that she was Blanche.

Daisy Drake was a good head shorter than the courtesan, and once she spoke, her clipped English bore no resemblance to Blanche's lilting French. And though the dress she was wearing hugged her form—an exceedingly pleasant arrangement of curves, even though they belonged to Miss Drake instead of Blanche—the gown was the plainest of muslin, a fabric no courtesan would dream of wearing. It had been merely a trick of the light in the parlor that was responsible for his mistake.

That and a longing to see Blanche again that bordered on obsession.

"I didn't agree to your being here," he said.

"Really? Then you'll have to discuss that with Mlle La Tour's agent. Oh, wait! That would be me." Daisy folded her hands, fig-leaf fashion.

A deceptively innocent gesture, he thought.

"Blanche has requested that I represent her in this matter," the infuriating chit explained.

"How on God's earth do you know a French courtesan?" he demanded.

"Through my great-aunt, Isabella Haversham," Daisy said sweetly. "Both Blanche and I are staying at Lady Wexford's home for the Season."

Of course. He'd totally forgotten the connection between the houses of Wexford and Drake. It was a tenuous, by-marriage sort of relationship, the kind maintained only by people who genuinely liked one another, since no actual blood tie bound them.

Daisy Drake in residence certainly explained how Lady Wexford heard about his project so quickly. Daisy probably put her up to inviting him to that blasted ball, probably urged Blanche to—No, Blanche was not the sort who could be cajoled into doing anything if it didn't please her. She was too strong-minded for that.

Blanche had no idea of the enmity between Lucian's father and all things Drake, else she'd never have chosen Daisy as her unlikely representative.

"Clearly, there has been a misunderstanding," Lucian said, aiming for a more conciliatory tone. "Blanche was supposed to send a gentleman as agent, one who could help with the work."

"I doubt she mentioned sending a gentleman, since she rarely has but one use for men," Daisy said with a raised brow. "Blanche says men try to intimidate women in matters of business, so she prefers to trust agents of her own gender to tend to such things."

"But she said she'd send someone who could help me." Lucian rubbed the small scar on his chin. "I know you're handy enough with a pike, but I confess I can't imagine you with a shovel, Miss Drake."

"If needs must, I suppose I could manage. As you can see, I've dressed in rustic fashion in anticipation of any contingency, but perhaps my talent would be better used in translation. I am quite fluent in Latin and can help you catalog your finds," she said airily. "And since you call Mlle La Tour by her given name, you may call me Daisy. It will be easier, since we'll be working quite closely together."

"Miss Drake," he said pointedly, "we will not be doing anything of the sort."

"Blanche will be most displeased," she said, folding her

arms beneath her breasts. "She was quite taken with the notion that I should be her eyes and ears here. She'll be frightfully put out when I tell her you have rejected the agent of her choosing. I wouldn't be surprised if she withdraws her funds."

"Then I'll find another partner." He turned to leave.

"Blanche will probably be so upset she'll refuse to see you," Daisy predicted.

That stopped him. He needed to see Blanche again, like a starving man craved food. Lucian turned and leveled a stare at the insufferable Miss Drake. "If my father learns you're on his property, he'll—"

"What? Have me arrested for trespassing?" She laughed lightly. "Unlikely, since you obviously intend to permit me to join you in your endeavor."

"Only under duress," he said icily.

Lucian was reluctant to admit, even to himself, that his father's hatred for the lord of Dragon Caern was excessive, given the nature of Gabriel Drake's offense. Other lords had spurned his father's request for investment in South Sea as well, but the Cornish baron had been Lord Montford's last hope.

Sometimes, Lucian suspected the earl teetered close to madness. Fear of seeing his father tumble into that dark abyss was part of what drove Lucian to improve the family fortunes, but it was certainly not something he'd confess to a Drake. Especially not this Drake.

"You don't understand—" he began.

"I know perfectly well that your father holds an unreasonable grudge against my uncle, but I don't see why that should extend to our relationship."

"We have no relationship."

She heaved an annoyed sigh. "I meant our business association, of course."

The sound of a raised voice echoed down the hall. By the

slurred speech and the crash of broken crockery, Lucian suspected his father was already in his cups, and noon still hours away. Lucian strode to the desk and rummaged through the top drawer.

"What are you doing?" she asked.

"Looking for a way to alter your appearance," he said as he finally found the glasses case he sought. The previous owner of the desk had mistakenly left them in it, and Lucian kept them only because sometimes it eased his own eyes to wear them if he read too much late at night. "If my father recognizes you, there'll be hell to pay."

"I doubt that he will," Daisy said as he settled the steel frames on her nose, distracting attention from her moss green eyes. She blinked over the rims at him. "After all, you certainly didn't."

He decided to ignore that jab. "But he might. Unlike my father, I'm not fixated on your family, and you do have a definite Drake look about you."

One after another, the Drake girls had assaulted London's fashionable set, their golden hair and golden fortunes the talk of the town. Lucian remembered hearing that Daisy hadn't managed to snag a husband, but given her proclivity for maiming and mayhem, perhaps that was understandable.

Some things even a boatload of pirate gold couldn't smooth over.

A loud crash sounded in the hall. His father was getting closer.

Daisy cast him a slightly cross-eyed look.

"Now, if you're serious about continuing as Blanche's agent, you'll leave the talking to me," he said under his breath as the earl staggered into the room. "Good morning, Father."

"Nothing good about it," Lord Montford said with a snort. He fixed a bleary-eyed glare on Miss Drake. "Who are you?"

Lucian stepped forward, partially shielding her from his gaze. "This is Miss . . . Clavenhook. Miss Clavenhook from Knightsbridge. She's come to help with the Latin translations."

"So, my son's dragged you into this mad business as well," the earl said. "Nothing in that field but extra heartache."

Lucian's lips drew together in a tight line. This conversation was a vicious little circle with no end. One they had already worn smooth with constant repetition.

"Better put your mind to courting, lad," Lord Montford said. "That'll come closer to filling the family coffers than mucking about in the mud. Lady Brumley and her daughter are coming to tea this afternoon. Don't be forgetting that. I'll expect you to attend them right sharp."

His father squinted around him at Daisy, raking his gaze over her form. Lucian sent up a silent prayer of thanks that she'd been prudent enough to dress in a manner that belied her wealth, no ostentatious frippery or jewels.

"You put me in mind of someone, m'dear," the earl said. "What's your name again?"

Ignoring Lucian's warnings, Daisy stepped neatly around him to dip in a low curtsy before his father. "I'm—"

"Miss Clavenhook, my assistant," Lucian finished, pulling her back to his side with a glare that demanded silence.

The earl laughed and chucked her chin. "Assistant, hmm? Didn't think Latin went with young ladies. No matter. Expect you're a fair treat without those spectacles."

He started to reach up to remove them, but Daisy put a hand to the owlish frames.

"Can't see a thing without them, more's the pity." She took Lucian's arm. "If you'll excuse us, milord, I believe we have work to do."

"Quite right." Lucian steered her toward the door. "Come along . . . Miss Clavenhook."

> *"Women have been gifted with a sensual nature, with a capacity for pleasure as acute as any man's, and an ability to beguile and seduce. To deny this is to deny our birthright as daughters of Eve."*
>
> *—the journal of Blanche La Tour*

Chapter Eight

"So, you did remember, after all." Daisy triumphantly squeezed Lucian's arm as they made their way over the uneven ground toward the excavation site. "I was sure you must."

"Remember what?" He waved away a bluebottle fly that buzzed near them, the insect weaving drunkenly in the sun-splashed midmorning. A small shower might spring up later, but for now, the weather was finer than a Londoner could hope.

However, the fair skies did little to improve his sour mood. Daisy would have to see to that herself.

"Clavenhook," she said. "That was my name in the play when we were children. Lady Rowena Clavenhook of the—"

"Of the Deadly Pike," he finished for her, rubbing his chin with a rueful expression.

"No, no, of the Castle Perilous." She made a small growl of disgust. "Will you never give that a rest? In truth, I think the scar gives you character." Daisy reveled in the warmth of his arm beneath her palm. It radiated through the thin fabric of his shirt and up her wrist to send the blood dancing in her veins with an effervescent fizz. "A small flaw like that is actually quite becoming. It makes you appear a dangerous man."

"Or a slow one," he said with a reluctant grin. "I obviously wasn't quick enough to get out of your way."

"Well, it doesn't appear you've been slow here," she said as they drew near to the Roman site.

Not only was there an impressive excavation pit, Lucian had constructed a long, low shed to house his finds once they were unearthed. The waist-high benches lining both walls groaned beneath the weight of dirt-encrusted objects.

Lucian handed her a small whisk broom and cloth. "Your domain, *Lady Rowena*. I apologize for the mess. I fear I've been less systematic than I should have been. I've been so intent on discovering the next tablet I've neglected many of the other finds."

"I'll need to catalog it all first." She eyed the disarray with mild trepidation.

"There's a small lap desk here somewhere. Please do what you can to bring order to this chaos." He started to go, but stopped short. "I should warn you that you may find some of the artwork . . . objectionable."

The lewd little phallic lamp and the exceedingly naughty mosaic flashed through Daisy's mind. Against her will, she felt her cheeks heat.

"Pray don't trouble yourself, milord," she said. "I am not easily shocked."

"No, I'm sure you're not," he agreed with a raised brow. "In fact, as I recall, you possess a healthy curiosity about such things. To that end, I wonder if you'd clean this object first."

He picked up a little statuette from the bench and placed it in her open palm. It was a representation of the goat-god doing a cloven-hoofed jig, his engorged penis all out of

proportion to the rest of him, despite having a bit of the tip
missing.

"I plan to take that to Mlle La Tour this evening," he
said. "I think she'll enjoy it, don't you?"

Daisy's heart tripped a beat or two. She was cleaning up
this lascivious little bit of antiquity so he could present it
to . . . her, in exchange for kissing lessons.

"Blanche will be charmed," she said.

"Good."

His smile was so blindingly white against his tanned face,
it made Daisy's eyes water to look at him. She sighed in
relief when he turned back toward the pit.

"Oh, and *Miss Clavenhook,* just so you know," he called
over his shoulder, using her assumed name for the benefit of
the boy who labored below in the dirt. "That's not life-size
either."

Daisy worked through the rest of the morning, sorting,
stacking, and rearranging the odds and ends. She grouped
the shards of pottery according to color, in the hope that
later she'd be able to reassemble the bowl or vase or amphora the pieces had once been.

She discovered the portable writing desk beneath a section of a mosaic depicting nymphs and satyrs. Most of the
mosaic was damaged beyond repair, but she was able to
discern a few body parts represented in the intact sections:
there a set of bared breasts, here detailed genitalia of both
sexes first in congress and then separate. She found a con-
fusing scene with only male figures and decided not to
scrutinize the mosaic further.

She tingled in strange places when she looked at it.

She turned her head surreptitiously to gaze from the shed
to where Lucian labored. The day was unseasonably warm,
so he and the boy who helped him had removed their shirts.
The muscles in his chest and broad back bunched and flat-

tened. His sun-darkened skin glistened with a sheen of male sweat. The sight of Lucian bare-chested sent a flutter through Daisy's belly. Even stronger tingles settled between her legs. She jerked her gaze back to her lap desk.

She noted each item in her small curlicue handwriting on the fresh paper and found that reducing the pulse-jumping images to mere words helped ease their effect.

> *Item: one bacchanalian scene with three figures, two male,*
> *one female, on black glazed pottery.*
> *Item: one frieze of woman with swan. Limestone.*

Reading about Leda dallying with Zeus in the guise of a swan was romantic. Seeing the act depicted so . . . realistically was another thing altogether.

> *Item: one . . .*

Daisy's quill hovered over the page, dropping a blob or two of ink in her hesitation. There was something different about the next pottery fragment. The detailed ornamentation was just as explicit as the others. A nude young man was reclining on his elbow while a young woman hovered over him, guiding his erect penis between her widespread legs. Their gazes were locked on each other.

The man was reaching up one hand to touch the woman's face. The gesture was so tender; it reverberated with power through the centuries and made Daisy's breath catch in her throat. She wondered if she'd been laced too tightly that morning.

No, it's just that these Romans were real people, she thought. *Doing the loving things real people do.*

"Only they apparently did so much of it, one wonders when they found time to conquer the world," she murmured.

"Perhaps this was why they conquered the world." Lucian's voice sounded behind her, and she started. "In order to have peace to enjoy the gentler pursuits. Art, music, the delights of love."

She slanted her gaze up at him. "I wasn't speaking to you."

"Oh." He looked pointedly around the long shed. "I see no one else here, so unless you have an imaginary friend, I have to assume you intended for me to hear you."

"You might assume so if I'd known you were there." He'd donned his shirt once again, but hadn't buttoned it properly. A deep vee of dark skin showed at the base of his throat. Daisy looked away from him. "Honestly, for a large man, you're quiet as a cat when you wish to be."

"Or perhaps you were deeply absorbed by something." He leaned over her shoulder and looked at the painting of lovers that had so captured her imagination. "Ah! Yes, quite . . . inspirational. I see why you didn't hear my approach."

She pressed her lips together in a tight line. "It's still very rude to eavesdrop on someone else's conversation—even if it's only with themselves."

He narrowed his eyes at her. "Someone else said something very like that to me recently."

Blanche. Surely he wouldn't connect the two of them solely on the strength of that one tiny gaffe.

"Well, whoever it was, milord, they were right."

"No doubt she'd agree with you," he said with a laugh. "Unfortunately, I'm expected for tea with Lady Brumley and her daughter, and I can't greet them covered in grime, so I need to clean up a bit. I would ask you to join me, but—"

"I'm not in need of a bath at present," Daisy said primly. Why did he feel himself at liberty to make such outrageous suggestions to her? At the same time, the thought of

Lucian's warm skin and slithering soap bubbles left her slightly light-headed.

He snorted. "What a charming imagination you have. I meant join me for tea."

"Oh." Her belly writhed like a bucketful of eels. It was an honest mistake. Hadn't he . . . She squinted at him. She suspected he wanted to see if he could catch her with his craftily worded noninvitation to tea.

"No, thank you. There's too much work to be done here for me to stop for tea and silliness. No need to trouble yourself on my account, milord." The last thing she needed was to have to watch Lucian dance attendance on Miss Brumley. "Besides, I know both those ladies and they me. If your father should join the party . . ."

"Our little charade would be at an end, Miss Clavenhook." Lucian took her hand suddenly, all traces of teasing gone from his expression. "Thank you for understanding."

He truly was worried about his father, she realized. Daisy had been quite young when she lost both her parents, but she still had the loving support of her aunt and uncle and her four sisters. And her great-aunt Isabella, of course.

Lucian had only his father.

"It's all right. But you might send out a pot of tea and a biscuit or two," she said. "We who are about to die of hunger and thirst might salute you, but we won't be able to continue to work without a little sustenance. And I'd like to keep working here."

The teasing grin returned. "Ah, the Clavenhook curiosity. Long may it wave."

Some of the images Daisy saw that afternoon explained a number of mysteries; others created even more questions in her mind, but she couldn't discuss the disturbingly erotic art with Lucian. In fact, she tried mightily not to even think about him while she sorted and arranged and fit pieces together into startling pictures.

But she did anyway. He rose in her mind's eye unbidden. It was as if Lucian were still peering over her shoulder.

Perhaps it was because she was now seeing depictions of the adventures of the flesh she'd only read about in Blanche's journal. Perhaps it was because the men in the artwork were all blessed with hawkish dark good looks, an echo of Lucian's Mediterranean heritage. Or perhaps it was the knowledge that she'd be giving him lessons in kissing that evening as Blanche.

Her insides twisted in confused circles.

She turned away from the pottery to the stack of wax tablets. Lucian had skimmed over them, hoping for a reference to the missing Roman pay wagon, but he hadn't done detailed translations of them. Household accounts and bills of lading seemed safe enough. She settled to the work, taking another sip of the tea Lucian obligingly sent out to her. She kept "Rowena Clavenhook's" steel-rimmed spectacles at hand in case Lord Montford should make an unexpected appearance.

A distant rumble warned of an approaching shower. Daisy decided the shed would offer enough protection for her to remain at work. But after only a short time, the Latin etched on the tablets began to blur as if she were actually wearing the ill-fitting glasses. Daisy's concentration kept wandering to the Montford parlor, where Lucian was courting Lady Clarinda.

What on earth would Lucian find to talk about with Clarinda Brumley? The girl was useless. She gave new definition to *shallow*. Surely Lucian couldn't be taken with her.

Clarinda was appealing enough, Daisy supposed, in a plump, German-partridge sort of way. Or perhaps what drew Lucian's interest was her dowry, which was reportedly even more ample than the girl's shapely bosom.

Men married for money all the time, exchanging their name and title for fresh infusions of cash or lands. Even Daisy's uncle Gabriel had set out to do it once, but he fell in love with a penniless girl and couldn't bring himself not to marry her. Daisy hated the way money intruded on what should be a matter of the heart.

Quite often, it was painfully obvious in well-moneyed matches that the transaction was purely financial, and yet the world didn't call the men involved whores. Daisy frequently complained of the inequity. But her great-aunt Isabella, who'd been called many things, simply reminded her that butting her head against that particular wall would only produce a headache without any effect on the wall whatsoever.

Still, it seemed weak-minded for Lucian to court a woman for her money. Even though the world in general would heartily approve, she couldn't imagine why he allowed himself to be bullied into it. After all, he was a man who wasn't afraid of manual labor—an activity fashionable folk *would* frown upon—and he was stouthearted enough to pursue his dream even when the Society of Antiquaries laughed him from their halls.

If Lucian had to marry for money, why not marry her?

The thought startled the quill right out of her hand. She'd nearly set herself to the idea of never marrying. The long march of days alone stretched ahead of her now. She might enjoy her freedom in the sunshine of her youth, but the light patter of rain now plinking against the shed's roof reminded her that life was not always fine. Dark days of illness or loss might rise to meet her. And to go through those times alone was not a pleasant prospect.

Still, a woman must have scruples.

No, she decided as she bent to retrieve the fallen pheasant feather. If she had to purchase a husband, she'd do without.

Besides, if Lucian wouldn't accept her funds for his project, he'd never accept her fortune for his name. Not so long as his father hated her family.

With a sigh, she turned back to the tablet she was translating. Her eyes flared when she recognized a name.

Caius Meritus. The ancient thief.

She bent over her work with absorption. Lucian must have missed this one. Her quill flew across the page. If she could translate it quickly, she might be able to dash up to the manor house before the rain began in earnest.

And before Lucian could seriously court Clarinda Brumley.

"When one marries solely for financial considerations, one is exchanging one's body for the sake of mammon. In what respect is this different from harlotry?"
— the journal of Blanche La Tour

Chapter Nine

"And so you see, my dear Lord Rutland"—Lady Brumley punctuated her speech with an aristocratic sniff—"you simply must come to the Duke of Lammermoor's masquerade next month. Everyone who is anyone will be there and I know for a fact you received an invitation because the duchess is a particular friend of mine. She assures me you were included, as a favor to me, you understand."

"Thank you, Lady Brumley," Lucian said with resignation. The rain lashing the tall windows ensured that his digging was at an end this day, but he might have spent the afternoon more profitably engaged in organizing his finds alongside his new assistant.

"It will undoubtedly be the event of the Season," Lady Brumley proclaimed, then leaned forward confidentially. "They say the king might even be in attendance."

That meant debutantes lined up like a row of tulips, each scheming mama preening her own bud to best advantage, and an opportunity for him to trot out his threadbare best.

Not a chance in hell.

"If my schedule permits," he said evenly, "I will certainly avail myself of the duke's hospitality."

He understood why his father was promoting this match between him and Clarinda Brumley. The money was the least of it. Lady Brumley's family was well connected to the

Crown, having been elevated to the peerage when King George I came to the throne. Lady Brumley had worked tirelessly to shed her Hanoverian accent, and now she wanted to ally her daughter with the scion of an old English house. Lucian could trace his Beaumont ancestors back to the Norman conquest, and his Italian roots were well regarded as highly romantic. A venerable English earldom and a nouveau riche fortune. A match between Lucian and Clarinda made perfect sense for both parties.

But it still made his gut wrench.

"Well, of course you'll be there," Lady Brumley affirmed. "Dear Clarinda would be highly disappointed if you weren't."

Which meant Lady Brumley would be highly disappointed, and the lady's public rages were the stuff of legend. Her daughter dimpled prettily and loosed a simpering giggle, as if on cue. Clarinda's one virtue, aside from her impressive bosom and even more impressive dowry, was extreme shyness. The girl hadn't said two words since they began this interminable tea.

Politeness dictated a smile, so Lucian gave her one, which resulted in such a deep blush, he wondered if she'd burst a blood vessel or two. As heir to Montford, he knew his duty was to wed and breed sons, but he shuddered to think what sort of tongue-tied male children Clarinda might bear.

Yet his smile seemed to loosen her floodgates. Miss Brumley began prattling on about her ball gown for the fete, undoubtedly the most cunning bit of French artistry yet to grace the British isle. Then when she'd exhausted her string of superlatives about her gown, she launched into an unprompted diatribe on who was coming to His Grace's ball and who was too deeply disgraced by some social faux pas to dare show their faces—metaphorically speaking, of course, since this was to be a masked ball. Lady Brumley smiled at her daughter indulgently.

Lucian vowed silently never to so much as quirk his lips at her again. Her words flowed so fast and furious, it didn't seem that she had time even to snatch a breath. Lucian wondered if Clarinda breathed through her ears when her mouth was busy.

His ears were saved by the unexpected arrival of his manservant at his elbow.

"My lord, Miss Clavenhook is waiting without," the ever sedate Avery said. "It appears she may have found something of interest among your Roman antiquities."

"Has she?" That was fast. And perfectly timed, too. If Miss Clavenhook hadn't been in reality Daisy Drake, Lucian could have kissed her. He stood with alacrity. "Your pardon, ladies. It seems my presence is required elsewhere. Most pressing. No help for it, I fear."

Lady Brumley's lips pursed sourly. "And just who is this Miss Clavenhook?"

"My assistant, madam. Expert in Latin translation, a rather bookish sort, frightfully nearsighted, but most helpful. Now, if you'll excuse me." He bowed over each of their offered hands. "Thank you for coming. Lovely to see you. Avery will show you out."

He finally made good his escape, but not before being obliged to reiterate his intention to attend the duke's blasted ball two more times. When he closed the parlor door behind him, he breathed a sigh of relief.

Daisy was waiting at the end of the long corridor, clutching something to her chest. She had those ridiculous spectacles perched on her nose.

He hid his smile behind a cough and strode toward her. It was deucedly thoughtful of her to keep up her Miss Clavenhook disguise in case his father should happen along. But no one would mistake her for a wellborn heiress at present.

A small puddle of rainwater pooled at the hem of her

sodden, mud-speckled skirt. Her blond hair, which had been artfully curled, now hung in limp, wet strands. Her lips had a blue tinge, and she was drenched to the skin.

But her smile was radiant.

"What have you found?" he asked.

"This." She thrust the tablet toward him.

He'd bet his fortune, if he had one, that she didn't have a clue how transparent wet muslin became. The thin fabric of her bodice clung to the tops of her breasts and followed the curves into the sweet hollow between them. Her flesh was rosy and glowing beneath the oatmeal muslin. Her corset was made of sterner stuff, confining and concealing the bottom half of her breasts. Her nipples were shielded from his gaze, but the slightly darker skin of part of one areola winked at him.

For a moment, he imagined dipping his hands into her bodice and freeing those bound breasts. Would they be soft and pliant in his hands? Would her nipples draw tight at his touch? His mouth went suddenly dry and his breeches were suddenly tighter.

"Lucian," her voice called him back. "Don't you see?"

That was the crux of the problem. He was seeing entirely too much at the moment. He gave himself a mental shake. As enticing as those breasts were, they were Daisy Drake's breasts. No good could come of unlacing that bodice.

"Oh, yes." He willed himself to look away from her and at the tablet.

"Here, *Caius Meritus,* signed by his own hand." She pointed to the signature mark at the bottom of the text. "It says . . . Oh, Jupiter! I can't read it upside down."

She turned it back around. "'Bought at auction: one female Celtic slave, answers to Deirdre, to serve the master's wife.' I thought you said Caius Meritus was a freedman. Why would he call someone master?"

"For form's sake, I imagine." Lucian took the tablet from her and ran his finger over the incised block. "Our man Avery refers to my father as 'the master,' and he's no slave. I suspect Meritus uses the word the same way, because the tablet I originally found declared the thief was a freedman. Seemed to be a particular bone of contention with the proconsul, Quintus Valerian Scipianus, that this Caius Meritus would serve the man who freed him so ill."

Lucian frowned down at the tablet.

"What's wrong?"

"Well, I know it's foolish, but I hoped you'd found something more. Something that gave us a clue as to where the hoard was stashed." Lucian sighed.

"But I did find something else about Caius Meritus. If we learn more about the man, perhaps we'll be able to figure out where he hid it," Daisy pointed out. "Did you think we'd find an ancient map with an *X* to mark the treasure?"

He chuckled mirthlessly. "No. I never expected this would be easy, else the Romans would have found it."

She tapped her forefinger on her lips. "Perhaps the theft wasn't about the money." Daisy's tone was suddenly more thoughtful.

"What do you mean?"

"Maybe Caius Meritus was motivated by something else."

"A whole year's pay for an entire legion?" Lucian said. "Of course it was about the money. What else could it be?"

Her green eyes went suddenly unfocused, and Lucian could have sworn he saw her thinking, little hypotheses being tried on and discarded like ill-fitting suits of clothing. He'd rarely seen men exhibit such intense concentration. A woman, never.

"How likely would it be for someone to steal that much and get away with it?" she finally said.

"You have a point," he conceded. "Not very, I imagine. Meritus must have known he'd have every Roman sword in the country after him."

"Then his motive wasn't to gain wealth." She folded her arms beneath her breasts.

Lord help him! One of her nipples eased above the confines of her corset, a taut pink bump in the smooth, wet muslin. His collar had suddenly become too tight for him to swallow. He tucked a finger in and gave it a tug.

"He did go to great lengths to hide the payroll till he could return and retrieve it." Lucian forced himself not to let his gaze wander from her eyes.

"Are you certain he meant to return?" Her delicate brow arched in question.

"Well, the tablet I found—"

"Which was written by someone other than Caius Meritus," Daisy put in.

He conceded the point with a nod. "The writer of that tablet was convinced he meant to."

"But if his motive was something other than wealth, he might not have intended to return," Daisy said.

"He had to know he might not outlive the deed," Lucian admitted.

His growing respect for her sharp mind didn't distract him from her pert nipple. It was as taut and inviting as Blanche's rouged ones. He wondered briefly if Blanche would let him practice kisses on anything other than her lovely mouth this evening. If she would, he had a definite idea where he'd like to start.

"What would drive a man to commit an act of such desperation?" Daisy mused.

She was so lost in thought she seemed not to notice that his attention was fading in and out as well. But Caius Meritus was not the object of his fascination. Her nipple was still above her corset, the darker skin visible beneath the wet muslin, but now it was perfectly smooth. Quiescent. Then, as if by magic, the little bump began to rise again.

"Love, perhaps?" she said.

"What?" That jerked his gaze back to her face.

"Perhaps Caius Meritus was motivated by love," Daisy explained. "Perhaps he had something to prove to someone."

"Does love entice a man to such lengths?"

"Love drives a man to all manner of stupidity. Have you forgotten Helen of Troy? Men have fought wars for love."

"That was lust, most likely." Lucian shook his head. "Not love."

"Then it was even more stupid."

"Well, if love makes a man stupid, I thank God I am not likely to be afflicted by it. However, I make no such claims for lust," Lucian said with a grin, and was perplexed by her scowl. Then he noticed her teeth chattering. "Come, let's get you into the study. Avery's laid a little fire there."

He put a hand to the small of her back and directed her into the tidy room. A lap robe was flung over one of the wing chairs, and he draped it over her shoulders. It shielded her from his gaze, and perhaps that was no bad thing. He derided himself for a cad. He'd been so caught up in the mysteries of her wet breasts beneath the thin muslin, he'd neglected to notice she was chilled from the rain shower she'd sprinted through to bring him this news.

"I'm sorry, Daisy." He used her name without thinking. "I should have realized you were cold and in need of a fire."

"That's all right." She snugged the rug around her with an almost feline grin. "You were distracted by my discovery."

He decided not to let her know he was distracted by something other than the tablet he held in his hands. Two somethings his hands itched to hold but shouldn't.

He heard the heavy tromp of boots and his father's voice in the hall. He couldn't make out the words through the thick oak door, but the tone was angry. His father was always angry these days. The stomping and growling faded as his sire moved on.

"Revenge," Lucian said softly. "Perhaps revenge spurred Meritus. Men are motivated by that dark emotion often enough."

Lord knew his father was. And Lucian had no clue what to do about it.

Chapter Ten

The sound charmed Caius toward the garden. The girl's voice was like a flute, all rounded and wispy, with air wrapped around the tone.

And sad.

In all his life—and as nearly as he could reckon it, he was around thirty years old—Caius had never heard such a lament. The song weaved its melodic fingers around his heart and squeezed.

He peered from the corner of the villa into the mistress's herb garden. The air was alive with the steady hum of tiny honeybees and the sweet scent of green, growing things. The new girl, Deirdre, was bent over, clawing at weeds, singing her sad Celtic song as she worked.

Then the song stopped and she straightened, arms extended over her head in a huge stretch. Her palla rose almost to her knees, baring shapely calves and delicate ankles. Her feet were naked, her toes and heels grass-stained. The fading sun flashed behind her, showing the separation of her thighs and a shadow of the dark triangle of hair under her thin palla. When she leaned down to grasp a long-stemmed cankerwort by its stubborn root, Caius saw the outline of her breasts swinging free.

The girl yelped suddenly.

Bee sting, Caius decided.

She stuck her finger in her mouth, sucking fiercely. The innocent gesture made his body respond in a not-so-innocent way. He'd desired women before, but none had ever made him stiffen quite so unexpectedly.

He'd never had a woman.

When he'd been a slave, his master hadn't permitted it. But now Caius was a freedman. If he wished, he might take a woman to his pallet. Though male slaves were in danger of emasculation if they were caught in unsanctioned coupling, a female slave was more prized if she proved fertile. He would bring the girl no harm if . . .

Without his conscious volition, he walked toward her. In the sparse amount of Celtic he'd gleaned from his dealings in the market, he told her to show him her finger. With care, he plucked out the stinger, still pulsing its venom into her reddened and swelling skin. He pursed his lips and blew softly on the spot.

"Better?" he asked.

Her smile washed over him like a breaker.

And he knew in an instant: he was a drowned man who just hadn't quit struggling yet. It was said to be not at all an unpleasant end once a man gave up.

Best to let the deep claim him.

*"The chase is far more important than the capture. A woman
will never hold more power in a relationship than when it
has yet to be consummated."*

—*the journal of Blanche La Tour*

Chapter Eleven

Daisy raced up the long curving staircase, lifting her skirts
and taking the stairs two at a time. Even before she reached
the safety of her suite, she was unbuttoning her muslin
overdress and calling out for Nanette to come quickly.

She didn't know how long she had till Lucian turned up
on her great-aunt's doorstep with that lewd little Faunus
figurine in his hand and lust in his heart, hoping to see
Blanche. But she'd bet her best frock she didn't have a quarter hour to spare.

"Oh, no, mademoiselle, if you wish to present yourself as
a woman of pleasure, you simply cannot rush your toilette.
It is not *done*," Nanette complained as she oversaw the hast-
ily prepared bath.

"He'll be here any moment, I know it," Daisy said from
behind the dressing screen where she plopped down on a
stool to yank off her stockings. They were a muddy mess,
but it had been worth it to see the pleasure in Lucian's eyes
when she showed him the reference she'd found to Caius
Meritus.

Besides, she'd sacrifice any number of stockings to pry
him away from the likes of Clarinda Brumley.

But she hadn't been able to rest on her laurels in the cozy
little study. Her simple muslin dress had barely dried before
the small fire when Lucian began to let her know—tactfully,

of course—that he had a previous engagement for which he had to prepare.

He didn't drop any names, but she knew he was thinking of his kissing lessons with Blanche La Tour.

With her!

She was pleased he seemed eager to see her as Blanche, yet it meant he rushed her out the door as herself.

She couldn't quite decide how she felt about that.

"Oh, no." She sneaked a peek behind the thick damask curtains down to the street below. The householders in the neighborhood were setting out their required lanterns in the growing dark, and Lucian was climbing down from the barouche with the Montford crest emblazoned on the side. "He's here."

"Ah, but it does no harm to a man to make him wait," Nanette said with a sly wink. The French lady's maid had been with her great-aunt for years, all through Isabella's scandalous and celebrated career as a courtesan. "In fact, whenever madame entertained a lover, she had a hard-and-fast rule that her gentleman must wait at least twenty minutes for her appearance, even if she had been awaiting his arrival for hours."

"On the theory that hunger is the best sauce?" Daisy guessed.

"*Oui,* mam'selle, you have it. *Exactement.* The appetite is increased with the waiting. It is how the game of love is played, *n'est-ce pas?*"

It seemed a little underhanded. Daisy preferred things more straightforward, but she couldn't quibble, since she was already engaged in a pretty flagrant deception herself. Still, playing Blanche was the most fun she'd had in years.

Wicked fun, she admitted, but fun nonetheless. An adventure worthy of the name.

Daisy sighed with pleasure as she sank into the warm hip bath and let Nanette scrub her back. Her belly growled softly, a reminder that she'd had only tea and biscuits since breakfast.

"Speaking of hunger, could we have a light supper served in . . . Jupiter! I don't even know where I'm to entertain him," Daisy said as she lathered her washing cloth with fragrant castile soap Aunt Isabella had had made especially. Even though soap carried a heavy tax, it was always plentiful in the Wexford household.

"But of course," Nanette said, "a courtesan always entertains a gentleman in her boudoir."

That made Daisy drop the washing cloth. She had to go searching for it by feel along the bottom of the copper tub. "I can't—"

"Of course not," Nanette said. "If you brought the gentleman to this room, he would immediately suspect something was amiss. A courtesan's chamber is arranged for entertainment. You have no couch, no chairs, no table for the cards, if he should wish to play."

Daisy didn't think Lucian had whist on his mind.

"Wipe the smirk from your face, *cherie*," Nanette advised. "I know you youngsters are taught that men are ravening beasts to be feared and avoided lest they throw themselves upon you at the least provocation, but it is not always so. Sometimes a man just wants a woman's company—a little tête-à-tête, a little harmless play. Perhaps the play ends up in bed, but even for the real woman of pleasure, such is not always the case."

"Really?" Daisy assumed men visited their mistresses solely for sexual gratification. Strangely enough, the idea that there might be a relationship aside from the bed seemed an even deeper slight to their wives.

"*Bien sûr.* A wife, she will prattle on about the household and the babies, always the problems and cares. But a light-o'-love, she talks about the man himself, his hopes, his dreams. Madame always said her gentlemen valued her friendship as much as her bed. But since your play is *not* to end in the bed, Madame has allowed me to set up the guest suite across the hall as the room of Blanche La Tour, ready for entertaining," Nanette said. "It never pays to do things by half measures, Madame always says."

"I suppose that will do." Daisy gnawed her lip thoughtfully. "I trust you, of course, Nanette, but I wonder if the other servants will spread tales of this little exploit of mine."

"Rest your mind, mam'selle. Jerome and I have been with Madame most of our lives. We never carry tales, and believe me, we would have plenty to carry should we wish it. But we owe Madame our living. How could we betray her? Lord Wexford's people, they feel the same. This house, she has many secrets, but she keeps them all, no?"

Daisy certainly hoped so. If word of this little farce ever came to light, she'd be ruined. Not that she minded so much for herself. Being unconventional had always appealed to her, even if it meant public censure.

But her family would be hurt, and there was her younger sister Lily to consider. It would be another couple years before she'd come out, and it wouldn't do to have a cloud of taint hovering over her because of Daisy's ill-advised romps. For fear of that, Daisy decided she'd end her association with Lucian as Blanche after tonight.

Then maybe he wouldn't be so hasty about showing her the door as herself.

"However"—the maid interrupted her thoughts, cocking a delicate brow at her as she helped Daisy rise from the water and towel off—"Madame wished me to remind you that you made her a certain promise."

"To guard my purity," Daisy recited. "Have no worries on that score. Lord Rutland is only expecting kissing lessons from his paramour this evening."

"Ah! But kisses quickly lead to other things," Nanette

said. "And kisses do not willingly confine themselves to the lips."

Daisy hadn't considered that. There were any number of places on her person that might enjoy the brush of Lucian's mouth. Clearly she hadn't read far enough in Blanche's journal. Several of the naughty Roman images rose up to taunt her imagination.

But this was just a play. Daisy might flirt with passion, but she had no intention of succumbing to it. She was in perfect control.

"Well, tell Isabella not to be concerned," Daisy said. "As you so wisely observed, this is how the game is played."

"The game of love, mam'selle," Nanette said with hooded eyes. "And sometimes the rules for that game sprout the wings and make to fly away. Come, *cherie*. I shall do your rice powder before you dress."

Lucian slapped his gloves against his thigh for the umpteenth time. What the devil was keeping her?

He didn't expect the earl or his wife to trouble themselves with him, but Blanche should have more consideration than to keep him cooling his heels in the Wexford parlor so long. He'd been working like a ditchdigger all day, except for when his father had him playing at gold digger with the Brumleys, and yet he managed to arrive on time, as promised.

He set the little Faunus statuette on Lady Wexford's Louis Quatorze side table. It mocked him with a leering grin.

"For one glimpse behind her mask, you'd wait too, old son," he grumbled to the goat-god.

His one regret in hurrying over here, he realized with surprise, was hustling Daisy Drake out of the study like an unwelcome guest. She'd proven her worth today by finding that little tidbit about Meritus. And her questions about the motive for the ancient robbery had set his thoughts racing in a new direction. Perhaps there was more to Daisy Drake than his experience with her pike hand proved.

Of course, as long as his father was on the rampage against her family, it wouldn't do for Lucian to try to find out. He was beginning to seriously worry for his sire. Sometimes, late at night, he'd wake and hear his father, drunk and loud in the study below his bedchamber. He wondered if a physician's leeches or purges would drain the venom from his father's soul.

Finally, the little French maid came to collect him, and he pocketed the Faunus statue. To his delight, instead of being escorted into some other parlor, he was led up the curving staircase to the second level of Wexford's grand residence.

The Promised Land, he thought, anticipation tightening his gut. The maid dropped a curtsy and flashed a knowing grin before a closed door on the long corridor, then bustled away.

His hand actually trembled when he reached for the knob. It was still a minor miracle to him that a woman like Blanche *gave* him so much of her time. Since he didn't have the coin to shower her with jewels as her other patrons had, he was determined to hold her interest by other means. He fingered the little Faunus in his pocket.

He hoped she'd find it clever instead of grotesque.

In the dim room lit by only a few tapers, Blanche was waiting for him. She lounged on the fainting couch, dressed in the most becoming dishabille. A beribboned camisole displayed her creamy décolletage.

Without nipples showing this time, he realized with disappointment. But Lucian decided in the next breath that it was good for a man to have a challenge.

He made a jaunty leg to her.

A lacy *casaque* flowed from her white shoulders to her hips. She seemed to have left off her hoops, for her long skirt completely covered her feet. No stolen glimpse of an ankle here, but he was more disappointed that she yet wore a wig and mask. However, when she extended her hand to him, he forgave her everything.

"Oh, Blanche, the day seemed so long," he said as he dropped a kiss on her knuckles, taking in her exotic jasmine scent clear down to his toes.

"Did it?" she replied in French. "And I feared the hunting of treasure would be so fully engaging, you would forget all about your promise to visit me."

"Nothing could keep me from your side." He knew she understood English, but she seemed intent on holding their discourse in his third language. It had been years since he'd dreamed in Italian, his mother tongue, but he feared his schoolboy French wasn't up to the task of dazzling this bird of paradise. But with any luck at all, they'd be communicating without need of words in no time.

Perhaps the French, like the mask and wig, was part of her allure. An air of mystery swirled about the woman like her expensive perfume. Lucian's pulse quickened.

"You did not find that which you seek?" she asked.

"No, not today." He suddenly remembered the goat-god in his pocket. "But we did find this. I promised you some naughty Roman art. I hope it pleases you."

She accepted his gift with a smile. "Pan, is it not?"

"Pan to the Greeks, Faunus to the Romans," Lucian explained, "but by either name, he's a randy little fellow."

"He is . . . gifted, no?" she said with a tinkling laugh as she drew a coy fingertip along Faunus's erection from its base to the broken tip.

Lucian swelled to rival the little horned god, imagining that same teasing stroke on his own skin. Lord, he'd never thought to envy a chunk of fired clay.

"Yet not without flaw," she observed, circling the broken tip of the statuette's phallus.

He swallowed hard, willing his voice to sound even. "It's rare to find a bit of antiquity that isn't a bit flawed."

"Or a person either."

"I think I found one." He leaned toward her. "You."

She laughed. "Perfection is not one of my gifts."

"I believe it is," he said. "And though I confess to extreme curiosity over your hidden gifts, I find the ones I can see nearly perfect."

"Only 'nearly'?" She swept her feet to the floor and patted the spot beside her on the couch.

"One thing would improve upon your perfection." He settled beside her without further coaxing. "Having you in my arms."

"Clever boy," she purred as she set the figurine of the goat-god on her silk-covered side table. "And yet, a woman should be wary of climbing to such a high pedestal as perfection. It seems a long way to fall."

"I'd catch you."

Her little tongue darted out and swept her bottom lip. His belly tightened in response.

"I believe you would," she said. "Let us make a test, shall we?"

And she slid her hands around him beneath his frock coat, sidling close. She tipped her head back. Behind her mask, her eyes, whose color he still could not determine for the dimness of the room, fluttered closed.

His mouth descended on hers by finger widths, as though he were an unworthy pilgrim approaching a shrine. When he finally covered her softness, pleasure washed over him like a warm flood. He gave himself to the wave without a second thought.

"Love is a game. The trick is to make sure both parties win. Or at least believe they have won."
　　　　　　　　　　　　　—the journal of Blanche La Tour

Chapter Twelve

Jupiter! Lucian needed no kissing instructions. As far as Daisy could tell, the man already knew perfectly well how to kiss. Either that, or he was the sharpest pupil in history.

He cupped both her cheeks and changed the slant of his mouth across hers, applying a little more pressure. Daisy let her lips part the tiniest bit and his tongue invaded her, hot and questing.

What would Blanche do?

She'd welcome him, Daisy realized as she twined her tongue with his in a warm, wet sparring. She suckled him and heard his low groan. He stole all the breath from her lungs and replaced it sweetly with his own.

Everything inside her went soft and liquid. She turned the tables on him and slipped her tongue into his mouth to explore. He mirrored the welcome she gave him.

She ran a hand up the indentation of his spine and he shifted closer. His hands left her cheeks, sliding along the sides of her neck and down to her shoulders. Very gently he pushed the frilly *casaque* off to slip down her arms.

Then his kisses wandered down to her jawline. Tendrils of pleasure followed in their wake. He kissed his way along her neck to the soft indentation at the base of her throat, his warm breath streaming over her chest and sneaking between her breasts. Her nipples ached.

She sighed his name.

"I like the sound of that." He nibbled his way up to her earlobe. "The way you said my name. For a moment there, you didn't sound a bit French."

Jupiter again! She forgot to pronounce it *Loo-see-ahn,* as Blanche would. At least, thank heaven, she'd used but a wisp of a voice, so the chances of his recognizing her were slim.

"And is it so bad, you think, that I am French?" she asked in Blanche's language, using the moment as an excuse to pull back from him to a place of relative safety. Not too soon, either. He nearly had her trembling with need.

"Not a bit," he said, his own tone ragged. "It's just that my French isn't the best, and it seems you use it to keep me at a distance."

If that kiss was distant, she was lost if he got close.

"I think you've demonstrated that you have no need of my lessons on the art of the kiss," she said, rising to her feet. She'd remembered at the last moment to insist on the high heels she'd worn before as Blanche. She tottered over and sat at the small table. "Please come and join me."

His brows drew together, and she wondered if he'd discerned her secret. Other than the brief slip when she practically moaned his name, she couldn't point to any un-courtesanlike behavior.

Then he rose from the fainting couch and took the other chair at the table.

"Nanette will be bringing a bite of supper for us soon," she informed him. "I do hope you have an appetite."

"That, mademoiselle, is not in doubt."

His rakish grin told her that food was the last thing on his mind. She opened the deck of cards and executed a perfect shuffle. Holding the cards felt safe, as though the fifty-two thin pieces of paper were somehow shields.

"You would perhaps enjoy a game while we wait?" she asked.

"Only if it's a game of chance," he said.

"And what will you wager?" Daisy wondered. If his financial state was as bad as she thought, gambling was not the wisest course.

"Right now, you and I are partners in my search for the Roman treasure, split in half when we find it," he said. "For each hand I lose, one percent more of the money we find will be yours."

"Ah! And if I lose, that one percent shifts to you," she guessed.

"No." A slow smile spread across his face. "I'll take my winnings now in satin."

"How do you mean?" she asked, thankful he couldn't see her puzzled frown behind the half mask.

He reached forward and gave the top ribbon on her camisole a tug. The knot gave and her bodice sagged open enough to bare the meeting place of her breasts above her pounding heart.

"Do we have a wager?" he asked. "Or are you afraid you'll lose?"

A true *fille de joie* wouldn't be able to resist such a naughty game.

"Ah! *Monsieur le Vicomte,* either way I win." Daisy shuffled the cards with more bravado than she felt and dealt the hand.

She lost the first round and, with resignation, started to untie the next ribbon.

"No, no," he said. "Allow me."

Very slowly he pulled the end of the bow, and Daisy felt her supportive camisole give a bit. More of her breasts spilled out. Still not as much as he'd already seen that first night at the masquerade, but enough that the heat of his gaze made her skin flush rosily.

And between her legs, her still-hairless folds began to ache. She shifted on her seat, but nothing eased the throbbing.

Before he drew his hand back, he pushed the edges of the

satin camisole aside, brushing her exposed skin with his fingertips as he did so. Now her nipples were scarcely covered. In fact, if the hard little points weren't holding up the fabric, she'd be bared already.

Another lost hand, or even a deep breath, and . . .

"There," he said. "Much better. No point in unfastening that contraption if the blasted thing stays in place."

"We did not wager on touching. Merely on satin," she reminded him.

"Perhaps we should amend the wager then," he said. "When I win, I may touch whatever I see."

Lucian drew his knuckles softly over the swell of her breast. A jolt of heat lightning streaked to her belly and stayed to simmer in an ever-tightening circle of warmth.

"Then we should adjust the wager the other way as well," she said. "How shall you feel if I lay claim to your breeches buttons with each hand that falls my way?"

He chuckled. "Ah! Mlle La Tour, either way, I win."

She'd blundered badly and she knew it, but she was momentarily saved when Nanette rapped at the door with their supper. If the maid noticed that Daisy was showing a good bit more skin than when she last saw her, Nanette was tactful enough not to show surprise. She laid out the fine china and silver for them, and left with a wink and a smile, but fortunately no comment.

Daisy lifted the silver chafing lids.

Oysters and chocolate. Aphrodisiacs both. As if Lucian needs that sort of encouragement!

Lucian helped himself to a couple of oysters while she poured tea for them.

"How did you find the assistant I sent 'round to represent me?" She dropped a lump of sugar into his tea and added a dollop of sweet cream.

"I take it you mean Miss Drake?" he asked, dabbing at his lips with a linen napkin. "She's competent."

Competent! Was that all the man could say for her?

"I understand she's an accomplished Latin scholar," Daisy said primly.

"Is that why you sent her?"

"Well, yes, of course," she said. "The dear girl did confess to me that she is extremely interested in Roman antiquities."

"I'm well aware of the *dear girl's* . . . curiosity about them," he said.

"Then, too, she's my hostess's great-niece, so it was the politic thing to do," Daisy said, wishing she'd never broached the subject.

"I was surprised that you didn't send a man who could help with the actual labor," he said as he selected a piece of chocolate and offered it to her.

She allowed him to tease the sweet treat over her bottom lip before popping it into her open mouth. Daisy closed her eyes and let the chocolate dissolve slowly on her tongue.

When she opened her eyes, she found him studying her intently. Not her nearly exposed breasts. She would have expected that. Lucian's gaze was fixed on her eyes. To divert him, she offered him a chocolate, taunting his mouth with it as he had hers.

"The money I sent will more than pay for laborers to do your digging. That way you and"—she barely caught herself before she said "I"—"you and Miss Drake can do the more scholarly work together."

"And it doesn't bother you that I'll be working closely each day with an attractive young lady?"

Attractive! Well, that's several steps up from competent, *at least.*

"Not in the slightest." Especially since the competition for his attention was herself. "Were you hoping to make me jealous, Lucian?"

"Never mind," he said. "I'm sure you're a stranger to such an emotion."

"*Bien sûr*. For one's heart must be involved in order to feel jealousy," she said, remembering the real Blanche's thoughts on the matter. "You and I . . . what we have is a pleasant diversion. Nothing more."

"Well, good," he said, agreeing with her assessment of their relationship more quickly than she'd hoped. "Then perhaps you'll advise me in a matter of the heart."

"*Oui?*"

"I plan to show a certain young lady that I admire her soon," he said. "Perhaps you can help me know the right way to go about it."

He wants me to help him woo Clarinda Brumley. Not bloody likely.

It wouldn't be very ladylike, or even very Blanche-like, to voice such sentiments, but she could jolly well think them as loudly as she wished!

"Here is what you should do." She leaned toward him, forgetting for a moment the way her bosom was poised for exposure. "Ignore the lady. If you are in the same room, do not even acknowledge her presence. Whatever you do, be as aloof as possible, and she will be panting in your wake in no time."

"By heaven, mademoiselle! You make it impossible to ignore you." He reached forward to circle an exposed nipple. When she started to pull back, he stopped her by splaying his whole hand over her breast, which was now quite bared. "We can touch what we see, remember."

"So we can." She willed herself to relax into his hand.

He continued his unhurried exploration of her breast, drawing his fingertips over her skin in featherlight strokes. She seemed to have grown a second heart, and it pounded between her legs. Daisy narrowly resisted the urge to squirm in her seat.

"How will ignoring her make her want me?" he asked.

"It is clear you are not a student of human nature, monsieur," Daisy said, trying to come up with a valid reason for such poor advice. Maintaining a courtesan's composure while he taunted her nipples nearly had her grinding her teeth. "Since the Garden, we have ever wanted that which is forbidden. If you are distant, the lady will see you as a challenge and act accordingly."

Not Clarinda Brumley, Daisy knew. That young lady had to be coaxed into each conversation, and if it were not about either fashion or gossip, it would be a short exchange indeed. If Lucian ignored Clarinda, she'd simply sit like an inanimate lump unless her mother pressed the issue.

And if Lady Brumley was affronted by Lucian's slight, so much the better.

"If you're sure," he said doubtfully while the pad of his thumb thrummed her nipple.

"Absolutely," she said, feeling like a plucked string. Her whole body seemed to vibrate in concert with her breasts.

One side of his mouth hitched upward. "Then I will implement your excellent idea. You really think it will work?"

"Indeed," she affirmed, her tone breathless.

"Upon your word, I'll try it, then," he said, pulling back his hand.

Daisy bit the inside of her cheek to keep from crying out for him to continue pleasuring her with his fingers. Who would have thought a woman's nipples were so sensitive?

Lucian pushed back his plate. "And now, mademoiselle, I believe we have a card game to finish."

Whether by accident or design, Lucian's luck soured. Daisy found herself fighting to control the trembling in her hands as she undid his breeches buttons. More than once, her hand brushed his hardened groin in the process.

What's he got in there? A lead pipe?

He was still covered by his drawers, but only barely, and he'd just turned up the losing hand.

He made a *tsk*ing noise with his tongue and teeth. "Looks like I can't draw a winning card to save my soul."

"Oh, my dear Lucian," she said. "I greatly fear this game is of no benefit to your soul whatsoever."

"Maybe not, but the rest of me enjoys it immensely." Lucian stood, the better to present his remaining buttons.

She willed her hands not to tremble as she unfastened one side of his drop-front fly. The thin cotton fell forward and the tip of him was exposed above the cloth.

She'd seen artistic representations of penises in terra-cotta. The little Roman lamp sprang to mind. And a few in granite, most notably the one on the nude statue in Lord Wexford's grotto in the center of his garden maze. There were even one or two displayed in quiescent form in the classical painting in Aunt Isabella's boudoir.

But this was the first one Daisy had seen in the flesh. Of course, she could see only the head, the dark skin pulled smooth around the tiny mouth at the tip. Already she could tell the little Roman lamp hadn't been anywhere near life-size. Lucian's penis leaned toward her of its own accord, straining at its cotton prison.

"Remember," he said, his tone husky, "in this game, what we can see, we can touch."

"From childhood, women are schooled to tell men no, to stop them from acting upon their baser instincts. If men are unable to control themselves and need women to keep them from succumbing to the rages of lust, why, I ask you, are we dubbed the 'weaker sex'?"

—the journal of Blanche La Tour

Chapter Thirteen

Daisy swallowed hard. To her surprise, she discovered her hand fairly itched to touch him.

But how to go about it?

A circuitous route seemed safest. She circled his navel with her fingertips. A narrow line of dark hair led downward, spreading when it reached his groin. She followed the trail. She teased along the tip of him, exploring the smooth head and the spongy flare.

When she brushed over the bit of skin just below the head, Lucian groaned. A small pearl of liquid glistened at the tiny opening.

There was undoubtedly a good bit more of him, but the flap of his fly was still fastened on one side. Daisy looked up at his face.

Lucian was gazing down at her. His snapping dark eyes were now hooded and hungry. He was having difficulty controlling his breathing.

"Will you play another hand?" she asked. "Or do you yield the next round to me?"

"I yield," he whispered. "God help me, I can do nothing else."

Daisy accepted his surrender with a smile and turned her

attention back to his groin. She slowly unfastened his last remaining button and let the cotton flap fall.

"Mon Dieu!"

"You're not seeing anything that surprises you?" A bit of worry crept into his tone.

"Not at all," she assured him. Daisy reminded herself she was supposed to be Blanche La Tour, courtesan. She should be quite familiar with the amazing mysteries of a man, but it was hard not to be impressed by him. "A woman is allowed to appreciate male beauty when she sees it, isn't she?"

He brushed her cheek with his knuckles and grinned down at her. "You are a wonder."

She stroked his full length, reveling in the smoothness and warmth of his skin. She cupped his bag, fondling the twin lumps hidden inside. His breath hissed over his teeth.

"I haven't hurt you?" she asked.

"No, but you drive a man to his knees." He suited the action to the words and dropped before her.

He leaned in and kissed her again, but this time, the kiss was tinged with urgency. His hands once again found her breasts.

"Will you yield the next hand to me?" He breathed into her ear between kisses.

"I yield." She palmed his cheeks and brought his mouth back for another kiss. "I can do nothing else."

He pulled at the next ribbon, but the satin fouled into a hard knot. He gave the front of the camisole a good yank, completely freeing both her breasts, setting them on the camisole's padded shelf.

He pulled back to look at her. "You're so beautiful."

Daisy's flesh glowed under his unabashed approval.

Then he flashed her a grin. "According to the rules set down, what we can see, we can touch. But we didn't say it had to be with our hands, did we?"

Her nipples drew tight. She wondered if the touch of his

mouth would still the ache or make it worse.

"No," she said in a breathless whisper, "we didn't say it had to be with our hands."

His kisses started at the base of her throat and moved south.

Daisy gasped when his mouth closed over her nipple. Blanche's journal had mentioned the pleasure to be found in having a lover suckle and tease one's nipples, but the courtesan had woefully understated the case. Bliss spread over Daisy's entire body, but she fought the downward pull in her groin.

She ran her hands over Lucian's head, wishing he hadn't lashed his dark locks back in such a neat queue. If he'd let it fly free, his wonderful thick hair would curl around her fingers.

Lucian kissed his way through the valley that separated her breasts and nibbled up to the other stiff peak. This time he bit down just hard enough to make her cry out.

His head jerked up. "I didn't hurt you, did I?"

"No." She gasped, clutching his shoulders for support. The ache between her legs was fast becoming unbearable. Lucian's little love bite sent a streak of pleasure to the region that was so sharp, it was a knife's edge from pain. "But that was positively wicked."

"I'm sorry."

"Don't be," she said with a smile. "I enjoyed it immensely. Are you certain you've no experience with this sort of thing?"

"Well, one hears things, of course, and I confess to having seen a few French postcards from time to time," he admitted.

Daisy had heard rumors of those explicit pictures that no legitimate post would ever carry. Like the anatomically detailed ancient Roman art, a wealth of sensual information was said to be conveyed on those little cards.

"But no words, no pictures can come close to actual experience." He held her close and rested his forehead against hers.

"Do it again," she urged.

He didn't need to be told twice. His mouth found her nipple again. The little nip sent the same jolt of white-hot urgency streaking through her. Daisy wondered if she'd missed the passage in Blanche's journal about love bites or if her experience had surpassed the courtesan's in this instance.

Lucian straightened to kiss her lips again, and she suddenly remembered his open fly. Her hands wandered from his shoulders, caressing his chest, his flat belly, and found his hot shaft waiting for her touch.

"Life-size is ever so much better than the pale imitations," Daisy said when he released her mouth for moment.

He jerked back and stared at her. "Why did you say that?"

Jupiter! She bit her lower lip. Even though she still spoke in French, Daisy had accidentally let something she'd say as herself slip out in the heat of the moment. She forced what she hoped was a gay, courtesan-style laugh.

"My dear Lucian! Miss Drake told me of the very naughty way you baited her about her interest in the Roman phallic lamp." She stroked his full length in an attempt to distract him. It seemed to work, for his dark eyes glazed over as she teased his taut skin with one hand and cupped his scrotum with the other. "It really was too bad of you."

"I think you like bad, Blanche." With a feral male growl, Lucian scooped her up and carried her to the bed. "You certainly bring out the wickedness in me."

He dropped her on the thick feather tick, and Daisy sank into the soft mattress. Lucian followed her, covering her body with his. His weight felt wonderful, as if he were claiming her. Somehow, her legs separated of their own accord and his hips settled between them. Only the thin fabric of her skirt shielded her throbbing mound. Propped on his elbows, he laved her nipples, suckling, licking and tugging till Daisy nearly cried out.

The wanting was so keen. A tear slipped from the corner of her eye to slide beneath the half mask and disappear into her wig.

Why hadn't Blanche's journal warned how powerful these urges were? Even Aunt Isabella's caution was far too tame for the wildness that surged through her. Daisy was stretched on a rack, but she didn't want the torment to stop.

Lucian kissed her lips again and then her cheeks. He ran the tip of his tongue along the bottom of her mask.

"Take it off, Blanche," he whispered. "Let me see your face."

That would never do. "No, Lucian. No man ever sees my face."

He raised himself higher on his elbows. "Never?"

She shook her head.

"Even your lovers?"

"Especially my lovers," she affirmed. "A woman must retain a part of herself, you know."

"You haven't a scar or some other disfigurement, have you?"

"Of course not."

"No carbuncle on your nose?"

She swatted his chest.

"Then why must you hide?"

"I'm not hiding," she said with indignation.

He traced her jawline with his fingertips. "Your skin is like satin. Surely the part under the mask must be starved for air and sunlight."

"My skin is fine just as it is," she said stiffly.

"Is it this soft all over?"

She smiled at him, thankful for the distraction that let her regain a bit of control. "I would leave that to you to discover, but we have well exceeded the bounds of our arrangement already. Our agreement was an exchange of naughty art for kissing lessons."

"Practice makes perfect." He descended for a deep kiss. Daisy followed him willingly to that hot, dark place where pleasure was the only law. When he pulled back up, she laced her fingers behind his nape.

"You are a master of the kiss, Lucian Beaumont," she said breathlessly. "I believe my work is done."

"Surely there is more to be learned about pleasing a woman." He nuzzled her breasts.

"Undoubtedly." The ache between her legs kept advancing and retreating. Now it was on the march again with a vengeance. Where had he learned how to torment a woman so thoroughly?

"I've heard it said that there is a place on a woman's body that, if touched, drives her wild," Lucian said. "Is this true?"

Daisy didn't see how she could feel any wilder than she did at the moment, but she allowed that it might be possible. She really needed to finish reading Blanche's journal. "Where did you hear such a thing?"

"At the clubs. Men talk, you know. Sometimes, it's all bluster, but you never know when they've dropped in a nugget of truth," he admitted. "Please, Blanche, is there such a place?"

She pushed against his chest and he rolled off her.

"There is, isn't there?"

"If there were, it would give a man more power over me than I wish him to have," she said, trying to sound as Blanche-like as possible. "Why should I tell you?"

"Tell me? I was hoping you'd show me." Lucian reached down and slid a hand under her hem. His palm moved steadily up her leg.

Daisy started when his hand left her thigh and settled over her sensitive, hairless mound. She fought the urge to arch into his touch.

"I'm close, aren't I?" he asked.

Daisy heard the blood rushing through her ears. Her head, her heart and her core were pulsing, throbbing in tandem. She had to regain control. How could she continue to masquerade as Blanche if she let him overwhelm her senses with nothing more than his warm hand?

"This was not part of our agreement," she said, willing her voice to sound even. "Kindly remove your hand."

He was still as stone for several heartbeats. Then he withdrew his hand and climbed out of the bed, tucking his shirttail back into his breeches. He strode over to the table, stiff-legged as a dog with his ruff up. Lucian retrieved his tricorn and cocked it on his head.

"Lucian—"

He turned to face her. "Is that all it ever is to you? Agreements? Trades? Goods received for goods delivered? Is there a heart beneath your lovely breasts, mademoiselle, or merely a ledger?"

"You know nothing of my heart." Daisy adjusted her camisole so her breasts were once again covered.

"Then it does exist," he said with a cutting tone. "I had begun to suspect it was as mysteriously missing as the Roman treasure I seek."

She wished suddenly that she weren't wearing a mask so he could see her dark frown. "Why are you so angry?"

"If you have to ask, you know far less about men than a woman in your line of work ought."

Jupiter! If Lucian didn't believe her ruse, he'd figure out her true identity in short order. There was only one other young lady in residence in Lady Wexford's home. Lucian would not take kindly to being deceived.

"And you know nothing of women if you fail to see the

chase as the highlight of the game," she said, calling up some of Blanche's very words. "A woman, even one in my line of work, enjoys being wooed. Once again, you rush in, Lord Rutland. If you would learn to please a woman, you must learn patience."

He studied the thick Persian rug beneath his feet for a moment. Then he looked back up at her and made a courtly leg in her direction.

"My apologies," he said. "You are a free spirit, Blanche. You own yourself. I understand that. I know I have no claim upon you."

He strode to the door and stopped with a hand on the crystal knob.

"But I wish I did."

He closed the door softly behind him.

Chapter Fourteen

Londinium, A.D. 405

The girl was there, just as Caius had hoped. He'd watched her surreptitiously for weeks. Each full moon, she sneaked out of her tiny cell of a chamber to perform some pagan ritual in the garden. He knew it was wrong to spy on her while she performed this rite.

But for the life of him, he couldn't bear not to.

She crouched for a moment, her head tucked nearly to her knees. Then she stood suddenly, raising her slender arms in the silver light. He thought he caught a whispered Gaelic chant.

Deirdre's back was turned to him, but he knew what was coming. Anticipation made sweat pop on his forehead. Languidly, she gathered most of her long hair up and twisted it into a knot on top of her head. The short curling hairs that escaped along her nape made Caius's soft palate ache. He longed to claim that tender skin with his lips.

The girl put a hand to the neckline of her simple shift and slid the coarse material off, baring first one smooth shoulder and then the other. A gray shadow along the indentation of her spine divided the perfect, moon-silvered skin of her tapering back. Her slender waist was revealed as the homespun continued its downward course. She eased the fabric over the flare of her hips.

Caius's palms burned to hold her inverted heart-shaped buttocks. His breath hissed over his teeth when she bent over to step out of her shift. For a blinding moment, he caught sight of the mysterious folds of her womanhood and the dusting of hair between her legs.

He touched himself, trying to still the ache. Nothing helped. He wanted the Celtic girl more than he wanted his next breath.

Then she began to dance. Moving to music he could not hear, she raised her arms and praised the moon with her whole body. Sinuous and slow, she circled the splashing fountain, turning gracefully on her toes, arching her back so her bare breasts were bathed in liquid silver.

Then the tempo changed and the dance became a frenzy. Her hips undulated as if she rose to meet an invisible lover's thrusts.

Caius thought he might die of wanting. The gardeners would find his body in the morning amid the lavender and rosemary, his member stiff and swollen with unfulfilled need.

Then Deirdre's dance stopped suddenly as she collapsed in a heap. She was so still, Caius wondered if she yet breathed. He stepped from the shadows.

And she raised her head to meet his gaze. A flash of knowing sparked between them.

Deirdre had danced for him. Not the moon.

He strode toward her, pulling his short tunic over his head and dropping it in the cool grass. She stood to meet him, but when he was an arm's length from her, she raised a forbidding hand.

"Do you love me, Caius?" she asked in her own tongue.

"Gods help me, yes," he whispered in the same language. "I do."

"Then I will have you," she said simply, and molded herself against him.

Her skin was warm and smooth and covered with a fine sheen of perspiration. Deirdre smelled of musk and earth and green growing things. He found her mouth and joined his breath with hers in a kiss tinged with desperation. His soul flowed out of his body and mingled with hers, a bonding too complete to ever sever without damage to both.

Without knowing how, he found himself atop her on the fragrant grass. He worshiped her breasts with his mouth, reveling in the small sounds of helpless pleasure that escaped her when he suckled and nipped.

She was wet and hot. Her legs wrapped around his hips as she urged him deeper. He lost himself in her dark womb and didn't care. He heard the rhythm of her secret music, moving in time with the silent Celtic rondelet.

His ballocks tightened as her wet sheath pulsed around him. He emptied his love into her, all his hopes, his desires, all he was; he gave himself without thought.

Afterward, they lay twined together without speaking. The stars wheeled in his head and the smiling moon blessed them.

"Women are ever painted as either saint or sinner. When will the world realize we are all both?"
— the journal of Blanche La Tour

Chapter Fifteen

The next morning dawned fair enough, but Lucian barely dragged himself out of bed. He blamed Blanche for his sleeplessness. She'd whipped him into an aching fury, then shoved him away like the heartless courtesan she was. He knew it was stupid to expect more.

The callow aspirations of inexperience.

She'd made no bones about the fact that she was a woman of pleasure. If he wanted a more intimate relationship with her, he'd have to produce the coin. Even though she'd seemed pleased by the Faunus statue, Lucian realized it would take something much shinier to induce her to reveal more of herself to him.

And yet he couldn't shake the feeling that there was more to it than just his lack of funds. Something else had made Blanche pull away. He'd bet his last good shirt she'd been as breathlessly excited by their explorations as he. He'd felt her tremble with need.

Was that usual for a courtesan? Surely one so well versed in the pleasures of the flesh would possess more self-control?

Or less.

She was nothing like he'd imagined a *fille de joie* would be.

Lucian tugged the bellpull for Avery.

"Good morning, sir." The butler appeared so quickly,

Lucian almost suspected Avery had taken to sleeping across his threshold like a faithful hound. "Will you be venturing out this day?"

Lucian knew Avery was wondering if he should lay out Lucian's only remaining decent suit of clothes. Since Daisy Drake had spoiled his other set by emptying her inkwell on it, he was left with only the black with pewter buttons.

"No, I'll be working at the site." Lucian ambled to his nightstand and poured some water from the pitcher into the basin. He leaned over and dashed a couple handfuls on his face. The bracing liquid drove the last cobwebs of fatigue from his mind.

"Very good, sir."

Avery disappeared into Lucian's threadbare wardrobe and emerged with a serviceable pair of breeches and a simple shirt. The butler handled the garments with as much aplomb as if they were the latest foppery from France.

"How do you do that, Avery?"

"Do what, sir?" He laid the garments across the foot of the bed and produced a small whisk broom from his pocket to give the breeches a quick brushing.

"Act as if things were as they used to be," Lucian said. "I know you're working harder than ever since the staff's been pared to the bone. We can't begin to pay you what you're worth, and yet you stay on, treating Father and me with the same deference, the same respect as when Montford was in its glory days."

"One does what one can," Avery said modestly. The tips of his ears flushed scarlet with embarrassment under Lucian's praise. "But if one may be so bold, sir, it has been my observation that whatever the underlying truth, things are as one perceives them to be. It has been my honor to serve the house of Montford all my life. I believe it to be a worthy pursuit, despite appearances to the contrary."

"A worthy pursuit." That described Blanche as well as

anything. A slow smile spread over Lucian's face. "You're a secret philosopher, Avery."

"Ah, young sir, you flatter me. Though I must admit I hold the venerable library at Montford one of the finest benefits of my position. I merely borrow the thoughts of greater minds," Avery said with a thin-lipped grin and a twinkle in his gray eyes.

Things are as one perceives them to be.

Lucian rolled that idea through his brain while he ate his breakfast porridge. He tried it on several different areas of his life to see if the observation would fit.

It certainly worked when one considered the nobility. His peers were no finer men and women than Avery and the rest of Montford's staff. In fact, he knew several titled gents who were downright scoundrels. And yet because they were *perceived* to be better, taught from the womb that they were somehow a class above, the perception became their reality.

"If I continue down this train of thought, I'll be on the road to sedition in short order," he muttered as he pushed back from the table and headed out to the excavation site.

As he neared the pit, he heard the scrape of shovels and the swish of brooms. Work had commenced without him, and from the sounds of it, there were several additional men laboring. On the far side of the site, Daisy Drake was crouched down, pointing into the pit. Her sunbonnet was of such ridiculous proportions, she resembled an oversize, beribboned mushroom.

"Careful, Mr. Peabody," Daisy said. "There's something protruding by your left foot. Switch to a broom till you've discovered what it is. Remember, carefully is better than quickly."

Even with the large bonnet, her exposed arms were pinking in the morning sun. Intent on her task of direction, she hadn't noticed Lucian's approach. Lucian crossed his arms over his chest and indulged in looking at her unimpeded.

Here was another case where perception might belie the truth.

She might be trouble with feet, but there was no denying Daisy Drake was an eyeful. Even when she was ordering about a group of workmen, her pale hands gestured with unexpected grace. She was round where Lucian liked a woman round. He suspected her corset didn't labor too much to narrow her waist. A Roman sculptor would have no complaint if Daisy were his model. Except perhaps that she was too fully dressed.

Ignore her, Blanche had advised when he asked how to go about showing a young lady he admired her. Daisy Drake was many things, but easy to ignore was not one of them.

Against his better judgment, Lucian *did* admire her. Too bad she was the niece of his father's bitterest enemy.

She tilted her head, and the bonnet hid the upper part of her face, leaving only her mouth and jawline in view. Lucian narrowed his eyes.

Was lack of sleep playing tricks on him? There was something about the full pout of her lower lip, the sharp point of her chin. He rubbed his eyes.

For just a blink, Lucian thought Daisy Drake could be Blanche La Tour's twin.

Or was he so besotted with the courtesan that he was seeing only what he wished to see?

Things are as one perceives them to be.

Surely he was mistaken. He searched his memory. Had he ever seen Daisy in the same room as Blanche? No, he hadn't. Still, that didn't prove anything.

He looked back over and found Daisy had dropped to her knees. She leaned over the lip of the pit, her posterior pointed to the sky.

A very unmaidenly pose. He'd wager his title she had no idea how erotically appealing she looked.

Blanche, on the other hand, would know full well what she was doing and milk the posture for effect. Daisy's attention was focused on something wedged in the strata of dirt below. She was so keen on whatever it was, she didn't concern herself with how she might appear.

Lucian had seen enough Roman art to imagine how she'd look with her skirt flopped up over her head, bare bottom smiling at the sun.

"Never a stiff breeze around when you need one," he muttered, tamping down that thoroughly rakish hope. Lucian walked around the pit and stood behind her for only a little longer than necessary. Then, since no breeze seemed to be coming, he cleared his throat.

"Oh!" Daisy righted herself and glared over her shoulder at him. "I see you've finally deigned to grace us with your presence, milord. Has it escaped your notice that half the morning is spent?"

"Seems you've managed well enough without me." Lucian strode forward to inspect the crew she was directing. "Who authorized hiring these men?"

"Your partner, Mlle La Tour," she said. "She thought her investment would pay their salaries, and their labor will free you to work on . . . well, to work with me on organizing your existing finds."

"And that was Blanche's wish?"

She squinted up at him. "Yours as well, I assume. Didn't you discuss it with her last night? Oh, you there!" Her gaze was dragged back to the pit. "Careful with that."

Daisy leaned down again, reaching for the newly excavated wax tablet. Her hoops swayed in the breeze. Her skirts pressed against her legs and conformed to the confounded wire contraption she had strapped to her hips, but she remained more or less decently covered. When she sat back upright, she was cradling the tablet.

"This is the third one we've found this morning," she said. She blew across the surface to try to dislodge some of the clinging dirt, but succeeded only in raising a billowing cloud of dust that had them both coughing and sputtering.

That settled it. He was definitely taking a slight resemblance between Daisy Drake and Blanche and multiplying it all out of proportion. Blanche would never risk dirtying her coiffure and gown in order to blow ancient grime from an old wax tablet.

"Here." He handed her his clean handkerchief. She wiped her eyes and then blew her nose soundly on it.

"I'll have it laundered and return it to you tomorrow." She slipped the hankie into a pocket pinned amid the folds of her skirt, then called down into the pit. "Mr. Peabody, please take charge of the others and remind them to be careful."

The new fellow tugged at his forelock and turned back to his task.

"Where did you find them?"

"Mr. Peabody was waiting here when I arrived this morning," she explained. "According to his letter of reference, he's served in similar capacity as foreman for several excavations on the Continent, Germany and Italy mostly. He'd caught wind of your finds and thought to offer his services."

Lucian frowned at the back of Peabody's head. "I'd rather hire my own people. This is a delicate situation."

"Ordinarily, I'd agree, but since you presented at the Society of Antiquaries, it's not as if you are working in secrecy," Daisy said. "Besides, where would you find someone with Mr. Peabody's experience?"

"Experience we cannot readily verify."

Daisy cocked her head at him. "He's already kept your

stable boy from hacking off the winged foot of an unsuspecting statuette of Hermes."

She turned and strode toward the shed. Daisy's words made sense, but doubt still niggled at him.

"Do you want to release them from service?" she asked when he didn't move to follow her.

As he watched, the team of workmen fetched up a delicate copper chain, the metal green with age. Peabody handled the find with as much care as Lucian would himself, placing it in a canvas-lined wooden tray and hoisting it out of the pit where Lucian and Daisy could retrieve it easily.

"There," she said behind him. "Are you satisfied?"

"I suppose."

"Come, then." She waved him toward the shed. "You and I have work to do."

Daisy massaged the bridge of her nose. Both she and Lucian had been working all day translating the newly discovered tablets. They stopped briefly for tea and biscuits when Avery brought out the refreshments, but even then, Lucian had spent the time poring over his notes, hardly speaking three words to her.

She glanced over at him. He'd cleared a space on one of the benches and was bent over a tablet, quill in hand, transcribing the contents of the ancient Roman manifest. His brow furrowed and his tongue was clamped firmly between his teeth in concentration.

I swear the man's ignoring me, Daisy thought.

Ignoring her?

In her guise as Blanche, hadn't she advised him to ignore the young lady he wanted to impress? Could it possibly be that he . . . ?

"Look here!" he said suddenly.

"You've found a clue about the location of the payroll?"

"No." His disappointment stripped an edge from his previous excitement. "But I have found another reference to our thief."

Daisy hopped up and strode over to join him.

"Oh! This seems to be a court docket of some kind," she said as she skimmed over the text. "Plaintiffs, respondents, pleas. Ah!"

Lucian ran a finger beneath the line in question.

"'Caius Meritus, freedman, requests permission to purchase the freedom of one Deirdre of the household of Quintus Valerian Scipianus,'" he read.

"That's the same name as the girl he bought for the proconsul's wife." Daisy settled onto the chair near Lucian and folded her hands on her lap. "Jupiter! Do you suppose he loved the girl?"

"The record on the tablet doesn't say anything about that," Lucian pointed out.

"Well, of course it wouldn't, would it?" Daisy said, warming to the idea. "In the process of reconstructing antiquity, some things must be inferred."

"Or fabricated."

"Why are you so certain he didn't love her?"

"My dear Miss Drake, you are assigning much more noble motivations to Caius Meritus than he may deserve. He was a thief, after all." Lucian's mouth curved in a crooked smile. "And a man doesn't have to love a woman in order to crave her company."

She narrowed her eyes at him. "Just as you don't love Blanche."

"My relationship with Mlle La Tour is not the subject under discussion," he said.

"And your motivations are ever so noble." Her tone dripped sarcasm.

His smile took a decidedly wicked turn. "Again, you infer that which is not in evidence."

Daisy narrowly resisted the urge to box his ears.

"You want evidence. Very well. Here is what we know. Caius Meritus bought the girl in the proconsul's name to serve in the ruling household. He subsequently attempted to purchase her freedom. It says here"—she stood and pointed to a row of characters on the ancient tablet—"that the request was denied. The only other thing we know about him is that he stole an entire Roman payroll. Is it such a stretch to imagine that these events are connected?"

"There's only one problem with your theory," Lucian whispered, leaning toward her.

"What's that?" Daisy whispered back. She leaned toward him, subconsciously mirroring his movement.

And was shocked to her curled toes when he slid a hand behind her neck and pulled her down for a kiss. His mouth claimed hers in a warm rush. When her lips parted for an instant, he was quick to send his tongue in for a scandalously sexual exploration of her mouth.

She felt herself go pliant as a reed by the riverbank. She could no more stop her body from rousing to him than she could stop her finger from bleeding if she pricked it with a needle. Moist warmth pooled between her legs.

But she didn't have to let him know it. She pulled back her arm and sent him a stinging blow to the cheek.

He released her at once.

"Why did you do such a thing?" Daisy demanded. His taste was still on her lips, his scent all she could smell.

"Because I wanted to prove my point."

"Which is?"

"I wanted a kiss, Miss Drake. So I did what most men would do given the opportunity. I stole one," Lucian said with smugness. "If Caius Meritus wanted the girl, why didn't he just take her and escape to the hinterlands? Why steal the Roman payroll instead?"

"Maybe she didn't want to go with him," Daisy said. "After all, I didn't want you to kiss me."

Her trembling damned her for a liar.

"Really? I could have sworn you didn't mind at first, but that's a discussion for another day, isn't it?" He stood and she stutter-stepped back to stay out of his reach. "Don't worry, Daisy. I'm not going to steal any more kisses to convince you." He strode to the open doorway, then stopped and turned back to her. His eyebrows hitched upward twice. "Not unless you ask me nicely."

His dark gaze was so knowing, she felt as if he'd suddenly caught her naked. His lips taunted her, and she realized she wanted him to kiss her again.

Very badly.

When she schooled him in kissing as Blanche, she'd created a monster.

A damnably attractive monster.

She pushed past him and stomped out of the shed, her shredded dignity trailing behind her like a broken pair of angel wings.

"There comes a point in every chase when the vixen must slow her pace, lest the hound lose the scent."
— the journal of Blanche La Tour

Chapter Sixteen

"Your face *is* flushed," the earl said as he stared down at his only son, who still lolled in bed.

Lucian had smacked his own cheeks several times before his father entered the chamber. Now he let his eyelids droop in what he hoped was a sickly fashion. "Please convey my regrets to Lady Brumley and her family."

"This is deucedly inconvenient." His father frowned at him. "Damned insolent of you to allow yourself to get sick. We accepted their invitation for a picnic and lawn bowling weeks ago."

You accepted the invitation weeks ago, Lucian amended silently. "I don't feel myself up to it, sir. Pray have me excused."

"It's all that mucking about in the dirt." The earl exhaled noisily but finally bobbed his head in agreement. "Well, you're no good to me this way, in any case. I'll make your apologies and send 'round the leech."

"Don't trouble yourself, sir. I'm certain this will pass." Even if Lucian were truly ill, they'd have to bind him to make him submit to his father's quack of a doctor, with his lancet bowl and evil-smelling purges.

If the physician had been able to help the earl quell his temper, Lucian might have thought better of him. The earl's melancholy was getting worse, his late-night drinking louder and more destructive. Lucian had had Avery hide his father's pistols for fear that he might harm himself. Last night, the earl nearly dismantled his study looking for the pearl-gripped pair. His shrieks and curses rattled the rafters when he couldn't find them.

When the morning dawned, Lord Montford shook off the black rage and donned his best remaining suit, chipper as a lark. Lucian chalked up the brightening of his father's mood to the prospect of a match between Lucian and Clarinda Brumley.

Lucian wanted to please his sire, but not at that cost.

If he'd judged his father to be his rational self, Lucian would have had no trouble standing up to him directly. But because he suspected the earl teetered on madness, Lucian was loath to do anything that might send him careening over the edge. Bedlam, the only hospital for those with troubled minds, had an evil reputation. Lucian didn't want to see his sire tossed into its maelstrom if he could help it. So he feigned illness instead of starting an argument.

Once his father left, Lucian threw off the bedclothes and dressed. He gave quick instructions to Avery to water the liquor in his father's cabinet, hoping to tone down his nightly drunkenness, and hurried out to the site.

Daisy would be there already, he was sure. No matter how early he appeared, she always managed to beat him there, almost keener about finding the treasure than he. She'd be head-down, puzzling over some translation or reassembling a bit of broken crockery.

He wondered if the girl ever slept.

In fact, now that he thought on it, she was looking a bit haggard of late. Dark smudges had settled beneath her green eyes, and more than once, he caught her nodding over her work in the drowsy midafternoon. He appreciated her dedication, but he didn't want her health to suffer for it.

In fact, there were many things he was beginning to appreciate about Daisy Drake—her quick wit, her scholarship and attention to detail, her creamy bosom.

Her lovely mouth.

He rarely looked at it without conjuring the memory of that stolen kiss. Perhaps it was his imagination, but he could have sworn he scented a slight whiff of jasmine when he claimed her lips.

Blanche's fragrance.

No, it was ridiculous. Daisy and Blanche could not be the same person. No respectable English miss would masquerade as a French courtesan. Daisy might be unconventional, but she was certainly respectable.

He peered around the corner of the open shed and found her in deep concentration over a pile of mosaic tiles. She was trying to re-fit them into the ancient plaster. A frown knit her pale brows together as her clever fingers worked.

He stared at her hands. Blanche had unbuttoned his breeches. She'd held his cock, caressed his balls and driven him nearly beyond reason. For a moment, he tried to imagine Daisy doing such a thing.

The notion was laughable.

In the simple muslin she wore to work amid the antiquities, Daisy's breasts were pressed together and up, the creamy mounds displaying her gender. Lucian had suckled Blanche's nipples, giving and receiving torment. He wondered if Daisy would tell him, as Blanche had, to nip her again.

He almost snorted aloud.

Daisy tipped up the portion of mosaic to get a better look at it, and all the little tiles spilled off onto the rough plank bench.

"*Maudit, merde et sacre bleu!*" Daisy swore with vehemence.

Lucian staggered backward. The French invectives might have poured from Daisy's throat, but the voice sounded exactly like Blanche's. He ducked back around the corner, his mind reeling.

Daisy Drake and the French courtesan Blanche La Tour were one and the same. He was almost certain of it.

Almost.

Frustration sizzling, Daisy scooped up all the tiny pieces and started over. As soon as Avery told her that Lucian and his father were expected to call on the Brumleys, she purposely picked a task that would occupy her for the better part of the day. Her annoyance over Lucian's social calendar spilled into her work on the mosaic.

"Good morning."

His voice nearly knocked her off the little stool upon which she perched. Lucian appeared in the doorway, his lean, masculine frame silhouetted by the morning sun, as beguiling as the fallen Angel of Light himself.

"Oh! I wasn't expecting to see you," she said. "Avery told me you were off to Lord Brumley's estate for a day of merrymaking."

"I had a change of plans," he said curtly.

"Clarinda Brumley will be disappointed."

"It will do her good not to see me," he said with a quick grin.

Daisy's belly clenched. He was ignoring Clarinda, just as she, as Blanche, had advised.

Jupiter! He must truly want the match then.

"What have you there?" He moved to stand over her.

"A mosaic," Daisy said. "I can't be sure I have all the pieces, but I believe it's a representation of Ariadne." She held a small tile up for him to see. "Doesn't that look like part of a spool of thread?"

He leaned down and squinted at the tile. His fresh, masculine scent washed over her, and Daisy forgot to exhale for a moment.

"I think you're right," he said, straightening to his full height. "Poor Ariadne. First she saves Theseus from the Minotaur with her neat little rope trick, and then the brute deserts her on Naxos."

"One might argue that's the way of all men," Daisy said sourly.

After all, Lucian tried to seduce her as Blanche, and forced a kiss on her as herself, while in the midst of a politically and financially expedient courtship with Clarinda Brumley.

"That's a cynical outlook." He pulled a face at her.

"I'd argue that it's realistic." Daisy stuck her tongue out at him in retaliation. Some things about their relationship had not changed a whit since they were children. "Nowadays, a woman must be prepared for a man to pledge his undying devotion and then keep a light-o'-love on the side."

Lucian cocked a brow at her. "For an English maiden, you seem to know a good deal about men."

"I know lots of things," she said tiredly. Blanche's memoirs were filling her head and stealing her sleep. "You might be surprised."

Lucian considered her carefully for a moment, then turned his attention to the remains of the Ariadne mosaic.

"Well, we ought not shed too many tears for Ariadne," he said. "There is a variation of the tale that says that after she was abandoned by Theseus, she caught the eye of Dionysus. Not a bad end for a mortal woman."

"You do know your mythology, don't you?" Daisy said.

"I know lots of things. You might be surprised." He leaned over her shoulder, picked up a tile and placed it in a likely spot. "I surprise myself sometimes."

Well, that's odd.

Did she imagine it or did he just sniff her hair?

"What's that fragrance you're wearing today?" he asked.

"I'm not wearing any," she said. "Too many bees in this field to douse myself with rose water."

"It doesn't smell like rose water."

Each evening, just in case Lucian should take it into his head to visit, Daisy donned her Blanche disguise. That included a liberal spritz of jasmine. She did her best to scrub it off each morning, but evidently Lucian's sense of smell was keener than most.

"Perhaps something's blooming nearby," she said.

"Perhaps." His dark eyes were hooded as he looked down at her. There was something different in his gaze, a sort of disbelieving fascination. He stared as if he'd never seen her before.

She wondered if she'd suddenly sprouted a second head.

"You look tired," he finally said.

"I don't think that's any of your concern." She swiped at her eyes with both hands.

No, she wasn't sleeping. She burned the candles down reading Blanche's journal each night. Ever since Lucian had asked about that secret place on a woman's body that when touched might drive her wild, Daisy had been searching for the answer. The French courtesan knew a good deal about her own body, and she recorded her observations with astonishing frankness.

When Daisy did a little exploring on her own, she quickly discovered that Blanche knew her subject exceedingly well.

So now Daisy knew. She was still innocent, but definitely not ignorant.

But did she possess the courage to play the next hand as Blanche?

She didn't know. Sometimes at night as she lay on her bed, her chest ached with longing. She might never marry;

she knew that well enough. She was old for it now, and she didn't like any of her choices. Better no husband than the wrong husband.

But she wanted to be touched. And she wanted Lucian to touch her.

"I haven't been 'round to see Blanche lately." Lucian's voice interrupted her thoughts. "We parted rather badly the last time. Bit of a tiff. How is she?"

"She's fine. Busy."

"Hasn't taken a lover, has she?"

"No, no, of course not!" Daisy snapped, then amended quickly, "She's on holiday, remember."

"Ah! That's right." He turned away to begin working on the tablet he'd started translating yesterday.

Daisy tried to focus on the mosaic, but the tiles kept blurring before her eyes. "Blanche misses you."

He stopped, quill poised over his paper, and turned to her. "Did she say so?"

Daisy nodded. *In for a penny, in for a pound* . . .

"She wanted me to tell you . . ." Her courage faltered.

"Yes?"

Heat crept up her neck and kissed her cheeks with flame. "That she is ready to show you something you wanted to know about."

A slow, sensual smile stole over his lips.

"That's very . . . unexpectedly good news. Please tell her I shall attend her this evening. Would eight o'clock be convenient, do you think?"

Daisy swallowed hard. "She'll look for you then."

Chapter Seventeen

The longcase clock in the study below chimed the hour. Daisy checked her appearance in the mirror over her dressing table for the umpteenth time.

"He's late," she announced to her masked reflection.

Lucian had dismissed the workers early that afternoon, sending her home as well shortly before teatime. Daisy wondered if he'd decided to visit Clarinda Brumley after all.

Daisy turned away and resumed pacing. She still wasn't accustomed to the tall platform shoes she wore as Blanche. They slowed her progress a bit as she circuited the chamber, clacking furiously on the hardwood.

She wasn't wearing hoops. Somehow, she couldn't bring herself to don something that might impede Lucian's investigations later. So the fabric of her gown brushed against her thighs as she moved. Occasionally, the satin rubbed her sensitive mound. The slightest touch sent a little shiver over her. Even the pressure of her own thighs made tiny muscles contract in her groin.

Since she'd tested the eye-popping revelations in Blanche's journal about that secret place that could drive a woman wild, Daisy's body had risen in rebellion, refusing to quell its demands. Isabella warned her of dallying with her body's powerful urges, but Daisy hadn't heeded her.

Lucian wanted to learn from her. Now she was armed with the knowledge he sought. Her belly jittered uncertainly. Did she have the courage to allow him to touch her so intimately, when the mere thought of it melted her like hot wax?

A light rap at the door halted her pacing. Nanette peeked in.

"Your gentleman, he is arrived," she said.

Daisy drew a deep breath. "Send him right up."

"But, mam'selle, he must be made to wait in order to fully appreciate the honor you give him," Nanette said. "Twenty minutes, at the least."

"Now, Nanette," Daisy said. *Before I lose my nerve.*

"It shall be as you say." Nanette rolled her eyes. "But if you want my advice—"

"I'll ask for it!" Daisy snapped.

The French maid's eyebrows shot skyward, and Daisy felt instantly contrite. Nanette had been nothing but helpful from the very beginning of this caper. Daisy was churlish to take her frustration out on the woman who was more friend than servant.

"I'm sorry, Nanette. You're right. But five minutes only. No more."

Nanette smiled impishly and laid a shrewd finger beside her Gallic nose. "*Oui,* mam'selle. Five minutes."

Daisy sank into one of the chairs by Blanche's card table. No, perhaps standing was better. The difference between her height as Blanche and her normal stature was one of the most convincing pieces of her disguise. She popped to her feet.

Daisy crossed to the mirror and turned this way and that, examining her reflection once more. She couldn't see a bit of herself in the exotic creature who stared back at her.

Except the eyes. Behind her mask, they were enormous, full of trepidation.

She was about to share a part of herself with Lucian, a part she hadn't even dreamed existed until recently. It was rather like discovering a treasure and then sharing the secret's existence with a fellow adventurer.

What if he didn't like the treasure she had found?

Her heart drummed against her ribs.

A quick rap snapped her head toward the door.

"Come," she breathed softly in English, then remembered herself and switched to French. *"Entrez, s'il vous plaît."*

The door slanted open, and Lucian stood bathed in the brighter light of the hall. She forced herself not to run to him. He bowed smoothly and then entered, closing the door softly behind himself. The room was plunged once again into dimness, lit only by a single candle and the small fire in the grate.

"Hello . . . Blanche," he said, hesitating over her name for a bit.

Had he been about to call her Clarinda?

Irritation bubbled in her chest. Daisy Drake in the morning, Clarinda Brumley in the afternoon and now Blanche La Tour by candlelight. How did the man manage to keep all his women straight?

Maybe she wouldn't be bringing him along on any treasure hunts this evening.

Lucian moved quickly to her side, but stopped shy of taking her into his arms. He leaned toward her, and Daisy closed her eyes in anticipation of his kiss. Her eyes flew open in surprise when she felt his lips buss her cheek instead. He stepped back an arm's length away from her and ran his gaze over her.

Slowly. Deliberately. As though he were memorizing her.

"I've missed you," he said simply. "I know I haven't visited you in a while, but please know you are always in my thoughts. I was an oaf last time we were together. Dare I hope you've forgiven me?"

He smiled at her, and Daisy's heart expanded in her chest till it threatened to burst through her ribs.

Then reality washed over her.

Always in his thoughts? Did that include the time he kissed her as herself? She'd have sworn he didn't have Blanche on his mind while his tongue was making love to Daisy's mouth. The man's duplicity was growing by the moment.

"Of course I forgive you," she said.

After all, this was nothing but a play. Her heart couldn't be hurt if she simply remembered that none of this was real. She was a modern woman. She was Blanche La Tour, who took her own pleasure without a by-your-leave from any man. The heart had nothing to do with it. She waved him to one of the comfortable chairs by her flickering fireplace, then settled into the opposite one herself.

"It is good to see you, Lucian. How does your excavation progress?"

A decanter of port was on the small table between the two chairs. She allowed him to pour a glass of wine for each of them while he told her of his most recent discoveries.

"But I regret to report that we are no closer to finding the treasure than when you and I first spoke," he finished with a troubled sigh.

"No closer? How can you say that?" Did he think she worked for nothing every day? "Haven't you learned more about the ancient thief Caius Meritus? Don't you have a new theory about the reason for the theft?"

One of his brows arched in question. "I see you've been in communication with Daisy Drake."

She bit her lower lip. She had to tread carefully or she'd tip her hand.

"*Bien sûr.* She is my agent in this venture, after all." Then on impulse, she added, "Tell me, now that you have spent more time in her company, how do you find Miss Drake?"

"How do I find Miss Drake?" He swirled the wine in his glass and inhaled deeply before tasting it. "Granted, my experience with the fair sex is thin, but everything in me warns against discussing one woman with another."

Daisy forced an amused courtesan's laugh. "There is no danger when the woman asks for your opinion."

"My opinion on Daisy Drake," he said with a crooked grin. "Candidly?"

"I would never have you be less than candid."

"Very well, but remember, you asked." He leaned back in his chair. "First, Daisy is whip-smart and doggedly hard-working."

"Commendable," she said with a sinking sensation in her gut. "But not very exciting."

"Oh, I didn't say that. She's exciting, all right." A broad smile spread across his handsome face. "You should see her when she's just come in from a rain shower. The dear girl has no idea how transparent wet muslin becomes."

Daisy very nearly spewed port out her nose. She covered her mouth with her hankie and coughed violently.

"Her breasts are nearly perfect, dark nipples that perk right up through the wet cloth. They remind me of yours, Blanche, and that's high praise," he continued, ignoring the sputtering sounds she couldn't suppress. "Yes, Daisy Drake is as exciting as they come. Oh, I'm sorry. Have you choked on something?"

He hurried to her side and leaned her forward to thump her back. Daisy waved him off.

"No, no, I'm quite all right," she assured him.

"Was that too candid?"

One more cough pushed through her throat. "Well . . ."

"Because if it was, I apologize. But you did ask how I found her, and—"

"So I did." Her cheeks flared with heat.

It was one thing to display her breasts as Blanche. For Daisy to have done such a thing without even realizing it was mortifying in the extreme.

Still, she had invited him here this evening with a definite goal in mind. All she could think about was Lucian's touch, her hope that he would be delighted with her little point of pleasure. And she could summon the daring to venture that with him only as Blanche. She grasped her courage with both hands.

"But let's not dwell on Miss Drake now," she said. "I assume she relayed my message to you."

"Yes." He dropped to one knee beside her chair. "She told me you were ready to show me something I wanted to know about."

Daisy nodded, not quite willing to trust her voice. She swallowed hard. If her tone quavered, perhaps he'd attribute it to her coughing fit.

"The place that drives women wild," she whispered.

Delight glinted in his dark eyes. "You honor me, Blanche, and I confess that curiosity about that blessed spot is driving *me* wild, but in truth—and I can't believe I'm saying this—there is something else I'd rather have you do."

She blinked, not sure she'd heard him properly. She was ready to share her deepest secrets with him, but he seemed to be turning her down. Something inside her wilted.

"What?" she heard herself ask.

"I want you to remove your mask," he said. "I do want to know all you wish to share with me, but most important, I want to know you." He turned one of her palms up and placed a soft kiss in the center of it. "Please."

Jupiter! If she took off her mask, this little farce would be up, and she was not ready for it to end. The way his father hated her family, Lucian would never dally with her as herself. That one kiss he'd forced on her was merely his insufferably superior masculine way of proving a point.

"I never reveal my face to my lovers. You know that." She pulled her hand away.

"Oh, so I'm to be your lover now?"

"I didn't say that."

"It was inferred." He gathered her into his arms. "Daisy Drake is keen on inferred meanings, you know."

"No, I wouldn't know," she said stiffly.

"And here I thought you and she were great friends." He kissed her lips, a light, teasing kiss. "How about if we manage things so I can't actually see your face?"

"And how shall we accomplish that?"

"We could blow out the candle and bank the fire," he said as he delivered baby kisses along her jawline. He finished the string of nibbles with a light nip on her earlobe.

She closed her eyes as pleasure sparked down her neck. "No, the moonlight is too strong."

"Blindfold me," he offered.

Several tantalizing possibilities popped into her head. Blanche had devoted an entire journal entry to naughty little love games involving blindfolding one partner.

"You won't peek?" she asked.

"On my honor as a gentleman, I shall not peek." He raised his hand to solemnize the oath.

"You won't remove your blindfold without my leave?"

"If I must remain forever in darkness, I shall not remove it until you give the word." The smile in his voice teased her ear, but she knew he would keep his promise. Lucian had always been a stickler for honor, even when he was a knobby-kneed boy brandishing a wooden sword.

"Then I accept your terms, sir." She rose and rummaged

through the drawer of her dressing table for a silk scarf to bind around his eyes. "Prepare to lose one of your senses, monsieur, but be forewarned: you may find your remaining ones considerably heightened."

His smile was sin incarnate. "I am counting on it."

"Love looks not with the eyes, but with the mind; And therefore is winged Cupid painted blind."

—*William Shakespeare*

Chapter Eighteen

Lucian settled into the wing chair and closed his eyes as the dark cloth blinded him. Her clever fingers brushed his hair as she knotted the fabric behind his head. He waited, but every inch of his skin simmered with expectation. This was her game. He'd let her take the lead.

For now, at least.

Her fingertips ran through the back of his hair, smoothing it down, her touch featherlight. He heard the rustle of silk as she came around to stand before him. Lucian was fairly certain the beautiful "courtesan" who now took his hands and raised him to his feet was in reality Daisy Drake.

But there was still a niggling doubt in his mind.

How could Daisy know so much about tormenting a man? She was, in many ways, an unusual young woman. From their encounter at the museum and her work at his excavation, he knew she possessed a healthy curiosity about things of the flesh. But she was also the wellborn daughter of a well-moneyed family.

Would she really have engaged in that wicked little card game with him? Was it Daisy Drake's hand that had stroked his cock, fondled his balls and nearly made him disgrace himself with a total loss of control?

He hoped to discover the truth of the matter this night, even without the use of his eyes.

She stepped closer to him. Her jasmine scent weaved an intoxicating summons through his brain. Yes, he'd definitely smelled the same perfume on Daisy, but muted. More like a memory of the scent rather than the actual fragrance. As if it had been grafted into her skin and become a part of her essence.

Her skin.

She allowed him to pull off her gloves. He took his time revealing her flesh to his touch. Drawing out the exploration clenched his gut and drew his balls tight. He played with her bare fingers, lacing his with hers, caressing the soft backs of her hands and supple wrists. He brought one to his lips and sampled the thin skin there.

Her pulse jumped when he lingered.

Would a true courtesan react so strongly to a simple kiss? Wouldn't her responses be jaded by frequent and much more erotic stimulation? His insides knotted in a confused tangle.

Or perhaps that heightened sensuality was what made a courtesan so desirable. His father had told him once that a top-tier bird of paradise could make any man feel like cock of the walk. A courtesan's passion was pure artifice, of course, but it was damned pleasurable artifice.

Lucian kissed and nibbled his way up to the crease of her elbow. She trembled beneath his lips, and he heard her sharp intake of breath.

Lucian would stake his soul that small gasp was no whore's trick.

"Have you removed the mask?" he asked.

"Not yet."

"Then allow me." His hands slid up her arms to her bared shoulders, up the satiny column of her neck.

She's too tall, he realized suddenly. His perception of Blanche was always as being much more delicate, but if he hadn't been blindfolded, this woman could look him squarely in the eye. The crown of Daisy Drake's head would fit snugly beneath his chin.

His belly spiraled downward. Was that disappointment? Had he been hoping she was really Daisy?

"You'll have to remove my wig first," she said, her voice breathless.

"Gladly." He tried not to let puzzlement creep into his tone. Would a courtesan have a catch in her throat over allowing a man to take off her wig? He lifted the powdered confection from her head, and she took it from him.

"I need to return this to its stand," she explained. He heard the tip-tapping of her heels across the hardwood.

Then there was a clatter and a loud thump.

"Blanche, are you all right?" He put a hand to the blindfold, but remembered his oath in time.

Silence.

"Blanche?" He'd give her another heartbeat or two and then the binding was coming off his eyes, oath be damned.

Then he heard muttered curses—the same string of invectives Daisy had used over the ruined mosaic—and then the scritch of fabric rustling, the scuffle of heels on hardwood.

"*Oui,* I'm fine," she said.

His hearing grew more acute with the loss of his vision. When she made the return trip across the room, her gait was different. Was he hearing a limp?

"Did you fall?" he asked.

"My skirts are too long," she said defensively. "I should have worn my hoops."

Or perhaps her shoes are too tall, Lucian thought. Could she be wearing a pair of those ridiculous Venetian platforms that had become so deucedly popular?

If so, maybe she wasn't too tall to be Daisy.

Her scent told him she was closer. He reached out a hand to find her and came into contact with a soft breast. She was dressed *en déshabillé,* as she'd been on the first night he visited her. He'd noticed before she blinded him with satin that her frilly corset ended in a half shelf beneath her breasts. Only the thin fabric of her chemise stood between him and her warm, smooth skin.

"There you are," he said.

"Here I am," she whispered, surprisingly enough in English. Blanche always spoke French to him, but without any voice behind the sound, he couldn't detect whether she breathed those words with an accent or not. She gave herself a slight shake. *"Je suis ici,"* she amended.

He stroked her slowly, and it almost seemed as if she leaned, catlike, into his touch. Her nipple hardened beneath his palm. He ached to slide his hand beneath her chemise and cup her breast. If he lifted his chin just so, he could peer beneath the blindfold enough to steal a glimpse of her breasts, ripe and round. The sweet hollow between them disappeared into shadow while the rest of her skin was kissed golden by the kindly candlelight.

He would have loved to stay right where he was and pay heartfelt homage to her lovely bosom, but he had business elsewhere. He gave her softness a slight squeeze and let his fingers wander north. Her skin was smooth beneath his questing hand. The pulse point at the base of her throat throbbed fast as a hummingbird's wing.

He traced her jawline with both hands, and his thumbs met at her pointed little chin. Daisy's face was also heart-shaped, broader at the cheekbones and tapering to a point that stopped just shy of sharp. Then he smoothed over her cheeks till he reached the feathered edge of the mask. He felt his way around to reach the bow behind her head, stepping closer to her. Her breasts pressed against his chest. He could feel the expansion of her ribs with each inhalation. She tilted her pelvis to meet his rock-hard one. It was almost as if her body melted into his.

Would Daisy Drake be so bold?

The ribbon holding the mask gave way, and he lifted it from her face.

"Do you need to put this on a stand as well?" he asked.

"No, I'll just lay it here on the table."

Was it just his imagination or did she traverse the short distance in little hitching hops?

"Are you sure you're all right?"

"I told you I'm fine," she snapped, and he heard the strange sound again as she returned to stand before him. "I'm back."

He reached for her, and this time he aimed higher. He couldn't be sure he could abandon her breasts a second time. His hands came to rest on her soft, bared shoulders. He leaned forward to kiss her.

She met him halfway, slanting her mouth on his. He palmed her cheeks, enjoying the feel of her nose against the side of his instead of the ticklish, feathery mask. Her lips parted softly. He answered the unspoken invitation, not rushing in this time, but slowly, savoring the taste of her mouth.

While remembering Daisy's.

Daisy had tasted of orange-spiced tea and sweet biscuits in the hot, dusty shed. This woman's mouth was tinged with wine, a full-bodied red that mingled with her heady jasmine fragrance enough to thoroughly befuddle him.

Shouldn't he be able to tell if he was kissing the same woman both times?

Perhaps he didn't have enough experience with kissing in general to know.

But her kiss was wonderful, whoever she was. Her lips were soft and pliant beneath his. And her clever little tongue darted in with a series of teasing advances and retreats.

Her hair was pulled back into a tight bun, since she'd been wearing a wig. He plucked out the pins as he continued to kiss her, letting them drop unheeded to the floor. He shook her hair loose and spread it over her shoulders and down her back.

As he kissed her, he ran his hands over her hair's length, testing his theory. About right for Daisy, he decided. The long locks curled softly around his fingers, as he imagined hers would.

Then he remembered the main reason for inducing her to remove the mask. He pulled back and let his fingers explore her face. He brushed his fingertips across her smooth forehead. He traced her brows with his thumbs, trying to create a mental picture of her face. Her eyelids trembled as he pressed a soft kiss on each one. He kissed the tip of her nose and was delighted to find that it turned up ever so slightly.

Just like Daisy's.

He gathered her in his arms and searched for her mouth again. He stole her breath and replenished it with his own. He suckled her bottom lip and then gave it a soft nip.

She moaned into his mouth.

He must be getting quite good at kissing, he decided. Encouraged, he did it again.

Her moan grew louder.

She pushed against his shoulders, and he suddenly realized she was moaning in pain, not passion. He released her and felt her nearly topple. He caught her and hugged her close to his chest.

"Ow," she whimpered.

"What's wrong?"

"I turned my ankle when I fell. I thought I could ignore it, but I can't. It hurts like the devil."

Lucian stooped and picked her up.

"Oof!" Her breath rushed out in a cross between a yelp and a yip. "What are you doing?"

"I'm going to carry you to your bed so you can get off your ankle."

"But you're blindfolded," she protested. "You might walk us into the fireplace."

"Are you giving me permission to remove the blindfold?" he asked.

"No!" Then she softened her tone. "No man sees my face, Lucian. It is my rule."

"And a deucedly inconvenient one at present."

"Nevertheless, you gave me your word."

"Very well," he said with a sigh. "Give me directions to your bed then, unless you want me to stand here holding you all night."

"Lovely as that sounds, it's not terribly practical. Make a quarter turn. *Bien*. Sidestep once to your right. Take three longish strides—Oh!"

His shin barked against the side slats of the four-poster and they both tumbled onto the feather tick, Lucian landing atop her crosswise at what felt like her narrow waist.

She made a woofing sound.

"Have I injured you further?" He scrambled to right himself.

The whimper dissolved into a nearly hysterical giggle. "No, I just . . . I had plans for us, you see . . . but now, of course . . . my ankle's throbbing and . . . Oh, Jupiter! I can't believe how atrocious my luck has been this night."

"Mine as well, but there will be other nights," he said, finding her hand and giving it a squeeze. And days, too, if he had anything to say about it. "Let me see about your ankle, then."

"No, Lucian, you promised." He heard the bed creak and imagined she'd sat bolt upright.

"I didn't mean I'd literally 'see' anything." He spoke with the same soft tone he'd use to calm a startled horse. He patted his hand across her body and splayed his fingers over her flat belly. "I merely want to check on your injury using my hands, not my eyes. Settle yourself."

He felt her lie back down.

"Very well," she said softly.

He moved his hand slowly, feeling the warmth of her skin through the thin fabric of her chemise. With regret, he forced himself not to linger over the juncture of her thighs. If she was injured and in pain, she wouldn't appreciate his exploration of that happy region.

Please, God, let there be other nights! He sent his prayer skyward as he settled a hip on the bed beside her.

Her thigh quivered slightly as his hand continued to slide down to her knee and onto her hard shin. When he reached the hem of her chemise, he turned it up, draping it over her knees. If only he weren't blindfolded, he'd be feasting his eyes on her slender calves and neatly turned ankles.

He discovered in short order that his fingers served admirably in his eyes' stead. She was wearing thin stockings. Lucian found the garter behind her knee and gave the ribbon a tug. He rolled the stocking down a delicate curve, past a small bump of ankle bones, and, oh! There was the cold, rough touch of her gem-encrusted shoe.

"Nothing amiss here that I can feel." He lifted her foot and slipped the shoe off. Before he set it on the floor beside the bed, he ran his hands over it and was delighted to find that the platform must have added at least six inches to her height. It certainly explained why she took a tumble.

And so much more.

"It's my other ankle," she said.

He reached for her right leg and pulled the stocking down. When his fingers reached her swollen ankle, she flinched.

"I'm sorry to hurt you," he said, "but if your ankle is swelling this much, we must remove the shoe and stocking quickly, while we still can. May I?"

"Please."

Trying to be as gentle as possible, he tugged off the

clunky shoe, then eased the stocking over her tight flesh. This ankle was twice its normal size and much warmer to the touch than the rest of her skin.

She might have broken a bone. Any thought of further dallying fled from his brain. "You need a physician, and quickly." He stood.

"Lucian, remember your promise. Oh, wait! I have it. Now you may remove the blindfold." Her voice seemed muffled.

He peeled off the dark cloth and looked down to see that she'd covered her face with a pillow. He stifled a laugh. So she still wasn't ready to give up the farce. Very well. It had been an enjoyable game of seduction and chance thus far, and now that he knew a few more of the rules, he fully intended to win the final hand.

Then his gaze traveled down her prone body to her poor ankle. Even in the dim light, he could tell her flesh was darkening with an evil bruise.

He bent over and lifted her hand to his lips. "I bid you farewell, my little French bird."

"Lucian, please tell—"

"Fear not. I will alert the staff to your situation. Please send word when you are ready to receive me once again. Rest assured, my dearest Blanche, I remain your devoted admirer."

Then he turned and strode to the door. Once it closed behind him, he sagged against it for a moment. An invisible hand squeezed his heart and wouldn't let go. The tenderness and concern that engulfed him now were just as potent as the passion she'd stirred in him before.

Maybe even more so.

Daisy—confound it!—Drake! Of all the women in the world, why on earth did it have to be her?

Chapter Nineteen

Caius finished tallying the last column on the bill of lading for the shipment due to leave on the next square-rigged vessel bound for Rome. Tin and amber, sealskins and thick wool from beyond Hadrian's Wall far to the north, where the savages still painted themselves blue for battle. This was a goodly haul for the greater glory of Rome.

Caius rechecked the final figure. Then he made his mark and laid aside his stylus.

He dragged a hand over his face. He received a small commission on each of the loads he assembled and oversaw. Perhaps next month, when the proconsul sat in judgment once again, Caius's stack of coin would be sufficient to induce him to release Deirdre from service.

On that happy day, Caius would make her his wife.

It couldn't come too soon. They still met by moonlight each night, their loving both wilder and more tender than Caius had a right to expect. They shared themselves, not just their bodies.

She told him of her childhood near a tiny island in the middle of the great river. Time out of mind, it had been a sacred place to her people, a place of forbidden magic. Since the Romans had outlawed druidism, the rites performed there had ceased, but the stones still stood, and the hidden cave summoned her to explore deep within "the goddess," as she called it. Deirdre had no magic, to her sorrow, but it pleased her to think the lordly Romans believed that little patch of ground so haunted they feared to set foot on it.

Last night, as Caius and Deirdre lay together in the fragrant garden, passion-spent and covered with a light sheen of sweat, she'd confessed that she might be bearing his child.

His child. He blinked back tears. Since he had been stolen from his Germanic village as a boy and pressed into the Roman's service, he never dreamed he'd ever father a child of his own.

If it was a boy, he'd name him Artos. It was close to the name that had been his own before the slave brand was burned into his shoulder. His new Roman name had been plastered on him that day, along with the numbing salve that sped his healing. In time, the brand's scar healed cleanly. Even though he later earned his freedom, his spirit had never completely recovered from the shock of slavery.

Now Deirdre's love was healing his vanquished soul.

Caius wondered where she might be working now. He knew it would be foolish to display his affection openly. Even asking to purchase her had won him some good-natured ribbing from his friends. But he felt a sudden need to see her, if only to bask in the light of her fleeting smile.

He left the countinghouse near the wharf and trudged back to the proconsul's villa. Deirdre might be in the lady of the house's suite of rooms, in which case, he'd not be able to find her. But she might also be working in the kitchen or, if he were very fortunate, in the garden. He might sneak a kiss or two there.

He found her behind the grape arbor, but all thought of stealing a kiss quickly fled. She was weeping. Silent shudders racked her frame. Brown spots of dried blood marred the white of her palla across her breasts and down lower.

"You're injured." Caius dropped to his knees beside her.

She shook her head. "The proconsul . . ." Her voice trailed away.

There were ligature marks on her wrists and ankles. And

a sore-looking love mark on her nape. The Roman governor had indulged in his favorite form of entertainment.

Ravishing a bound victim.

And this time Scipianus had chosen Deirdre. Caius hugged her close and let her sob. Hatred fisted in his chest.

"He—"

"Hush." Caius cradled her head against his heart. Best to let her cry away the pain. Reliving the ordeal by speaking it aloud would only hurt them both.

Especially since there was nothing to be done but hope the proconsul lost interest in her quickly. If she stopped struggling, if she didn't cry out, he'd turn to one of the smooth-bottomed little boys who mucked out the stables, or maybe the new goose girl.

But Deirdre couldn't keep silent. "He's going to do it again tomorrow. He said so."

In halting tones, Caius told her how to feign indifference so the proconsul would cease molesting her. It was information bought with a price. He'd been very young when Scipianus became his master.

Instead of realizing Caius shared her pain, Deirdre grew indignant. "You won't do anything to stop it?"

"What can I do?" She belonged to the proconsul, like his horse or his hound. Caius hated it, but unless Scipianus agreed to sell her, he was within his rights to use her as he pleased.

"You could be a man." Her chin trembled. "You could kill him."

Before Scipianus became a politician, he'd been a soldier. Barrel-chested and beefy-armed, he was a formidable fighter, made even more fearsome by callous cruelty. Caius still occasionally woke drenched in sweat and trembling from a night terror of the proconsul. Caius was a boy again, tasting stale garlic breath, feeling thick fingers on his member, the fist that tightened on his young balls. . . .

Caius might hate Scipianus with every fiber of his being.

But he feared him even more.

Life was all that mattered. Years of slavery had taught him that. Survive and there was hope, even if it was but a slim one. The weight of law was on the proconsul's side. If Caius killed Scipianus, neither he nor Deirdre would see the next sunrise.

"I cannot kill him," he admitted. Shame curled around his heart. "Please, Deirdre, say something."

She looked at him with naked loathing, then turned away.

"Don't you see?" He grasped her shoulders and made her face him. "If I kill the proconsul, they would put us both to death as well."

And it would be a terrible death. Public and protracted and painful.

"Among my people, dishonor is worse than dying," she said softly.

"You're not among your people. This is the Romans' world," he said. "But we will get through this somehow. I will see you free. I promise."

"I hate you," she said simply. "And I will free myself."

She rose shakily and walked away without a backward glance.

"In the dance of courtship, there are times when one must withdraw in order to see if one's lover will follow or breathe a sigh of relief and turn away."

—the journal of Blanche La Tour

Chapter Twenty

Lucian closed the ledger book cataloging his finds. He didn't want to chance a fire in the shed housing his collection of Roman objects, so he didn't allow a lamp, always stopping work when the light began to fail. He glanced out the open door of the shed. Mr. Peabody dismissed the rest of the workers and began tidying the site for the night.

Lucian pulled the note he'd received that morning from his pocket and read the neat curlicue script once more.

My dear Lord Rutland,

He chuckled at the stilted formality before reading on.

With regret, I am unable to assist you at your excavation this day. As you know, Mlle La Tour suffered an injury to her ankle, and I am attending her until she is recovered. Pray do not expect me to return for at least a fortnight. Knowing you wish Mlle La Tour well, I remain, along with dear Blanche, of course,

Your partner in this Roman venture,
Miss Daisy Drake

"Oh, yes, Miss Drake," he mused as he slipped the note once again into his breast pocket. "You're my partner, for good or ill. And I'm sure we both wish Blanche exceedingly well."

Last night, Lucian had stayed, hovering in the parlor, while the physician ministered to the injured "courtesan." Lady Wexford took pity on him shortly after midnight and let him know the doctor didn't think any bones were broken. The leeches had been effective in relieving the swelling. However, Blanche had suffered a serious sprain and would be incapacitated for several days.

Daisy's note explaining her absence made him smile. He wondered how much longer she'd be able to keep up this deception. It would prove amusing to watch her try.

His team of workmen had unearthed another wax tablet. He intended to take it to her this evening, since her Latin was far superior to his own. He wondered if she'd agree to see him as herself or if she'd insist on playing Blanche behind that beguiling feather mask.

He didn't know which he hoped for.

Part of him didn't want to unmask her. His father might heartily approve of Lucian dancing attendance on a French woman of pleasure, but the earl would be beside himself with rage over a liaison between Lucian and Gabriel Drake's niece. Since Lucian wasn't sure how he was going to handle his father's displeasure, he was willing to play along with Daisy's double life for as long as she wished.

Perhaps once Lucian found the treasure, the change in the Montford fortunes would also change his father's unreasoning hatred of Drakes. Lucian hoped so. Otherwise, he'd have an unpleasant choice to make. He'd become so accustomed to mollifying his increasingly difficult father, he dreaded the confrontation that was sure to come.

Lucian dragged a hand over his face as the sun slid beneath the horizon. Soft twilight began to fade around him. The workers were climbing out of the pit and ambling away, their coarse, good-humored speech a pleasant sound as they passed the shed.

Mr. Peabody was still rattling around in the site. Lucian stood and stretched. The foreman was certainly taking his time about closing up shop.

Then he saw Peabody's head jerk furtively, first right, then left. Lucian froze, knowing he was invisible in the darkness of the shed. The foreman stooped and picked up from the dirt something that glinted for a moment in the dying light. He shoved the item in his pocket before Lucian could make out what it was. A bit of ancient jewelry, perhaps?

Mr. Peabody climbed out of the pit and strode away.

The blackguard was stealing! Anger boiled in his Italian veins. Lucian started after Peabody, ready to give the lout a good thrashing, but Daisy's voice in his head made him skid to a halt.

Perhaps it's not about the money.

So then why? Daisy's infusion of cash had assured that the workers were well compensated for their labor. Surely Peabody realized he risked his position for pocketing that small item.

What could he have found that was so important?

Lucian locked the shed door and silently followed Mr. Peabody into the deepening night.

Along broad thoroughfares and down crooked alleys, Lucian tailed his foreman. He maintained a discreet distance between himself and his quarry until Peabody turned down a bustling street lined with public houses. When the thief ducked through a door under the sign of a unicorn, Lucian stopped, unsure how to proceed.

If he entered The Unicorn, Mr. Peabody was certain to spot him. Even dressed in his work clothes, Lucian was far better turned out than most of the men who entered the pub. He would stand out among the salt of the earth as a gentleman out of his element. If he didn't follow Peabody, the man would probably find a fence for his stolen goods in the seedy-looking establishment and emerge with only a handful of unremarkable coins in his pocket.

"Alms, good sir," a piteous voice bleated nearby. "Penny for a blind man."

A bundle of rags propped against the sagging building had spoken. The man's eyes were covered with a filthy bandage. His torn and stained coat might once have been fine, but now its color and fabric were obscured beneath a layer of dirt and traces of previous meals. The hand extended toward Lucian was crusted with grime, the nails black and broken.

Lucian decided he'd never consider himself poor again.

"I've no penny, my good man," Lucian said. "But I'll buy that coat from you for two shillings, if you're willing."

It was twenty-four times what the man had asked for. More than enough to outfit him with an entire new set of used clothing and feed him for a week.

"For that much, gov, you can have me hat as well." The beggar peeled out of his coat with alacrity, loosing an almost visible cloud of stink.

Lucian donned the disreputable coat, turned up the collar and prayed mightily that the man hadn't been infested with lice. The slouchy hat sported a greasy ring around the inner band, but no evidence of any little beasties. Lucian jammed it on his head, promising himself a hot bath as soon as he returned home.

He shuffled into the smoky pub and swept the room with his gaze. There! In the far corner, Peabody was seated with his back to the door, hunched forward in deep conversation with two other men.

Lucian worked his way around the dim room and found a seat in a booth near them, careful to keep his face turned away. The barmaid brought him a pint without being asked and accepted his coin without comment. The coat's

stench had the added benefit of making all the other patrons keep their distance. He nursed his drink and strained
to hear the low conversation behind him.

"No, no," one of the men was saying. Lucian couldn't
identify the speaker. A whispered voice might belong to
anyone. "This little bauble does us no good at all."

"But I'll lay me teeth it's gold, right enough," Peabody
hissed.

"It's only a trifle," the other man said, with a bit more force
in his voice. Was there a hint of a Scots accent in his tone?
"What good will it do us if ye lose your position before
ye discover the location of the mother lode?"

Anger swelled in Lucian's chest. So, someone was trying
to finesse the Roman treasure out from under him using
Peabody as his eyes and ears. He fought the urge to turn
and confront the men. Beating them to a bloody pulp was a
satisfying thought, and Lucian had been pugilistic cham-
pion in the fledgling sport at Oxford. But he didn't know
how many confederates the men might have in The Unicorn. Better to learn more now and seek to best them later
on ground of his choosing.

"Don't ye see, mon?" There was no mistaking the accent
now. The man was still speaking softly, but Lucian thought
he recognized the voice. "The true king willna be served
by half measures. Think of the reward to the man who
brings him a worthy tribute in Roman coin."

The true king?

Lucian had learned in the schoolroom of the failed Scottish rising in '15. Could these men be planning another
attempt to place James Stuart on the English throne?

Lucian listened as the voices sank to muffled mutterings,
but his ears pricked at occasional words. *Bloody German* and
usurper surfaced with regularity.

He sipped his ale, letting the sharp bite of the liquid cool
his anger. If Peabody and his associates spoke so openly, this

pub must be a hotbed of sedition, and he was wise not to disclose himself.

The punishment for treason hadn't changed since the Middle Ages: hanging, drawing and quartering. It was a heinous enough end to turn the stoutest man's bowels to water. And to make a thinking man consider carefully before he decided to try to overthrow his king.

But once a man made such a dire decision, he might do anything. Because he had everything to lose.

"Then what would you have me do?" Lucian heard Peabody ask.

"Take this back and pretend to find it in the morning. It's too distinctive for us to sell it without young Rutland hearing of it."

Lucian cast a quick glance behind him and saw a flash of gold as Peabody stuffed the Roman trinket back into his pocket. The angle was wrong for him to catch a clear look at the other men's faces.

"Keep your teeth together and your eyes and ears open," the obvious brains of the outfit said. "Especially when there's a tablet found. Report back only when Rutland discovers the location of the treasure."

Lucian hid beneath his hat's brim as Peabody stood and stalked out of the pub. The other men made no move to leave, so Lucian decided to remain as well.

"Will he do, you think?" the second man asked.

"Well enough, if he keeps his sticky fingers in his own pockets," the first said loudly.

Hearing his voice clearly for the first time, Lucian was certain of the man's identity now. It was Sir Alistair Fitzhugh, head of the Society of Antiquaries, and to all appearances a reputable knight of the realm. What was he doing involving himself in such an enterprise?

"But we'd do well to keep an eye on Peabody. If he'll steal for us, he'll steal from us," Alistair said. "Sometimes men of good conscience are forced to deal with such riffraff for the sake of their cause, eh, Brumley?"

Lord Brumley. The loudest detractor at his presentation was now trying to steal Lucian's find. He almost laughed aloud at the irony.

"So have you secured our other partner yet?" Brumley asked.

Who else would be mad enough to join these lunatics? Lucian leaned slightly toward the sound as he took another pull of his ale.

"Not quite," Alistair admitted. "But it won't be long. After all, it was the German king who granted the exclusive charter to that South Sea group."

The hair on the back of Lucian's neck stood on end with foreboding.

"Without a royal monopoly, the earl would never have invested and subsequently never lost his shirt. He was duped by the usurper. I have only to hammer that nail in a bit harder and he'll see the light. If Peabody fails us, Montford will force his son to give up the location of the treasure."

Lucian choked on his ale.

His own father consorting with Jacobite sympathizers. Discovery would mean the earldom would be stripped from Lucian's family. He'd lose his viscountcy as well. They might be pinched at present. If his father were branded a traitor, Lucian might as well get used to wearing this ragged coat.

Lucian's gut churned. The loss of title and being plunged into abject poverty were far from the worst of it. If the earl were sucked into this doomed plot, his poor deluded father would die horribly.

No matter what happened—even if meant he never found the Roman treasure—Lucian couldn't let his father wander down that dark road.

He pushed away his half-drunk mug of ale and slipped out of The Unicorn as silently as he'd slipped in.

"Anticipation is a whetstone that sharpens desire."
—the journal of Blanche La Tour

Chapter Twenty-one

Daisy closed the heavy edition of *Moll Flanders* and leaned her chin on her palm. Her own life was too much of a tangle for her to feel any empathy for the misadventures of Daniel Defoe's hapless heroine. Besides, Defoe tended to moralize a bit too much for the comfort of Daisy's conscience. She imagined that worthy Puritan author would have a good deal to say about her masquerade as a courtesan and the fleshly adventures she and Lucian had almost shared.

It was the *almost* that brought a sigh to Daisy's lips.

"Are you in terrible pain, sweeting?" Isabella glanced up from her own book. She and Lord Wexford had been playing a companionable game of chess earlier in the far corner of the parlor. Isabella looked lovely in the soft lamplight and was thoroughly enjoying trouncing her good-natured husband. But then Lord Wexford's valet had arrived with a note, and Geoffrey excused himself early. Isabella had been wearing a scowl ever since. Daisy didn't think her great-aunt had turned a page in the last quarter hour.

"No, the willow-bark tea seems to dull the ache." Daisy's injured ankle was propped on the tasseled pillow of the cunning Turkish-style ottoman.

"Then why the sigh?" Isabella asked. "You're far too young to have such cares."

Daisy exhaled noisily. "It's just . . . well, now that I'm no longer able to be Blanche, I can't be myself either. I mean, with this stupid sprain, I can't even go to work at the excavation and—"

"And see Lucian Beaumont," Isabella finished for her.

"Exactly." Daisy shifted her foot to find a more comfortable position. "And yet, I have a feeling that given the choice he'd rather see Blanche than me."

"Why do you say that?" Isabella asked. "Haven't you and he enjoyed working together by day?"

"Yes, we have a jolly enough time, and I think he tolerates me well now, but—"

"But he presents a different side of himself to you when he thinks you are Blanche?"

Daisy nodded.

"Do you like him less by day?"

"No, I like him rather too much by day or by night," Daisy admitted. "Oh, Isabella, what's wrong with me? I believe I'm actually jealous of . . . of myself!"

"Then perhaps it's time you put away your competition for good," her great-aunt said. "Retire Blanche La Tour. Playing at courtesan is a dangerous game for even one night, and you've managed it for several. So far you've escaped relatively unscathed."

"My ankle would beg to differ."

"I meant your heart, dearest," Isabella said gently. "You haven't allowed the game to run away with your heart."

Daisy wasn't so sure of that.

Isabella cast a long look in the direction of Lord Wexford's exit. "Once your heart is in play, the rules change." She seemed to give herself a slight shake. "As far as Lucian's presenting you with a different face when you are in Blanche's shoes, we all do that. Like a chameleon that blends into his surroundings, we become what others expect of us."

Isabella stood and paced over to the long windows. She gazed out, her graceful arms crossed so it almost seemed as if she were giving herself a hug. "It doesn't happen often, but if we are extremely lucky, we find someone with whom we can simply be ourselves."

"That's just the trouble. Lucian doesn't like me as myself."

"I wouldn't be too sure about that, but I suspect we'll find out soon enough."

"What makes you say so?" Daisy asked.

"Because Lucian Beaumont is walking up to the front door as we speak."

"Oh, no! Call Jerome quickly. He has to bear me back up to Blanche's room." Daisy tried to reach the bell that was just beyond the grasp of her fingers. "Ring for Nanette and see if she can help me—"

The sharp rap of the brass knocker sounded, followed by the butler's muffled greeting.

"Hush, darling," Isabella said. "Let us see whom he is here to see first. If he asks for Blanche, I'll tell him she's not up to seeing him. If he asks for you, well, that should tell you something, shouldn't it?"

"Why should Blanche be able to hide? What if *I'm* not up to seeing him?" Daisy's belly quivered, and she lowered her elevated foot to the floor.

"Can you rise unassisted?"

Daisy nodded. "As long as I keep my weight on the other foot."

"Good girl," Isabella said. "I won't allow him to stay too long."

"That's all right, Jerome," they heard Lucian say. "I know the way to the parlor."

The click of his shoes on the marble entry made Isabella turn her head to the doorway. "Good evening, Lord Rutland." She extended a gracious hand to him that allowed Daisy to rise to her feet without his notice. "How kind of you to visit."

"How could I not when our mutual friend is unwell?" Lucian bussed his lips over Isabella's knuckles.

"Mlle La Tour is not receiving guests this evening," Isabella said. "I'm sure you understand."

Lucian cast Lady Wexford a charming smile. "She's recovering well, I trust."

"Resting comfortably," Daisy said, slightly miffed that he hadn't even glanced in her direction yet.

"I'm glad to hear it." Lucian turned his dark eyes on Daisy. "However, I'm not here to see Blanche. I'm here to see you, Miss Drake."

"Oh?" Her heart did a little jig against her ribs.

"Yes." He pulled something from his waistcoat pocket. "We found another tablet late this afternoon, and I thought perhaps you might help me translate it."

"Oh." Her heart flopped helplessly to her toes.

"I appreciate your assistance." His smile broadened into something almost wicked. "Unless, of course, you're too busy attending Mlle La Tour."

"No, Blanche has already retired for the night." She tossed a pointed look at Isabella.

"If you'll excuse me," her great-aunt said, "I believe I'll see if Nanette can brew a spot of tea, and I'm sure we have a scone or two. Lovely to see you, milord."

"Well, shall we repair to the table and begin?" Lucian strode over to the small table where the chess match had lately been held and pulled out a chair for her. He shot her an inviting grin. "*Tempus fugit,* you know."

"Time can fly just as well from here," Daisy said, lowering herself back onto the settee before she lost her balance. Standing stork-legged was not her strong suit, and unfortunately she'd be able to traverse the length of the room only in short hops. "Bring the tablet and join me."

She patted the spot on the settee next to her.

"Good idea! A much friendlier arrangement." Lucian settled beside her. "Here's the tablet."

"A much friendlier arrangement," he says, and then it's "here's

the tablet," all business. *Blast the man!* Daisy turned her lips inward for a moment to bite back the words. *Would it kill him to notice me for once?*

Daisy took the ancient tablet and squinted at the marks in the gritty wax.

"Some of it's damaged," Lucian pointed out.

"I see that." About a quarter of the wax was bashed in, with no writing on the uneven surface. A faint curved line ran along the edge of the damage. Daisy curled her own fingers into a fist and set it into the indentation. "Well, whoever did this had a larger hand than I, but it appears someone was upset enough to slam their hand down on this tablet when the wax was still soft. Doesn't that suggest a finger imprint?"

Lucian leaned in. "I think you're right. The bottom of the tablet bears Caius Meritus's mark."

"So it does," Daisy agreed. "Let's see what Mr. Meritus wrote that made someone so angry, shall we?"

She bent her head to the work. After several minutes, she became conscious of Lucian's gaze on her. She turned to face him. "You're staring at me," she said.

"Forgive me." He reached up to tuck an errant curl behind her ear. A little tingle shivered over her in the wake of his hand brushing her earlobe. "It's just that from this angle, you remind me of someone."

Daisy didn't dare ask who. "Shall we attend to the tablet instead of my profile?"

"Fine, but you don't need my help. Your Latin is better than mine," he admitted.

"So that's why you're here."

"What are you angling for, Daisy?" he asked. "Do you want me to admit that I missed you today? If it will make you happy, I will."

Only if it were true. "What about Blanche?"

"What about her? Does Blanche miss me, you think?"

He leaned toward her. His crisp masculine scent, fresh and clean, tickled her nostrils.

"I . . . I didn't think to ask her." She turned back to the tablet to avoid the pull of his dark eyes. If she were dressed as Blanche, she'd have palmed his cheeks and drawn him down for a kiss. As herself, she didn't dare, so she focused her attention on the ancient wax.

"What do you make of it?" he finally asked.

"It seems to be a ledger of profit and loss." Daisy pointed to one column. "Here we have sales of wool and amber, so that represents profit. And on this side, a shipment of wheat was consumed by rodents and . . ."

"And what?"

"There's something about Deirdre, the slave girl." Daisy's voice sank to a whisper. "I think it was Caius Meritus who slammed his fist down on this tablet."

"What makes you say that?"

"Well, we know Caius tried to purchase her freedom, so he must have had some feelings for her."

Lucian shrugged. "That's a fair guess. What does it say about her?"

" *'Mortuus per suus manus,'* " Daisy said. "Dead by her own hand. The girl killed herself."

"We enter this world alone. And it is certain we shall step into the great dark by ourselves. But while we are here, the joy of having someone choose to spend part of their precious life with us . . . is unspeakable."

—the journal of Blanche La Tour

Chapter Twenty-two

"This is dreadful," Daisy exclaimed. "Of course, I understand that all the people we study in antiquity are long dead, but in my mind, they seemed to take on a life of their own. For Deirdre to take her own life . . . she must have been horribly unhappy."

"I'd expect slaves generally are," Lucian said softly. "I know I would be."

"But Caius tried to buy her freedom." Daisy ran her fingertips over the uneven wax, then jerked them away suddenly. For a moment, she felt searing pain emanating from the tablet. Sometimes a vivid imagination was no fun. "Wouldn't the hope of freedom have kept Deirdre from such a dire act?"

"Perhaps she had no liking for Caius. Just because a man fancies a particular woman, it doesn't signify that she will fall into his arms," Lucian said. "Seems to me I recall Lord Thornheld took a shine to you a few Seasons ago, and yet here you are, still on the marriage market."

"Ugh! I wish you wouldn't put it like that." She grimaced at him. "You make me sound like a spoiled apple languishing on the grocer's shelf."

"Not spoiled," he teased, his dark eyes snapping. "Ripe, perhaps, would be more appropriate."

She swatted his chest. He caught her hand and held it much longer than necessary. Something in his gaze shifted from teasing to tantalizing in a heartbeat. Fire burned behind his dark eyes.

Her belly fluttered uncertainly. He'd looked at her like that only when she was disguised as Blanche. His scorching gaze made her resolve as herself melt just as quickly as it had when she was playing the courtesan.

"I'm glad you didn't accept Thornheld," he said in all seriousness.

Lord Thornheld was considered no end of a catch for a young woman with no *milady* before her name, but Daisy found the middle-aged rake grasping and boorish. Thornheld made her flesh pebble with goose bumps—the "Ew! I've stepped in a cow pie!" sort of goose bumps—whereas Lucian made her skin tingle in a very different way.

"I had no idea you took note of such things." Daisy was both aghast that he brought up the unfortunate one-sided attachment and pleased that he had been aware of her in London society at all.

"I may cultivate the image of a recluse," Lucian acknowledged, "but that doesn't mean I don't make it my business to know what's happening among polite society."

Business. Yes, Lucian would probably consider the joining of two houses merely business. She decided to steer the conversation back to the tablet.

When she placed her hand on the ancient wax again, she fancied she felt a faint buzzing, as if she'd covered an angry bee with her palm.

Had Isabella slipped some laudanum into that willow-bark tea?

"These items we unearth, they certainly do speak, don't they?" she said.

"Each find tells a tale," Lucian agreed. "Or at least raises new questions."

"When I was a girl, a troop of Gypsies camped near Dragon Caern." Daisy shut her eyes, conjuring the memory. "An old woman there told fortunes and such. Frankly I think it was all rot, but she did say something that has stuck with me."

"What was that?"

"That the things we surround ourselves with capture a bit of our essence, absorbing the events of our lives like a sea sponge sops up a spill." Daisy turned to look at him. "And when something horrible happens, the things that clutter our homes become imprinted with the strong emotions."

"Doesn't sound very scientific," Lucian said dubiously.

"No, but I wonder." She laid her curled fist into the hollow indentation in the wax and this time felt no tingling buzz. Still, the sense of tragedy weighed her down like a heavy woolen mantle. "I wonder if sometimes the rocks cry out in a language only the heart hears."

"I think I know what you mean," Lucian said. "Certain places make us feel certain things. A sunny meadow lifts the spirit. A dark alley raises the hairs on one's neck. A cathedral leads us to worship."

"Exactly. You may think it silly of me, but I feel something from this tablet." Daisy paused to find the right words. "A deep, brooding rage."

Lucian covered her hand with his. His brows drew together in intense concentration. Surely he must sense the simmering ire, too.

"I don't feel anything," Lucian finally admitted. "Except the softness of your skin," he added with a wink.

She pulled her hand away and glared at him. He was patronizing her, but she plowed ahead in the firm belief that she was right.

"Given what we've learned empirically about your Romans, it's not difficult to infer that there must have been a romantic relationship between our thief and the Celtic slave girl," Daisy said firmly. "Once Caius Meritus secured

Deirdre's freedom, I half expected to find a record of their marriage eventually."

"Every woman's happy ending." Lucian lifted a cynical brow.

"That's not true, and you know it as well as I," Daisy said, thinking of her great-aunt's distracted scowl earlier. Until that moment, Daisy hadn't even considered the possibility that Isabella's late-in-life union with a much younger man had brought her anything but happiness. "Marriage doesn't necessarily result in happiness for either party, but one can hope."

"Is that what you hope for, Daisy?"

He leaned toward her, sliding an arm along the back of the settee behind her.

"Seems to me I recall your saying something once about people coming into this world with the same wants and needs since Eden." She drew a shallow breath.

His warm masculine scent curled around her brain, making coherent thought a serious effort. His thigh rested only a finger's width from hers. She remembered his leg's rock-hard musculature, as well as his rock-hard cock under her palms. She had to remind herself to exhale.

"Surely you hope to find happiness as well," she managed to squeak out.

He smiled wickedly. "Some would argue that a man's definition of happiness is considerably different from a woman's."

"Hmph! I suppose you are referring to the happiness you found with Mlle La Tour," she said testily.

"Are you sure you want to discuss my adventures with that lovely woman?" He let his hand slip from the back of the settee to rest on her shoulder. The warmth of his palm radiated through the thin fabric of her *casaque*. She fought the urge to lean into his touch. "Such knowledge can be dangerous to a young lady of quality."

"Knowledge is not something to be shunned."

"Ah, as long as you made reference to Eden, I feel compelled to point out that that's what Eve thought as well. And look where her quest for knowledge led us." He stroked her forearm absently with his other hand. "What is it about the forbidden that calls to us so strongly?"

"Is that what you like about Blanche, that she's somehow forbidden?" She turned her head to look up at him and felt his breath feather warmly over her lips.

"Really, Daisy, a gentleman shouldn't discuss one lady with another."

"Blanche would be pleased to hear you describe her as a lady," Daisy said, her voice a mere whisper.

"And how would you know that?"

"Ah," Daisy said, fascinated by the play of his tongue against his teeth and lips. "Blanche and I are very close. Almost inseparable."

A smirk tugged at his mouth. "I daresay you are."

"I'm certain Blanche wouldn't mind if you told me what you like about her."

"I don't think it's possible for me to explain to you what I like about Blanche," he said. "I think I have to show you."

His mouth descended to hers, and before she could protest, he covered her lips in a kiss that warmed her to her toes. Any thought of resistance died without so much as a whimper. Even the throb of her sprained ankle faded in the heat of his kiss. All that mattered was the smoldering touch of his lips, his tongue, on hers.

Her hands found his lapel and tugged him closer. His kiss deepened at her encouragement, and he explored her mouth with his tongue. His hand cupped her cheek, caressed her jaw and then slid along her throat. Daisy's world spiraled down to their warm, wet mingling of breath.

He was kissing *her*—Daisy—not Blanche. Oh, he'd done it once before, but that was only to prove a point. But this was a real, honest-to-goodness kiss.

No, make that an honest-to-wickedness kiss! Jupiter! The man certainly has learned quickly, she thought dimly, remembering his first abortive efforts when he thought he was kissing an experienced courtesan. Now she'd bet Lucian Beaumont's lips would beguile the most jaded woman of pleasure alive.

When his hand slipped lower to toy with the exposed tops of her breasts, she gasped into his mouth. He pulled back to look down at her.

"Do you want me to stop?" he asked, his fingertips teasing along the top of her bodice. Her skin danced beneath his touch.

"That depends. Lucian, are you amusing yourself with me only because Blanche is unavailable?"

He laughed loudly. "No, Daisy. My relationship with Blanche has run its course. If I return to her again, it will merely be to bid her a fond adieu and wish her extremely well. You, Miss Drake, have completely captured my attention."

Her lips twitched in a small smile. "Then don't stop."

Yet part of her was saddened that he tossed Blanche aside so easily.

Botheration! Living in two sets of skin is a difficult enterprise!

"Are you offering to teach me what you've learned from Blanche?" she asked.

His hand settled beneath her breast. Her nipple tightened into an aching point. She was sure he must be able to feel her heart hammering.

"What I learned from Blanche," he repeated softly. "Mostly I learned that people are far more complex and surprising than we credit them with. That one never knows exactly what is afoot in another mind. But if you and I continue down this road, I hope to learn what transpires in yours. I want to know all your secrets, Daisy. Does that scare you?"

"No," she said with only a slight gulp.

"I confess it gave me pause at first." He grinned at her.

"I don't frighten so easily. Kiss me again. And quickly," Daisy said. "Before my great-aunt returns with your tea and crumpets."

Isabella stopped so suddenly in the doorway to the parlor that Nanette nearly ran the tea tray into her derriere. There on the settee, Daisy and Lord Rutland were locked in an embrace.

The passionate tableau was more than Isabella had experienced in all her years of marriage, but she remembered what it felt like in minute detail. The first rush of longing, the drumbeat of desire, the heat, the chase—Isabella put a hand to her cheek and was mildly surprised to find it feverish to the touch.

He's eligible and presentable, and Daisy seems to like him well enough, Isabella thought as she waved Nanette back around the corner. *And it looks as though she took my advice about retiring Blanche.*

As a former courtesan herself, Isabella had no stones to throw over anyone's behavior. If Daisy wanted to dally with the man, she wasn't about to gainsay her. And if scandal ensued, they could always marry. Daisy carried a hefty dowry, and young Rutland held a venerable title. A well-moneyed match always made society forget to count months on the first pregnancy.

Surely Daisy would be happy with him. After all, such a vigorous display in the parlor boded well for his ardor in the bedchamber.

But for a marriage to work, it must function in all the rooms of the house. Heaven knew, she'd discovered the truth of that little gem to her sorrow. Isabella hoped for more for her great-niece.

In the hallway outside the parlor, she cleared her throat noisily and gave Nanette a loud, "And for pity's sake, don't drop the tea service. Who knows when the next shipment of fine china from Cathay will arrive?"

By the time she and Nanette rounded the corner to enter the parlor for the second time, Daisy and her new beau were perched at opposite ends of the settee, their faces flushing rosily.

The telltale blush of lust. Ah, yes! Isabella thought as she settled herself to pour. *I remember it well.*

Chapter Twenty-three

Londinium, A.D. 405

Caius Meritus made his mark in the wax, signifying his authorship of the monthly report due to the proconsul. His stylus dug into the soft surface much deeper than usual. Caius laid down the sharp instrument and flexed his fingers. He fought the urge to run screaming through the villa. Every time he closed his eyes, all he saw was his hand stabbing the stylus into Quintus Valerian Scipianus's black heart.

If only wishing would make it so . . .

It had been a week since Caius found Deirdre, her body silvered in the moonlight, stark against the dark water in the fountain basin. Water tainted with her life's blood.

Just as she said she would, Deirdre had freed herself.

He pulled her cooling body from the fountain, too late to save her. All he could do was cradle her till the sun rose. Her limp form stiffened in his arms as he whispered his love, his grief, his plea for her forgiveness.

Perhaps it was better that she couldn't hear him.

She might have scratched his eyes out rather than bear his touch.

He spent the money he'd saved to purchase her freedom on a fine gold necklace to bury with her. He doubted her spirit would rest easy, but perhaps the gift would help. He didn't want her to wake in the land of her gods a pauper.

He tried to resume his life. His first instinct was to withdraw, to retreat into the bland mask of servitude and close down his heart. He didn't deserve a woman anyway. If he wanted to survive, he must continue his service to the proconsul as though Deirdre didn't matter.

But she did matter.

And after a week of numbing grief, Caius decided survival was highly overprized.

Now the only thing keeping his chest expanding for its next breath was the thought of revenge against the man who'd driven his love to her last desperate act.

He looked down at the wax tablet that cataloged the region's output for the glory of distant Rome. Deirdre was reduced to a mere scratch or two on the report. A loss to be recorded, assuredly, but not given too much significance in the long scheme of things.

Caius slammed his fist down on the tablet.

Even if he thought he could manage it, killing the Roman proconsul would end the man's suffering far too quickly. Caius had to find a way to disgrace him, to destroy him in the eyes of Rome, to ruin him. And then leave him to struggle on in a world that would despise him till he drew his last pathetic breath.

But how?

The proconsul entrusted all his correspondence to Caius. Scipianus was too busy buggering the newest little stable boy to bother with official business. Caius broke the seal on the latest dispatch and unrolled the scroll. Unshed tears made his vision waver uncertainly.

Caius pinched the bridge of his nose and blinked hard. The message on the scroll came into sharp focus, and he read the missive quickly.

This was it. The way to strike Scipianus where he would feel the blow most keenly.

An entire year's pay for the Legion was due in next week. The proconsul was tasked with its safety and equitable distribution. If Caius were to make the payroll disappear—and he knew in a moment of blinding clarity exactly where to hide it so no one would ever find it—Quintus Valerian Scipianus would be shown to be ineffective and weak. He'd lose his rank, his wealth, his stature with the fighting men who guarded him. Every Roman hand on the island kingdom would be against him. Even if Scipianus survived the wrath of his own men, he'd forever be shadowed by a cloud of suspicion.

It was perfect.

It would inflict a festering wound upon Scipianus that would never heal.

But as much as he loathed the proconsul, Caius's deepest contempt was for himself. More than anyone else, he'd failed Deirdre. Her blood stained his hands.

Once he made certain Scipianus knew who was the author of his ruin and why, Caius didn't care what happened to him. Death—even a vicious, hard death—would be welcome as a warm, soft pillow.

"In the game of love, cheating is not encouraged, but it is sometimes the only way to win."
———*the journal of Blanche La Tour*

Chapter Twenty-four

Lucian squinted at the newest wax tablet Mr. Peabody brought him. He wished Daisy were here. His Latin was adequate—after all, he'd puzzled out the original ancient record that revealed the existence of the Roman treasure—but Daisy's facility with the dead language far exceeded his own.

"Do ye any good, gov?" Peabody asked, peering over his shoulder.

"Give me a moment. It may be nothing." They'd unearthed plenty of unremarkable lists of shipments and trade goods. Of course, antiquities scholars would find them fascinating, but when one was on the trail of treasure, bales of wool failed to excite.

There was no mark on this new tablet that indicated the writing was done by Caius Meritus. The thief had thoughtfully labeled each of his tablets with his name in the lower right corner. The fist that formed these letters was less refined than Meritus's neat script, but a word for a legionnaire's pay, *salarius,* leaped off the tablet at Lucian. Caius Meritus was named several times. The rest seemed less like a Roman report and more like gibberish. Something about a wet tongue, of all things, and a pagan blade pointing to the goddess's sheath.

Definitely something to take to the inestimable Miss Drake, he thought with a chuckle. *Blade and sheath. Pretty obvious sexual references when you add the bit about the tongue.*

Daisy had been curious about Roman visual arts. What would she make of its lascivious love poetry?

"Well, what's it say?" Peabody wanted to know.

"Nothing of import." Even if it were significant, Lucian would never tell Mr. Peabody. "We're done for the day. Tell the fellows to collect their pay and go home."

As Peabody obeyed, Lucian rose from his makeshift desk among the stored antiquities. Cataloging the finds was tedious, meticulous work, and he was too restless to force himself to it any longer this day. He missed Daisy's sunny presence in the midst of the ancient dust. And her methodical knack for bringing order to his chaos.

In the case of his antiquities, at least. Elsewhere in his life, she wreaked her own brand of anarchy.

He was eager to be by her side. Yet he felt the need to take something with him, lest it look as though he were courting her. Suppose *she* thought he was courting her?

Am I courting her? he wondered. Some might think it a logical assumption. But he couldn't risk word leaking back to his father. Sharing a newly discovered bit of antiquity gave him an excuse to see Daisy strictly on business. Yes, he would take the latest tablet. The naughty one . . .

Lucian stood watch as Mr. Peabody and the rest of the men climbed out of the excavation pit. He'd kept a sharp eye on the foreman since he'd caught the man palming that ancient necklace, but Peabody hadn't stolen anything since. The man had actually made quite a show of pretending to find the gold links and amulet afresh, and turned it all over to Lucian directly.

As he'd been ordered to do.

Lucian still wasn't sure how he'd keep his father from becoming involved in the Jacobite plot, but he'd already enlisted

Avery's help in watching his sire. The butler was charged with reporting immediately to Lucian whenever the earl expected to receive either Sir Alistair or Lord Brumley.

Of course, Lucian didn't share his fears with Avery, but the butler could be counted upon to follow direction without troubling himself over why. Between the two of them, Lucian hoped they could keep his father from folly.

Lucian hitched up the gig and sped to Daisy Drake's door. He gave himself up to pleasant daydreams as he contemplated how he'd spend his newfound wealth. The country estate in Kent was in even worse repair than Montford. He knew a dozen tenants whose modest residences needed new roofs, and the place could do with its own mill. With the proper investment and sound management, the earldom would thrive once again. Finding the treasure was his chance to do well for his father and himself and do good for others at the same time.

He pulled the gig up to Lord Wexford's sumptuous town house and handed the reins to Jerome. Lucian rapped sharply on the front door. He was ushered in and directed toward the parlor.

Delightful possibilities danced in his head. Daisy's kisses had been just as abandoned as Blanche's. As he rounded the corner, he was greeted by the sight of Daisy and Lord and Lady Wexford seated at the gaming table in the corner.

"Oh, there you are, Lord Rutland," Lady Wexford called. "We've been hoping you'd call."

"Actually, milady," he said as he made an elegant leg to her, "I need to see Miss Drake." It did his heart good to see Daisy's eyes light with pleasure at that. "My workmen have uncovered another tablet and—"

"Oh, rubbish!" Lady Wexford said dismissively. "If this is about something that happened a millennium ago, surely it can wait a bit longer. Join us, won't you please? We've a serious difficulty here and need your help."

"Of course, madam. How may I be of service?"

"Dear Geoffrey has been trouncing us mercilessly at hazard." The former courtesan pouted prettily at her younger husband.

"We've been desperate for a fourth player so we can switch to whist," Daisy explained. "Your arrival saves us from further humiliation."

"Ah! It's gratifying to be needed." A card game wasn't on Lucian's agenda, but he forced a pleasant smile and seated himself opposite Daisy. A wicked impulse made him ask, "Why didn't you invite Mlle La Tour to play? I'm sure being cooped up in her boudoir with nothing to do is tiring in the extreme. Why don't I nip up to her chamber and carry her down so she can join us—Oh!"

Someone—he couldn't be certain whether it was Daisy or her great-aunt—gave his shin a sharp kick under the table.

"Mlle La Tour?" Lord Wexford's even brows tented on his forehead.

"Yes, dearest, you remember. My friend from Paris," Lady Wexford said smoothly. "She came for your birthday ball and has stayed on for an extended visit."

Her husband nodded vaguely. "Ah, yes, of course. There were so many guests at that fete; I must have met her then. Odd that I haven't seen her about since."

So, his lordship was not privy to Daisy's masquerade as the French courtesan. The Wexford residence was a rambling, imposing one. Lucian supposed it might be easy for the earl to absent himself often enough not to know who else was sleeping under his roof.

"Blanche is . . . a very private person," Isabella said. "Her professional life is so demanding—always a whirlwind of parties and entertainments—that when she's on holiday, she sees very few people."

"Not even her host, it seems," Lord Wexford said with a frown.

"I believe Mlle La Tour intends to return to France as soon as possible," Daisy said quietly.

"I daresay she does." Lucian couldn't resist adding, "Once her ankle heals, of course."

This time, Lord Wexford's pale gray eyes flicked over first his wife, then Daisy.

"Two women with sprained ankles in the same household," he mumbled. "What are the odds?"

Lucian turned to Lady Wexford, a mischievous spirit urging him to goad her. "Don't tell me you've suffered a similar injury."

Daisy glared daggers at him. Evidently, there was much Lord Wexford didn't know about his own household.

"I'm afraid *I* took a bit of a tumble on the stairs," she said. "Nothing to trouble over. And I'm certainly recovered enough to enjoy winning a card game. Will you deal, Lord Rutland?"

As the evening wore on it became obvious that Lord and Lady Wexford were not going to leave them alone together. "Blanche La Tour" might entertain a man in her boudoir, but Miss Drake was not going to be allowed to entertain one in the parlor unless she managed it under the watchful eyes of her hosts.

The double standard confused Lucian because Lady Wexford, at least, must have been privy to Daisy's little deception. The earl and his wife were unconventional peers by all accounts, and the whispers that swirled about them were not confined to Isabella Wren's former occupation as a top-tier courtesan.

"Makes a body wonder, don't it?" Clarinda Brumley had speculated once her tongue had loosened that one time he'd been unable to avoid taking tea with her and her mother. "A handsome fellow like Lord Wexford marrying 'La Belle Wren' instead of just keeping her, especially since she's obviously past the age of bearing him an heir. Oh! I shouldn't say such things!"

Then she went on to titter about several theories on the unusual pairing. Veiled slights to Lord Wexford's manhood were the kindest of the rumors. Lucian routinely ignored gossip and did his best to think of something else while Clarinda prattled, but some of it trickled in like the rain found its way through Montford's leaky roof. The rumors of outlandish goings-on in the Wexford household were at odds with Geoffrey Haversham's conventionally dim view of Daisy receiving gentlemen callers unchaperoned.

But Daisy Drake was a guest in his home. Lucian must conduct himself according to Wexford's rules if he wanted to see her.

And he did want to see her—more desperately than he'd ever lusted after the French courtesan Blanche La Tour, even though she and Daisy were one and the same.

Blanche had been a boyish dream.

Daisy was real.

So Lucian played whist in Lord Wexford's parlor and took turns reading aloud from *Moll Flanders*. He even allowed them to coerce him into a recitation from *A Midsummer Night's Dream* that soon became hopelessly muddled with a soliloquy from *Twelfth Night*, but the merry company declared it a shining success in any case.

Finally, when the earl and his wife settled for a game of chess, Lucian managed to corner Daisy for a private conversation on the sofa.

"This is not what I envisioned for this evening," he said quietly.

"Nor I."

"I suppose your great-aunt doesn't trust me not to pounce upon you if she leaves us alone," he said with a wicked grin. "Can't say I blame her."

"That almost sounds like a threat."

"More like a promise."

Daisy laughed and he joined her, satisfied for the moment just to bring color to her cheeks.

"You know, this evening reminds me of happier days," he confided. "When I was a boy, my mother organized quiet family times like this. Even Father enjoyed them."

Daisy cast him a doubtful look.

"Oh, he wasn't always such a dour fellow," Lucian said. "I remember him being a lively man, quick of wit, and a fair treat on the clavichord. He and Mother would sit side by side at the keyboard, playing four-handed duets and singing together."

"Really? It's hard to imagine your father enjoying himself."

"Well, he did," Lucian said, caught up in the memory. "Mother had a soft soprano, but it was a very true voice all the same." He chuckled softly. "She had the devil's own time keeping Father's off-key tenor in check."

"Then your father and I have something in common, I fear," Daisy said. "I try mightily, but I can't carry a tune in a bushel basket."

"Don't fret, Miss Drake," he said with a knowing grin. "You have other talents."

"Since you constantly remind me of the incident with the pike, I don't think you're referring to my theatrical skills."

"I was thinking of your kisses," he whispered.

She smiled at him, her cheeks pinking again. "I thought perhaps you meant my Latin. You said you found something today," Daisy prompted.

"Oh, yes." The pleasant pursuits of the evening had driven the wax tablet from his mind. Now he pulled the carefully wrapped package from his waistcoat's deep pocket. "Not written by Caius, but he's mentioned. Several times."

Daisy took it from him and held it to the light of the candelabrum. Her brow furrowed as she read.

"Perhaps I should warn you"—Lucian lowered his voice to a whisper—"it seems a bit . . . risqué."

"Then I shall read to myself," she said with a grin.

"Where's the fun in that?"

Her grin flattened. "Oh!"

"What?"

"I think . . . I think this may be what you've been looking for," she said, all traces of teasing gone. Her finger skimmed along the old wax. "The writer seems to be the proconsul, Quintus Valerian Scipianus. He tells of capturing Caius Meritus on the river as he was trying to escape."

"Must mean the Thames."

Daisy nodded. "He used what he calls 'standard methods of interrogation' on him. Oh, dear. That doesn't sound very pleasant."

"Remember, Caius Meritus was a thief. He stole from every Roman on the British isle."

"I know," Daisy said. "But I hate the idea of his torture."

"What information did he give up?"

"It seems he would only repeat a love poem," Daisy said with a puzzled frown.

"Is it recorded?"

"Yes. Looks like there's a rhyme scheme. Oh, I'll never get the pentameter right."

"Best you can manage," Lucian encouraged.

"Let me see if I can render it correctly." She stared at the tablet for a few moments.

"O, whither is the cherished flown?
Up the long, wet tongue, I veil my own."

A scarlet spot bloomed on Daisy's cheek. "Oh, this next part is wicked."

"Better read it quick then, or I'll be tempted to stand up and use it for my next recitation," Lucian threatened with a sly wink.

"Oh, all right, but I want you to remember that my interest in antiquities is purely academic."

"Never thought otherwise."

"Liar," she accused with a grimace. "Very well. Here is it is:

> *"Her legs she spreads.*
> *And ankles crossed, my treasure she wraps between her knees.*
> *Where pagan blade points to goddess sheath,*
> *There shall my love be pleased."*

Daisy cocked her head at him as if to say, *I told you so.* He waggled his brows at her, since she seemed to expect a reaction. She rolled her eyes and continued.

> *"Spent, wasted, ravaged, lost,*
> *Too soon my love is o'er,*
> *Spent, wasted, untold cost,*
> *It rests forevermore."*

She heaved a sigh.

"Is there no more?" Lucian asked.

"Just that as he died, Caius Meritus swore the poem told where the Roman payroll was hidden. It seems none of the proconsul's advisers could puzzle it out." Daisy turned to him, a look of quiet sadness on her little heart-shaped face. "I think perhaps he was raving."

"No!"

Lord and Lady Wexford both looked up from their chessboard at his outburst. Lucian flashed them an apologetic smile.

"No, Caius Meritus is riddling." His tone was softer, but

there was a spine of steel in it. He hadn't come this far, spent money he didn't have, just to meet a dead end. All his plans, the changes he intended to make to the estate, the change he hoped to see in his father, even his budding relationship with Daisy, everything hinged on finding the Roman hoard. "The clues have got to be there, hidden in the poem."

"But if the Romans didn't understand—"

"The Romans were angry." A muscle ticked involuntarily along his jaw. "Angry people miss things."

Daisy turned her lips in on themselves for a moment. "Be careful you're not angry, too."

He drew a deep breath. "I'm not angry. I'm determined. There's a difference."

Daisy still looked doubtful. "If Caius was riddling, it's tucked in a rather awful poem. I can't see much here beyond love lost."

"The payroll was lost, too," he reminded her. "A riddle is just a way of hiding information in a web of words. What can be bound, can be unbound. And one way or another, I'm going to untie this knot."

"One wishes at times that love were like a cunning pair of shoes designed for one pair of feet. Alas! Sometimes, it simply won't fit."

—the journal of Blanche La Tour

Chapter Twenty-five

"Rutland is well spoken; I'll give him that." Lord Wexford closed his wife's bedchamber door behind him.

It was Thursday. The servants expected him to spend an extended period of time in Isabella's room tonight, and, given his delicate situation, it wouldn't do to ignore their expectations.

"Does your great-niece like him then?"

"Geoffrey Haversham! Have you misplaced your eyes? Of course she likes him." Isabella removed her powdered wig and began pulling the pins that bound her hair into a tight little knot. "How could you miss that?"

"I'm afraid I've missed quite a bit of late," Geoff said.

He crossed the room and began helping his wife remove the pins from her silky hair. He watched her in the mirror as she lowered her arms and closed her eyes, a satisfied smile lifting the corners of her lips. He picked up the brush and ran the boar bristles through the length of her silver tresses. Isabella loved it when he brushed her hair. It wasn't much, but he could do this for her. Gladly.

"Yes, I even missed the fact that I seem to have a mysterious houseguest," he said. "So, who is this Blanche La Tour?"

Isabella's eyes snapped open. "It doesn't matter. She's going away very soon."

"All right." He bent and dropped a pecking kiss on her bare shoulder. "Keep your secrets, Bella. Lord knows, you keep mine well enough."

He might have imagined it, but a shadow seemed to pass behind her eyes. Then just as suddenly it was gone, and she smiled at him.

"Love, they say, covers a multitude of sins," Isabella said sardonically. "Between the two of us, my dear, we must have hit all the seven deadlies many times over."

"Without doubt," Geoff agreed amiably.

Isabella stood and presented her still-straight back to him so he could unlace her stays. A lovely little domestic thing to do. It pleased him as much as it seemed to please her. His nimble fingers flew down the row of eyelets, tugging her free of her whalebone prison.

How many men had fantasized about unlacing the notorious courtesan Isabella Wren? Wondering what passions she might initiate them in, what exotic techniques for pleasuring she might possess? A night with La Belle Wren was reputedly the stuff of legends, a man's dearest desires fulfilled.

Geoff wished it meant something to him.

Isabella turned to face him, holding up her dress. The line of her neck, the swell of her breasts, everything in him that appreciated beauty enjoyed the sight of his lovely wife.

Everything but that all-important six inches.

"You could stay the night, Geoffrey." She stepped closer and let the dress fall. "Not that I expect . . . I mean, we could just . . . be together. Hold each other."

Damn. He hated to hurt her.

"Bella." He drew her into his arms and hugged her close. She misinterpreted the gesture and melted into him. He pulled back. "I'm sorry. I . . . have plans."

The shadow was definitely back. "Vincenzo?"

"Yes, but it's not what you're thinking," he said. "He

hardly ever gets a chance to go out for a bit of diversion, so I thought I'd take him somewhere and grab a pint. We'll just be two men having a drink together."

She forced a smile. "Careful, darling. Isn't drunkenness another one of those deadly sins?"

"Drunkenness is the least of my vices, and besides, I don't think it even made the list. I believe you're thinking of gluttony," he said, catching one of her hands. Geoff ignored the tiny veins that had begun to show on the backs of them. He knew Isabella's soul was still young and beautiful. What did this crude flesh have to do with anything? He kissed her palm. "You knew what I was when we married."

"Yes, and you knew what I was," she replied with an arch of a silver brow. She was still every inch the courtesan, but her smile seemed genuine. "So you can't blame a girl for trying."

He laughed. "Ah, Bella, if I were capable of loving a woman, believe me, it would be you." He cupped her cheek and searched her face for a moment. "I do love you, you know, in my way."

"And I love you, Geoff," she said, her violet eyes shining. "Even though there are those who might say I've known too much love."

He kissed her cheek and strode to the door.

As the latch clicked, he thought he heard her say, "And yet, not enough."

Lord Wexford and his valet, Vincenzo, climbed out of the hired cab and entered The Unicorn, the worst-looking of the lot on a crooked lane of disreputable establishments. Geoffrey raised a scented hankie to his nose to cover the stench of the place.

"Put that thing down," Vincenzo hissed. "Unless you want the pickpockets to mark you."

Geoff shoved the handkerchief into his deep turned-back

cuff. The last thing he needed was for anyone to mark him, let alone pickpockets. That was one reason he'd allowed Vincenzo to dress him several notches beneath his station. In this shoddy attire, no one would recognize him as the Earl of Wexford and wonder what he was doing out and about in the company of his valet instead of his wife—or, at the very least, one of his peers.

The other reason to tone down his dress was to level the playing field a bit between himself and the only lover Geoffrey Haversham had ever had. Vincenzo had been with him since he was a lad, serving him, dressing him and, later, teaching him what it was to love a man.

Even though Vincenzo was surly at times, Geoff did love him.

They made for a booth in the far corner and settled in. An indecently clad girl brought them tankards and flitted away, pouting when neither of them deposited a coin between her ample breasts.

No one should put their sexuality so blatantly on display, Geoff thought. In some ways, his opinions lined up neatly with those of the Puritans of the previous century. He smiled at the irony and sipped his ale.

"Ugh! That tastes like—"

"Horse piss," Vincenzo finished for him sourly. "What did you expect in a place like this?"

"You picked the place."

"Yes, and we both know why."

Secrecy and shame. Sometimes, Geoff thought those twin Ss were branded on his forehead. First, he had to hide his nature to protect his father. Then when the old earl died and Geoffrey took his place, he was under intense pressure to wed and beget an heir.

He settled for half a loaf. Marrying Isabella Wren accomplished several things. It increased Geoffrey's stature as a man with an intensely desirable wife, one who had resisted matrimony for years in favor of a courtesan's freedom. Lack of an heir was squarely laid at his older wife's feet. In that case, there was nothing wrong in naming his younger cousin as heir apparent. He and Isabella had been dear friends for years. They shared common interests—the opera, poetry, philosophy. His marriage to Bella made imminent sense, to his mind.

But it made Vincenzo surlier than ever.

Now they sat together in stone-faced silence in what surely must be the most odoriferous pub in all London.

Sometimes, Geoff thought, there was no place on earth where he could be truly happy. He took another sip of the ale. The horse piss tasted slightly better.

After his third tankard, it was pure nectar. Vincenzo still wasn't talking much, but the fellows in the booth behind them more than made up for it. In fact, Geoff put his finger to his lips when Vincenzo finally started to speak so he could continue to follow the conversation on the other side of the rough planks.

". . . and if I throw my lot in with you, what compensation might I expect?"

"Do ye have debt? Ye'll find them canceled if ye owe someone who supports the bloody German." The man's slight brogue pricked Geoff's ear. A troublemaking Scot. "Do ye need income? When the true king takes the throne, your worries are over. He'll come with rich rewards in his hand."

"A man in my position always garners a few enemies. What if I have scores to settle?" the first voice asked, his tone cultured and condescending, with just a slight slur to indicate a few too many upended pints.

Obviously a peer of the realm.

And talking treason to boot. Geoff wished he'd taken the seat occupied by Vincenzo. He might have a chance at recognizing the speaker. Still, his valet knew a good many members of the House of Lords by sight. Vincenzo frequently accompanied him to sessions of that august body to serve as courier should need arise. Geoffrey mouthed, *Who is that?*, to Vincenzo. His valet understood the silent question, standing and stretching to snatch a quick look at the men in the next booth.

"Who among us hasn't suffered under the hands of the Hanoverian's lackeys?" the Scot continued. "Whoe'er has done ye dirt will feel the sole of your shoe on his neck."

Vincenzo leaned forward and whispered, "Montford."

Lord Montford! Why, wasn't he Rutland's father? The young man had sat in Geoff's parlor and behaved for all the world like a model English gentleman while his sire consorted with Scottish rabble-rousers.

"Gabriel Drake in Cornwall," Montford said. "I want him ruined. Destitute. Deported as an indentured servant, if it can be managed."

"Aye, that it can, and so he shall be."

"Very well," Montford said. "I will discover what progress my son has made. The Roman trove, if such there be, is pledged to your cause. As am I."

And all his house, Geoff thought. If a lord committed treason, he might bear the worst punishment, but the rest of his line would suffer as well. Even if they weren't privy to the sedition.

But what if Rutland knew exactly what his father was doing? He certainly was keen on finding that Roman treasure.

Geoff knew full well that a man might behave exactly as polite society expected and yet keep a secret so volatile it had the potential to destroy all he touched.

"Come," he said curtly to Vincenzo. Moving quietly, Lord Wexford made his way past the bleary-eyed serving girl and belching patrons and into the inky night.

He'd let things slide in his own house, given Isabella too

free a hand in dealing with her great-niece. Well, that would end this instant.

There would be no more receiving Lord Rutland in his parlor, no more trysts between him and Miss Drake. No more of her running off to muck about in the dust with filthy antiquities. Whatever devilry the girl had been up to was coming to an abrupt halt. She was Geoffrey's houseguest. By God, the girl was his responsibility. He owed it to Gabriel Drake to protect her while she bided beneath his roof.

Treason was not something with which to trifle. The plot would unravel. That was a certainty. Geoffrey was a firm believer in the divine right of his sovereign. And a failed coup tainted all the conspirators irreparably, even those who merely brushed against it.

Besides, a respectable house could afford only one damning secret at a time.

"I believe Eve's eyes were opened not when she took a bite of the apple, but when she first decided to pluck the fruit for herself."

—the journal of Blanche La Tour

Chapter Twenty-six

"Go away!" Daisy plopped belly-first onto her bed.

"I'm not going away, and I must say, it doesn't become you to behave as though you were a child." Isabella's voice sounded from the other side of Daisy's recently slammed bedchamber door.

"Perhaps if I weren't being treated like one, I'd take your opinion more to heart." She blinked back the tears of rage.

Lord Wexford had been a veritable storm cloud when Daisy appeared for breakfast that morning. The thunder in his voice surprised her almost more than it scared her. He was usually such a mild and mannerly fellow, Daisy wouldn't have believed him capable of such sternness. She hadn't been given such a blistering set-down since she set the solarium tapestry on fire, quite by accident, when she was twelve.

The earl had informed her in no uncertain terms that Lord Rutland would no longer be received in his house. And Daisy was not to return to the Roman excavation under any circumstances. All ties were to be severed between her and Lucian Beaumont or Lord Wexford would drop his exceedingly important affairs in the House of Lords and personally escort her back to her uncle's home in Cornwall.

And if that eventuality occurred, he promised Daisy would not find it a pleasant trip.

Daisy had responded in kind and said a great many things she wished she could stuff back into her mouth when she saw the expression of hurt on her great-aunt's face.

Of course, the miserable scene wasn't Isabella's fault. But how dared that prig of a husband of hers order Daisy not to see Lucian again! It wasn't as if he were her guardian, for pity's sake. And it wasn't as if Lucian and she were courting. Not really. A few kisses did not a declaration make.

Not as long as they weren't caught at it.

In any case, if Uncle Gabriel trusted Daisy to manage her own affairs, what business was it of Lord Wexford's?

Still, she ought not be rude to her great-aunt.

"Isabella?"

The silence from the other side of the door was deafening.

Daisy swiped her eyes and dragged herself off the bed. She trudged to the door, favoring her sore ankle only a little, and opened it. Isabella was standing there, arms folded beneath her breasts with an air of resignation.

"Well?"

"Come in," Daisy said. "Please."

"You know, dear, you don't do yourself any favors by flying into a rage. I know that pirate who raised you has the devil's own temper, but even Gabriel Drake knows when to control himself and when to unleash the beast." Isabella swept into the room and settled into one of the two wing chairs flanking the hearth. "I know you won't credit it, but Geoffrey means well."

Daisy laughed mirthlessly as she sank into the other chair. "If he meant well, he'd at least give a reason for his high-handedness."

Isabella pursed her lips, a sure sign she knew more than she was about to say. "In this instance, I fear you'll just have to trust him. Sometimes, knowledge can be a dangerous thing."

Daisy scoffed. "I can't believe you said that. You, who have always championed a woman's right to learn, to pursue whatever field of study caught her fancy. Whatever happened to 'Ignorance is not always conducive to bliss'?"

"That's about a woman's right to understand how her own body functions—a totally different subject." Isabella waved the objection away. "Dearest, please trust me when I tell you there are things afoot here that will endanger you more if you are cognizant of them."

Daisy looked askance at that. "Things that will not endanger you, since it is obvious you know of them?"

"Geoffrey is taking steps to ensure—You're pulling me off subject. We are talking about you, my dear. The point is, while you are a guest in our home, Geoff feels responsible for your welfare. He's an honorable man, Daisy. And sometimes honorable men must do unpleasant things to serve the greater good."

"How is the greater good served by my not seeing Lucian?"

"Until Geoff can sort this whole thing out, you'll simply have to trust that it is and be satisfied with that." Isabella sighed. "Do you believe I love you?"

"Of course."

"Then you know that if I could offer you a more thorough explanation, I would." Isabella's shoulders hunched in an apologetic shrug. "I'm sorry, sweeting."

"May I at least be allowed to write to Lucian? You know, to say good-bye?"

Isabella cocked her head, considering the request. "I think perhaps we could manage that, but I'm sure Geoffrey would insist upon approving any correspondence you sent to Lord Rutland."

Resentment fizzed along Daisy's spine. "Very well. I'll have something to post within the hour." She stood, signaling her wish for solitude. "If you'll excuse me . . ."

Isabella came and kissed her cheek before gliding over to the door. "I know you care for the young man. Perhaps there will come a day when circumstances change."

"Perhaps," Daisy said, unconvinced. As long as she was kept in the dark at present, how could she feel any hope for a change in the future?

Once Isabella left, Daisy stared at her writing desk for a long while. What could she say to Lucian that would pass muster for Lord Wexford and yet be truthful?

Several crossed-out and wadded-up attempts later, Daisy hit upon a plan. She sharpened the end of her quill and started with a fresh piece of paper.

My Dear Viscount Rutland, she wrote.

"My very dear viscount, indeed," she said softly.

> *I regret to inform you that I will be leaving London shortly. I find I deeply miss my family in Cornwall.*

Heaven knew that much was true.

> *I am dreadfully sorry not to be able to continue to assist you with your endeavors, but am confident that you will find success. There is no one who deserves it more.*

She couldn't begin to name all she wished for him.

Now, how to end it? She screwed her face into a frown. How could she put into words what she felt for him and still pass Lord Wexford's demanding eye? She could scarcely mention their torrid kisses or the fact that he'd all but promised to pounce upon her if he managed to catch her alone. Finally, she settled for:

I trust you will remember me with fondness for the sake of the time we've shared, both as children and as adults. As always I remain

Very truly yours,

"Don't I just wish I really were his," she said.

Daisy signed her name with a flourish and went down to tell Isabella and Lord Wexford that she would be returning to Dragon Caern on the next available coach.

Of course, once Daisy Drake left, Blanche La Tour would shortly be returning to London. Daisy had access to her own funds. It was high time she used them.

No one told Blanche whom she could see. Or whom she couldn't.

> "*The moment when lovers step back and say, 'I know you and I won't turn away,' is the moment real lovemaking begins.*"
>
> —*the journal of Blanche La Tour*

Chapter Twenty-seven

Relentless as an executioner delivering forty stripes, rain lashed the tall palladium windows of the Montford library. A jagged fork of lightning brightened the low sky for a brief flicker, and then the day sank again into dreary grayness.

Lucian rubbed the back of his neck. It was far too nasty out to do any more digging, but there was little point, in any case. He'd already found the last piece of the puzzle.

But after two weeks of intense study, he still had no idea how it all fit together.

Perhaps if Daisy . . . No, he ordered himself sternly. He wouldn't pine for a girl who obviously didn't care enough for him to even say good-bye properly. As soon as he'd received her note, he slapped a saddle on his horse instead of bothering with hitching up the gig and rode hell-for-leather to Lord Wexford's residence with little heed for the uneven cobbles and less for the foot traffic that scurried out of his path. He might have saved himself the panicked ride. He was turned away at the door.

Daisy was already gone.

It made no sense.

And neither did Caius Meritus's cryptic love poem.

Lucian painstakingly retranslated the tablet himself, taking into account Daisy's view of it, and spent every waking moment poring over the document. But every time he re-

read the blasted thing, the bit about a wet tongue called to mind Daisy's kisses, and he slipped into reverie. Her mouth was a whole world of delight, slick and warm. A man could lose himself in her kiss and never wish to be found.

Then if he managed to drag himself back to the document before him, once he reached the part about "her legs she spreads," he was utterly lost again. That one time, when she was disguised as Blanche, she'd allowed him to reach under her skirts and rest his hand, however briefly, on her blessed soft mound. That intimate skin was smooth and beguiling, but hadn't yielded to him.

What delights would he have discovered if he'd been able to convince her to spread her legs? The bare thought rendered him hard as iron.

The ping of a steady drip in the corner yanked him back from his imaginings. Avery, ever quiet and unobtrusive, had slipped into the library and placed a tin bucket under the worst leak. Now instead of a widening but silent puddle on the old Persian rug, Lucian was treated to an incessant reminder of why he desperately needed to find the Roman hoard before the place fell in on them.

The double doors of the library swung open and his father stomped in.

"What are you doing there, boy? Why aren't you getting ready?"

"Ready for what, sir?"

"The Duke of Lammermoor's masquerade, of course," his father said. "Lady Brumley told me specifically that you promised to attend, so I hired a costume for you."

"Father, you shouldn't have done that," Lucian said. "If you'd bothered to ask me, I'd have told you I have no intention of going to any silly masquerade when I have so much work to do."

The earl glared down at the single sheet of paper on the desk. Before Lucian could put it away, his father snatched it up. Unfortunately, the page contained both the Latin and the English version of Meritus's poem. His father was no scholar, but he read English well enough.

The earl chuckled softly, then burst into full-throated guffaws. "Work? This sounds more like play, lad."

"You don't understand. The poem has a deeper meaning. It's the key to the treasure's location."

"There's definitely treasure between a woman's legs, all right." The earl laughed all the louder. "Deeper, yes, indeed. The deeper the better. If you're after spreading some slut's legs, there's no finer place to do it than a masquerade. Just make sure it's Clarinda Brumley's you're spreadin', though. We already know what kind of dowry she's hiding between her thighs."

"Father, you may as well know it now. I have no intention of wedding the Lady Clarinda. Not ever."

Even if it sent his father to Bedlam, Lucian had avoided this unpleasant truth long enough. To his surprise, the earl didn't erupt in the fit of temper Lucian expected.

"Then how do you intend to do what's needful by the estate?" his father asked, his tone rumbling with danger. "With this Roman nonsense?"

"Yes." Lucian stood to look him squarely in the eye.

For once, his father's skin wasn't flushed with too much drink. His gaze sparked with intelligence, though Lucian sensed barely contained rage behind the earl's gray irises. "You're certain of it?"

"There is a treasure hidden, sir," Lucian affirmed. "And I will find it."

"Keep me apprised of your progress then. I have some plans for this treasure when you locate it. You're not the only one who cares about Montford, you know." Lucian started to protest, but when the earl narrowed his eyes, madness glinted behind them. His father cut him off with a dismissive gesture. "But if you do not find it, I expect you to consent to the match with the Brumley chit. You can begin by dancing attendance on her at the ball this night."

"Sir, I have ever been a dutiful son to you, but what you ask is impossible." Lucian set his jaw. "I will not do it. My affections are . . . otherwise engaged."

"Otherwise engaged? Your affections be damned." A red flush crept up his father's neck, and a vein bulged on his forehead. Lucian almost wished the earl would explode in anger to release the pressure that was obviously building, but he continued to speak with soft menace. "Don't tell me you're nursing a fondness for that French whore."

"No, sir. The lady in question is no whore."

"Courtesan, then, but it's the same thing, and certainly not worth losing a fortune over." His father pulled out his snuffbox and took a pinch, a luxury they could ill afford, but one Lucian couldn't deny him. Not if the white powder calmed his father. "Rut her blind, if you must, but a bint on the side should not detract a man from marrying well."

"And did you keep a mistress when you married my mother?"

The snuffbox clattered to the floor, and the earl's fist came flying before Lucian had a chance to duck. It connected squarely with his jaw, and he tasted the coppery tang of blood where his teeth cut into the inside of his cheek. When his father reared back for another blow, this time Lucian caught the earl's fist and held him immobile. The manual labor of digging for the past months had strengthened Lucian, and when he tightened his grip, the earl winced.

"You will not strike me again, Father." Lucian's tone matched his father's for silky menace.

Avery burst into the room, bobbing and darting about them like a wren on a narrow windowsill, looking for a spot wide enough to settle upon. "Beggin' your pardon, milord, young sir."

When Lucian and his father turned to glare at him, Avery gave them a stiff bow and held out a much-polished pewter tray with a sealed note on it. "This came for you by special courier just now, Master Lucian. One is dreadfully sorry to intrude, but since the writer didn't wait for the regular post, one thought it might be important. And, perhaps, timely."

It didn't feel timely to Lucian. He was ready to have it out with his father once and for all. Whether or not Lord Montford was going off his cracker, Lucian was *not* going to marry Clarinda Brumley. The sooner his father got that little tidbit into his brain, the happier they'd all be. He nearly waved Avery away, but he caught sight of the script on the outside of the note.

It was definitely written by Daisy's hand.

"I'll take that." Lucian released his father with a slight shove. The earl cradled his bruised fist and shot his son a look of pure malice, but didn't move to interfere.

Lucian strode away to have a bit of privacy, broke the seal and ran his gaze over the familiar round script. Being without her for a fortnight had left a dull ache in his chest. Now the ache faded. He should have trusted Daisy. A smile spread across his face. Then he tossed the note into the small blaze in the grate, lest it fall into unfriendly hands.

"What sort of costume did you hire for me, Father?" Lucian asked. "It seems I will be attending the duke's ball this night, after all."

Once all the debutantes went home, the Duke of Lammermoor's masquerade was no less wild than the last one Daisy attended. It almost seemed the same cast of characters from her great-aunt's bacchanalia was in attendance. But this time, Daisy was in a stranger's home, not her great-aunt's.

She felt like a circus performer swinging high above the crowd, flying without a net.

Daisy willed herself not to shrink from the pointed stares of the men she wandered past. She'd managed to sneak Blanche's red tulle dress, feathered mask and ridiculously high heels out with the rest of her belongings for her supposed trip back to Cornwall. It was deucedly inconvenient that she'd forgotten to include the white powdered wig and, more important, the filmy fichu to cover her exposed nipples. She walked slowly to hide her slight limp.

In the last couple of hectic weeks, Daisy had been busy. She traveled as far as Oxford with a widow and her daughter for company, just in case Lord Wexford should check on her progress toward Cornwall. Then she pleaded illness and bade them to travel on without her. Once they were gone, she left Daisy Drake at the dusty roadside inn as well and returned to London as Blanche La Tour. She presented a draft on her account at the Bank of London made out to herself as Blanche. The skinny clerk frowned, but since Daisy's signature on the draft matched the one on file, he reluctantly turned the funds over to the veiled French-woman. She found a suitable house to rent, hired a discreet staff and settled in on a quiet, yet fashionable street and bided her time, trying to decide the best way to contact Lucian as Blanche.

The duke's masquerade seemed made-to-order. Of course, she'd received the invitation as Daisy, but it was a masked ball, so she expected to slip in easily. She hadn't realized she was missing that essential piece of her costume until her new lady's maid helped her dress for the ball. There was no time to run out for another fichu, so she had to brazen the evening out, exposed nipples and all.

Now, if only Lucian made an appearance . . .

Finally she decided she'd have better luck trying to find

him if she stayed in one place and let the dizzying crush wander past her. She'd already turned her ankle once on these confounded platform shoes. She didn't want to do it again.

She found a bit of space near a curtained alcove and leaned against the wall. After a moment, she heard soft moans and a rustle of silk from behind the damask drape, then a whispered, "There . . . oh, God, yes! Just like that."

Daisy ground her teeth, trying to ignore the grunts of exertion coming from the alcove.

The sounds of passion made her belly clench. She was acutely aware of an empty sensation. An ache began as a distant drumbeat and now throbbed in tandem with her quickening heart.

The clandestine lovemaking had already started all around her. Isabella was right: costumes allowed people to behave outrageously with impunity.

Daisy was ready to be outrageous, ready to put to the test all the delights she'd read about in Mlle La Tour's journal, but she had to find Lucian first. Ignoring her body's growing arousal and trying to seem bored and unapproachable, she sipped her champagne and let her gaze wander the room.

No somber Puritan anywhere in sight.

But there was an elegant and deadly-looking highwayman eyeing her intently from across the room. From his rakish plumed hat to the lethal rapier at his hip, he exuded masculine energy.

There's one thief who might take whatever he pleased from a woman and she wouldn't complain a bit, she thought. But when he started her way, Daisy's heart fluttered.

It was one thing to admire the fine line of a man's form and another to want his attention when she was looking for someone quite different. How could she find Lucian if she were fending off advances from this gentleman-turned-robber?

He made a courtly leg to her, doffing his hat to reveal a head of thick, dark hair.

She whipped out her fan. It didn't completely cover her bosom, but it was better than nothing. *"Bon soir, monsieur."*

He didn't answer. Instead he stepped toward her, tipped her jaw up with one finger and regarded her steadily. Behind his black mask, fire burned in the depths of his dark eyes. Like a hare caught in the gaze of an adder, Daisy couldn't move as he lowered his mouth to hers. He kissed her softly, then with more insistence, tasting and sampling, sliding his tongue between her parted lips to smooth over the slick roof of her mouth and tease her tongue back into his.

Jupiter! It's Lucian. She'd kissed him often enough as both herself and Blanche; now she'd recognize his kiss anywhere.

She let her fan drop on its wrist cord and grasped his shoulders, tugging him closer. True, he was kissing her as Blanche instead of herself, but at the moment, Daisy didn't care. All that mattered was his blessed mouth on hers. His hands found her waist and pressed her to his hard body. She rocked her pelvis against him, but instead of easing the ache in her groin, the action made it worse.

Then he reached for the curtain and edged her toward the alcove.

"No." She pulled her lips free with monumental effort. "Someone is there already." She forced herself to speak French to him, sagging against his chest. She inhaled his scent and smelled her own arousal, musky and sweet, as well. "Where can we go, Lucian?"

He took her hand. "His Grace has a fine library." His smile was bright in the dimness of the great hall. "And I know how much you love books . . . Daisy."

"Despite what the world believes about courtesans, pleasure is the true currency of love. Its coffers are replenished only by giving without thought of remuneration."
—the journal of Blanche La Tour

Chapter Twenty-eight

Lucian led her unerringly, communicating through only the pressure of his hand on hers, through the labyrinth of merrymakers and dancers. When they finally turned away from the more populated parts of the duke's imposing residence and down a wood-paneled hall, the noise of the ball dimmed to a dull rumble. Daisy skittered to come even with him.

"How did you know"—she panted with the effort of keeping up with him—"it was me?"

He smiled down at her, his gaze raking her pert nipples. They tightened further under his scrutiny.

"Let's just say you have certain memorable attributes." His smile flattened. "And you're limping."

Lucian scooped her into his arms and carried her down the dim hallway, past the suits of armor and waist-high Ming vases.

"How long have you known?" She draped her arms around his shoulders and pressed feverish kisses to his neck. The sweet saltiness of his skin made her mouth water.

"That you're limping? I noticed just now. Those shoes ought to be outlawed."

She swatted his chest. "No, I mean how long have you known that I'm Blanche?"

"Since the night you turned your ankle," he said. "I suspected before then, but that night you let me touch your face, and I knew for certain it was you, Daisy."

She'd been willing to let him touch far more that night. Instead he asked to feel her naked face. She'd felt disappointed at the time, but now happiness welled in her chest.

"Guess I'm not as clever as I thought. You must think me shockingly fast."

"Beyond shockingly fast," he said with a grin. He bent his head to kiss the curve of her breast, his warm breath teasing her nipples into aching points. "And I mean that in the best sort of way. I'll never complain so long as you're only this shockingly fast with me."

He pushed through the tall doors into the duke's dark library. Long shafts of moonlight spilled through the two-story windows to the polished oak floor. At any other time, Daisy would have been enraptured by the rows of books, by the spiral staircase in the corner that led to the upper collection, by the wall-size map of England behind the massive burled wood desk. But now, all she could think of was the man who carried her as easily as if she were a child, and yet made her feel all woman when he turned his dark-eyed gaze on her.

He lowered her gently to her feet. Then he took off his plumed hat and tossed it to the desk. He unbound his mask and let it drop.

"Now you," he encouraged.

Daisy pulled off the feathered mask and met his gaze. Lucian wanted *her,* not Blanche. She hugged that delicious knowledge to herself and decided she'd strip naked if he asked it of her.

"Let's get those infernal things off," he said.

She blinked hard, thinking he'd heard her exceedingly naughty thoughts.

"Before you fall again," he amended.

"Oh! The shoes, of course."

He knelt and she lifted her hem enough to expose her feet and ankles. She balanced on her good leg while he undid the shoe on her sprained ankle. It was still bound with a length of cloth for support. He eased the shoe off and brushed his fingertips around her sore spot, his touch gentle, yet arousing. When he caressed her instep before lowering her foot, a tickling streak of pleasure shot up her leg and settled in her groin.

"Can you stand on it?" he asked.

"For a bit." She lifted her other foot so he could remove that shoe as well. If he asked her to fly, she'd make an attempt.

When he was finished and she stood in stocking feet, he rose up, sliding his hands slowly along her legs, lifting her skirt and bunching the fabric over his arms as he came upright. Starbursts of sensation danced along her skin.

"You're so smooth," he said, as he covered her bare sex with one hot palm. "Now, where was I?"

"Right there." She scarcely breathed. His fingertip slipped into her intimate folds as he held her. A shimmer of pleasure sparked between her legs, coursed through her, then returned to circle her most sensitive spot.

He bent to kiss her again, then nibbled his way down her neck to her breasts. She threaded her fingers through his dark locks as she'd itched to do since she was a girl. Her nipples drew up taut and aching in anticipation.

His warm breath feathered over her breasts, doubling their sensitivity before he claimed them, licking and suckling. He thrummed her nipples with his tongue; then, when Daisy thought he couldn't please her more, he used his teeth in a love nip.

Delight arced from her breasts to her womb. Her mound ached under his hand. She rocked her pelvis against his touch, but that only increased her longing.

"Spread your legs," Lucian urged as he switched to her other breast. "Open to me."

It wasn't a request. It was a lover's demand, and she complied with joy. He invaded, gently exploring her tender places.

Breathless awareness prickled her whole being as he spread her intimate folds. She was so slick and wet, his fingers slid from one tiny valley to the next with ease. The whole world spiraled down to his hand on her, touching and exploring. Daisy gasped when he passed a glancing caress over that tiny bundle of flesh Blanche's journal had described as "the seat of bliss."

"Oh, that's it, isn't it?" he asked, returning to the pea-size bump. "The place that drives women wild?"

Daisy nodded, not trusting her voice. The little spot between her legs throbbed.

He returned to circle it with his middle finger, maddeningly, teasingly avoiding direct contact.

She shuddered in frustration.

Then he slid his finger farther along her folds and entered her, now rubbing over that special place with the pad of his thumb. She spread her legs wider, granting him deeper access.

"You feel wonderful," he whispered into her ear. "But I want to look at you."

Without waiting for her response, he grasped her by the waist and lifted her to the duke's glass-smooth desktop.

She leaned back on her elbows as he lifted her skirt and spread her legs wide. The scent of her arousal wafted around them. Her breath hitched uncertainly, but Lucian's nostrils flared like a stallion's, and the wild light of a rutting creature flashed in his eyes. As she watched his face, he struggled to master himself and contain the beast.

An exceedingly wicked part of her hoped he'd fail.

But he maintained control and very deliberately bent to place a kiss high on the tender skin of her inner thigh.

"You're like . . . like a flower," he said with wonder as he parted her outer folds and then drew a fingertip along the delicate inner ones. "All soft and dewy and fragrant, with your secrets safe inside."

He pressed a kiss on her, then stayed to dally using his hands, lips and tongue. Her eyes rolled back in their sockets, blinded by pleasure. She writhed. She moaned. She couldn't have remained a sedate and proper lady for worlds. She knew no law but delight.

Every woman in London, with the exception of her great-aunt perhaps, would admonish her to feel shame at being handled and ogled and finally devoured. But Daisy felt only joy at Lucian's obvious delight in her. She'd longed for his touch, yearned for him to discover all her secrets and find them fair.

But he seemed to be going round-robin a bit, missing that extrasensitive spot with each pass. She squirmed to shift herself into his path. It helped some, but the ache was quickly building to frustration.

Besides, she wanted to divine all his secrets as well.

Much as she hated to halt his investigations, she had her own to attend. She sat up and grasped his head, easing him up, even though her groin throbbed in protest.

"I haven't hurt you?" he asked, his expression dazed.

"Oh, no."

"Then why did you stop me? Was I doing it wrong?"

"Not exactly. Your touch is wonderful." She ducked her head shyly. "It's just that you're missing the spot sometimes. But I think we're on the right path. As Mlle La Tour says, 'The journey is at least as important as the destination.'" She kissed him and tasted herself on his lips. "I want to drive you wild as well."

"You do, Daisy, you do," he assured her. "You're the most vexing creature on God's earth."

"And I'm sure you mean that in the best possible way," she said with wicked smile, toying with the buttons of the drop fly of his breeches.

"Absolutely." He surrendered to her invasion.

She worked at unfastening his breeches and undergarments, knowing this time what a delightfully thick phallus awaited her under the linen. But her fingers weren't quick enough, and he rushed to help her. He strained against the fabric. She drew him out, one hand palming his scrotum, the other caressing the length of him, lingering over the bit of skin near the base of the head that seemed the male counterpart to her special place. She circled it teasingly with her thumb.

"Harder," he said, teeth clenched. "I won't break."

She grasped him firmly and slid her hand up his full length.

"Oh, my love," he said with a groan. Lucian reached up and cupped her cheek, forcing her to meet his gaze. She saw tenderness, bridled male strength and desperate need.

It made her melt.

She guided him to her opening, spreading her knees wider and scooting as close to the edge of the desk as she could to allow him access. He kissed her as he entered her, his tongue and his hard shaft easing in, moving in tandem.

He didn't stop when he reached her thin hymen. A shard of pain lanced her for a moment. She made a little moan, but he grasped her hips and pushed forward. The pain receded as she closed around him, drawing him deeper.

"It's wonderful," he said.

He began to move, slowly at first and then with gathering vigor.

"Lie back," he ordered. She was unhappy to let go of

him, but she did as he bade. Then he splayed one hand over her belly as he continued to rock into her. His hand moved south and she decided, in matters of the flesh at least, that it was safe to obey Lucian unquestioningly.

"I want another chance to find the right place." He stroked between her legs again.

Daisy gasped.

"That it?"

She could only nod while he moved inside her. The heat, the friction, the joy of his hardness against her softness—there was almost too much for her senses to take in at once.

A fresh surge of moist warmth bloomed inside her. She raised herself on her elbows to watch him. Their gazes locked. A muscle ticked along his jaw. His mouth was drawn tight in a rictus of effort.

Then something inside her began to coil, tightening almost unbearably, and she grasped at the edge of the desk to anchor herself. She chanted his name, a talisman against the madness growing within. Her legs tremored as he plundered her, pushing her closer to some unseen end.

Then the coil snapped and she unraveled like a frayed whipcord, her body shuddering with the strength of her release. He arched and pressed deeply into her. As she pulsed around him, his seed spurted into her like a hot fountain. She collapsed back onto the desk and stared upward, unseeing. Lucian came to rest atop her, his head between her breasts. They lay quiescent together, her hand stroking his head, his breath warming her nipple.

When Daisy read the thoroughly detailed description of a woman's "seat of bliss" in Blanche's journal, she'd done some exploring on her own, touching herself tentatively but she'd never ventured past a sense of titillation and unfulfilled desire. It seemed Blanche had not been as forthcoming in the details of ecstasy, after all.

It was just as well. Daisy wouldn't have believed her.

Her heart still galloped in her chest, but her breathing was returning to normal. Daisy blinked several times. The duke's ornately painted ceiling wavered overhead, and then the classical scene slowly came into shadowy focus.

"Jupiter!" she whispered.

"Lucian," he corrected, and gave her breast a soft nip. "Though if you choose to think of me as a god, who am I to argue?"

"Swear by thy gracious self / Which is the god of my idolatry / And I'll believe thee."

—*William Shakespeare*

Chapter Twenty-nine

Daisy gave his hair a playful tug. "You conceited oaf!"

"Conceited oaf? How can you say that when you were practically singing my name a moment ago?"

"I don't sing," she said.

"You were mightily close to it," Lucian said, drawing lazy circles around one of her nipples. It started as a supple pink mound but crested under his touch to a stiff peak.

He'd softened inside her but not slipped out. She clenched around him once, and he hardened in an instant. Her body responded to his quickening with a dull throb.

How was he able to make her need him so quickly?

"Want to give me second chance?" he asked. "This time I'll try to make sure you remember my name."

She chuckled and rocked herself against him, wishing she could feel all his bare skin against hers, but there was a masked ball going on not a hundred steps away. This was the best they could manage for now.

"There is no danger of my ever forgetting your name," she assured him.

But in only a few moments, he led her back into the madness of lust so utterly, she was within a pinch of forgetting her own. He drew their loving out this time, driving himself into her, claiming her, stretching her thin on a rack of need, pulling back when he sensed she was close and then restarting till she pleaded for him to let her go.

Finally, he released her into the bright white light of completion.

When she came to herself, she was flat on her back on the Duke of Lammermoor's desk once again, still looking up at the painting of assorted classical beings.

"Well?" Lucian propped himself on his arms and grinned down at her.

"You are amazing," she said softly. All her joints felt wobbly and loose. Her muscles were so relaxed, she didn't possess the will even to sit up. "Where on earth did you learn that?"

"Blanche was a good teacher as far as kissing goes," he said. "But I picked up a bit from all those mosaics and vases. Roman art is pretty explicit, you know."

"Yes, very explicit," she said distractedly, staring upward over his shoulder. "It's Jupiter."

She felt his belly jerk in surprise.

"I'm talking about the ceiling, silly." Daisy raised herself enough to drop a kiss on his forehead. "Take a look, Lucian. It's the god Jupiter and a group of naiads and dryads. And there's something else."

He glanced over his shoulder at the ornamented vaulted ceiling overhead, then straightened and glowered at her. "Next time we do this, I'm going to make sure there are no paintings on the ceiling to distract you."

"Next time," she repeated, her heart skipping like a spring lamb. She pressed a kiss to the base of his throat. "Oh, yes, there definitely needs to be a next time. And then perhaps we can arrange matters so you'll be in a position to admire the ceiling. But look at that, Lucian." She pointed upward. "Do you think you could light another candle or two? I think there's something important here."

He tucked his shirt back into his breeches and, grumbling under his breath, lit candles. When he held it aloft and looked up, he began to see what had captured Daisy's attention. Along with the representation of Jupiter, there was a large figure on one side of the painting—a water god with a long tongue lolling from his mouth. The tongue became a river, and Jupiter and his coterie of nymphs were sailing a pleasure craft on it.

"'O, whither is the cherished flown?'" Daisy recited.

So Lucian wasn't the only one who'd obsessed enough over Caius Meritus's love poem to have committed it to memory.

"'Up the long, wet tongue, I veil my own,'" Lucian finished. "The tongue is a metaphor for a river. Caius Meritus took the treasure upriver."

"And not just any river." Daisy's tone grew more excited by the moment. "*The* river. The Thames. When the tide is right, a small barge can go fifty miles inland with very little effort. Caius could never have traveled so far in a wagon, not with every Roman on the isle searching for him."

"You're right," Lucian said. "When he was apprehended on the river, he must have been riding the tide back out."

He looked up at the huge map of Britain on the wall behind the duke's desk, then back at Daisy. She was sitting up now, leaning back on her palms, gazing at the ceiling. Her lips were kiss-swollen, and at some point in their passion, he'd left a love mark on her white neck. Her nipples peeped rosily above the frothy lace bodice of the courtesan's red dress, and her skirt was still hiked to her spread knees. One stocking sagged to her ankle. Her heels drummed absently against the walnut desk. Lucian had never seen a more wanton or beguiling creature in all his life, and she seemed not to even realize she was.

Somehow, he had to make her his. Permanently.

He'd have to make sure she never wore that costume in public again. In fact, when he escorted her out of the library, he was going to drape his highwayman's cape over her. But he hoped she'd wear that red gown for him again.

Many times.

His gaze settled on her bare knees, and a new thought coursed through his brain. " 'Her legs she spreads.' "

Daisy pulled her knees together reflexively.

"No, don't." He stepped between them and rested his hands on her thighs. "I very much like your legs just as they are."

He kissed her again and, with supreme effort, finally pulled back. "If the wet tongue means a river, what if the *she* in Caius's poem is also the river? 'Her legs she spreads' could mean a fork."

Daisy nodded slowly. " 'And ankles crossed, my treasure she wraps between her knees.' "

He grinned and snugged her legs around him. "Don't you love it when poetry has double meanings?"

She smiled back at him, hooked her ankles behind him and squeezed him with her thighs. It felt wickedly good. Then her smile faded and a frown knit her brows. She released him and gave his shoulders a slight shove. Daisy hopped down and padded around the desk in stocking feet. She lifted her long skirts to keep them from trailing the ground without her tall shoes and gazed up at the map on the wall.

" 'Between a river's knees' might mean an island. You know, the way the water flows on either side and then joins again. 'Ankles crossed,' you see." She traced the snaking line of the river with her finger. "But the Thames is simply pockmarked with little islands. Which one?"

"I think Meritus has told us." Lucian came around the desk to stand behind her, slipping his arms around her waist. He dropped a kiss on her bare shoulder and inhaled her heady jasmine scent. " 'Where pagan blade points to goddess sheath.' What would the Romans consider pagan?"

"Druids," Daisy said. "There must be an island with roots in druidism."

"There may be several," Lucian admitted. "Even though the Romans outlawed the Celtic religion in the first century, it's hard to legislate people's beliefs. I've no doubt that even by the time Quintus Valerian Scipianus was proconsul, there were still hidden centers of druid worship."

"To this day, there's a spring near Dragon Caern where the local folk leave offerings of grain to the god of the place," Daisy said. "Uncle Gabriel says it does no harm, and the people seem to need to do it."

Lucian stiffened at the mention of her uncle. He'd listened for so long to his father's rants against Gabriel Drake, the ingrained resentment was as hard to relinquish as the simple folks' need to worship the Old Ones.

"So, of all the islands that may have an ancient connection to the Druids, how will we discover which is the one Caius used?" She clapped her hands together. "Oh, I know. The Society of Antiquaries might have some useful information in their reference library."

"No," Lucian protested. After hearing Sir Alistair and Lord Brumley plotting their treason, the last thing he wanted was to let them know he'd made progress on the Roman hoard. In fact, he intended to let all the workers go on the morrow with the tale that he'd failed to find what he sought. That should throw Mr. Peabody off the scent.

"If there's a chance the Society has the information we need, why ever not?" Daisy demanded.

Lucian couldn't very well explain that his father was in danger of becoming embroiled in a treasonous plot with men from the Society. So far, Avery hadn't warned of any contact by the traitors, but his father came and went at all hours. There was no way to know for certain whether Fitzhugh or Brumley had approached his father without Lucian asking the earl point-blank. Given his strained relationship with his father, Lucian wasn't prepared to broach the subject with him.

Oh, by the way, you haven't taken up with any treasonous wretches lately, have you, Father?

Wouldn't that just curdle the earl's milk?

"I can't go to the Society." Lucian couldn't bring himself to tell anyone, not even Daisy, that he feared his father might be tempted into sedition. He reached for the first plausible excuse that came to mind. "The last time I darkened their hall, I was shouted down as a charlatan."

"But now you can prove you're not," Daisy noted.

"At this point, we still have merely conjecture. The only way to prove we're right is to recover the treasure." Lucian pinched off the candle flames one by one, throwing them into stark shades of gray.

"And how will you find out where to search if you don't inquire at the Society of Antiquaries?" she asked with deceptive sweetness, bringing their conundrum's vicious little circle to its full end.

"I don't know." Lucian knelt to help her fasten the buckles on those ridiculous shoes. "But I mean to find out."

And he meant to find a way to end his father's hatred of the Drakes once and for all. He might defy his father in the matter of wedding Clarinda Brumley, but given the depth of his father's loathing, Lucian's taking Daisy Drake to wife would be too much to expect the earl to accept.

Unless Lucian found another way, there was little hope for him and Daisy. And life without her at his side was too much for *him* to accept.

"Though it cannot be denied that a man is an exceedingly useful ornament for a woman's arm, there are times when she must venture alone."

—the journal of Blanche La Tour

Chapter Thirty

Lucian's note arrived shortly after she broke her fast, letting her know that he had an appointment with the gentleman who held the classical studies chair at Oxford. The professor was in town and had invited Lucian to meet him at White's later that day for coffee and a circumspect chat. Lucian's letter was brimming with hope and enthusiasm.

And left her completely in the dark. His choosing an exclusively masculine haunt like White's in which to meet meant she could not accompany Lucian. She couldn't even "accidentally" cross his path.

"How like a man," she grumbled to herself.

And if the professor had no knowledge of ancient druidic sites on the Thames, the day would be totally wasted. Of course, Lucian promised to call on her at her new home later this evening to let her know what he'd learned.

That promise sent her musing about whether lovemaking in her thick new featherbed would exceed her experience on a duke's desk.

It bothered her a little that Lucian hadn't made any declaration of affection for her. She could hardly count the brief "my love" uttered in the extremes of passion, but there was time yet. There was endless new ground for them to explore together, and she had no doubt that if Lucian didn't love her now, he soon would.

Blanche La Tour virtually guaranteed that any woman who followed her sensual advice would have a man on his knees in short order.

But it was hours until nightfall, and she had little to occupy her, since she could no longer work at the excavation site. Daisy Drake had supposedly returned to Cornwall, so she couldn't very well call on her friends.

And Blanche La Tour had none, except Isabella, of course. Even though the former courtesan was a firm believer in romance, Daisy didn't trust her great-aunt to understand why she'd defied Lord Wexford's order not to see Lucian again.

She drummed her fingers on the arms of her chair. Like a bolt from Jupiter's blue, an inspiration struck her.

"Send for a chair, Mr. Witherspoon," she called out to her new butler. Riding in an enclosed sedan would effectively shield her from society's view, and she might travel about London in perfect anonymity. Especially this early in the morning, when most of the upper crust were still abed.

Lucian might not relish the idea of being tossed from the Society of Antiquaries, but Daisy was accustomed to it. One more time could not ruffle her dignity any further. And she might pique Sir Alistair Fitzhugh's interest enough that he would help her find the information she sought amid the tall stacks of musty books and scrolls that made up the Society's library.

Wouldn't Lucian be surprised when he turned up at her door this evening and found she had already solved Caius Meritus's riddle?

"So he gives us all the heave-ho," Mr. Peabody said, wringing his grimy hat in his grimier hands. "Weren't no use pickin' away no more, he says."

Sir Alistair's thick brows beetled as he leaned back in his desk chair. The Society of Antiquaries provided him with a sumptuous office on the second floor in which to conduct its business. He might not be entitled to a *milord,* but he was surrounded with the trappings of one by day.

"Did Lord Rutland seem upset?"

"No, his lordship were happy as a cricket." Peabody scratched the top of his head. "Course, the lads were sad on account of us losing our positions, but Lord Rutland give 'em all good letters o' reference and a tidy little sum. As severance, he said. So they all cheered right up."

Sir Alistair rubbed his chin. *Rutland's found something.*

"'Cept some of 'em weren't happy 'bout not ever seeing her no more."

"Her?"

"His assistant," Peabody explained. "Miss Clavenhook. She were a fair treat, and no mistake."

Clavenhook. Alistair couldn't place the name. He stood and strode to the window and looked down on the bustling street below. Along with the street sweepers and the merchants scurrying to open their shops, a fashionably dressed young woman was emerging from an enclosed chair. She looked up and down the street, then started toward the front door of the Society at a brisk, unladylike pace.

It was that infernal Drake chit again. Did she never tire of rebuff?

"Only I don't think Clavenhook was actually her name," Peabody said. "Once or twice, His Lordship called her something else, but I weren't never quite close enough to really catch it."

"What did she look like?" Fitzhugh asked.

"Like a lady, gov," Mr. Peabody said. "Skin like a pail o' milk, golden curls, bright green eyes, but a bit too sharp, if ye take my meaning."

That certainly fit Miss Drake. As far as Sir Alistair was concerned, brains were wasted on women. Daisy Drake had been lurking about the museum the day Rutland first spoke publicly about his hopes of finding the Roman treasure. "Are you sure you don't recall the name?"

Peabody's eyes rolled heavenward. "It were a bird name, I think. Swan? Mallard?"

"Drake?"

"Aye, that's the one."

Sir Alistair sighed. If she was working in concert with Rutland, Miss Drake bore closer scrutiny.

"Always neat and tidy," Peabody droned on, "even in the dust o' that shed where she sorted out His Lordship's lewd pictures and such."

"Lewd pictures?"

"You know, mo-say-icks and such-like," Peabody said with a leer. "Say what ye want about that art stuff. To my eyes 'twere nothing but more nekkid bodies than a brothel."

"Yes, well, that will be all," Sir Alistair said, anxious to shoo Peabody out of his office before Miss Drake made her appearance. He doled out a small stack of coins into Peabody's open palm. "Take the back stairs and speak to no one on the way out."

By the time Miss Drake's sharp rap sounded on his office door, Sir Alistair was seated behind his imposing desk and, to all appearances, deeply embroiled in a newly discovered illuminated codex.

"Come," he said curtly.

He looked up at his visitor and tried to register surprise. Politeness dictated that he rise, so he did, but took no pains to hide his displeasure at seeing her. If he was going to gain information from her, he had to treat her as he always had, or she might become suspicious.

"Miss Drake, it pains me to have to tell you each time, but frankly you must accept the fact that the Society of Antiquaries will not receive female members."

"I'm not here to petition for membership," she said, seating herself opposite him, though he had not invited her to do so.

"Oh?" He settled back into his chair.

"I was wondering"—she paused, and her gaze flitted up and to the left for a moment, a sure sign of prevarication if ever he'd seen one—"if you could settle a dispute my ladies' sewing circle is having."

"My expertise does not include slip stitches and French knots," he said frostily.

She laughed as if he'd uttered a witticism. "Of course not. This is a question concerning history, a dispute that I'm fully certain you will be able to settle. You see, some of the ladies have become interested in"—she leaned forward as if imparting a wicked little secret—"druidism."

Sir Alistair frowned, intrigued despite himself. Perhaps it would be prudent to let her believe him interested.

"I have certain information on that subject at my disposal, though it seems an odd topic for women to trouble themselves about. What do the ladies wish to know?"

"Well, a disagreement arose about whether many ancient druid sites of worship have been discovered."

"More than ought to be," he said stiffly. "Filthy pagans, the lot of them."

"Yes, quite. But still, the Celtic past is part of our nation's history and therefore subject to inquiry," she said, sounding by the moment less like a member of a sewing circle and more like a scholarly adversary preparing for a verbal joust.

Most unwomanly, Alistair thought.

Miss Drake rose. "If you do not know anything about druids, you might as well say so."

"I didn't say that." He'd overplayed his hand a bit. Time for a more conciliatory tone. "There have been a number of unusual discoveries throughout our isle—barrows, standing stones, and such-like. They seem to be scattered about willy-nilly."

He strode to his bookshelf and pulled down the dog-eared copy of Edlington's *Age of Magic or The Mysteries of Druidism and Other Pagan Religions Explained*. He needed to tread cautiously to avoid putting her on guard.

"Did the ladies have any particular place in mind?" he asked.

She hesitated for a moment. "Well, several of the ladies have country estates upriver, and they wondered if there were any druidic sites near the Thames."

"Oh, assuredly," he said as he thumbed through the old tome and found a faded map. He spread the book on the desk before him and turned it around for her to see. "Look here." He pointed to the Celtic symbols dotting the page. "Each of them represents a curious find indicating an ancient sacred spot."

Daisy's face screwed into a frown. "I never dreamed there'd be so many."

"Where are your friends' estates? Perhaps if I knew the precise locations of interest, we might narrow the field a bit?" he ventured.

"Actually," she said as she peered at the map, "I think they were interested in the ones that are to be found on islands in the Thames."

Alistair bit back a smile. He was getting warmer. If need be, he'd take a punt and search every stinking isle on the entire length of the whole stinking river.

"Weel, then," he said, his brogue slipping out in his excitement. "Have your ladies in the sewing circle aught else to go by in your search?"

"Not really," she said, sitting back in her seat. She reminded Alistair of a whist player who knew she was holding a winning hand, yet feared he might peek at her cards. "Unless perhaps some of the islands have Celtic names?"

"Assuredly, there are some," Sir Alistair said. "Even the name of the River Thames comes from the Celtic, *Tamesis.* Let's just see here."

He swiveled the book back around so it faced him and rattled off a half dozen or so whose place-names he recognized as having old roots.

"Do you know if any of the islands with Celtic names also have remnants of a druid presence?" she asked.

"Any island with an oak grove or a high spot might fit that description."

"I see." Her frown said she didn't. "I wonder if you'd be so kind as to lend me that excellent book, just for this evening, mind. I solemnly promise to return it to you on the morrow."

"Impossible, Miss Drake," he said. "What you request is a right reserved for members of the Society. I would be overstepping my authority to allow this copy of Edlington to leave the premises in your care. However, I can see this is important to you." He turned the map page back to face her. "Is there a particular Celtic phrase you're hoping to find in a place name?"

"How very astute you are, Sir Alistair," she said, cocking her head at him like a robin eyeing a bug on the cobbles. "One hears all sorts of things, you know. One of the ladies, of course—I shan't tell you which one—said she'd heard that there was an ancient site that had . . . rather intimate connotations. Something to do with a 'pagan blade' and a 'goddess's sheath.' "

She blushed rosily.

"There you have it, miss," Sir Alistair said. "The very reason women are barred from the study of such things. Much of the ancient world's ways were bound up with fertility rites and such. Totally inappropriate for a lady's tender sensibilities. Aside from the fact that ye haven't the mind for such study."

The blush faded and two angry indentations formed between her brows.

"I assure you, sir, there is nothing amiss with my mind," she said stonily. "In fact, I believe your bluster is the result of your not being able to answer a mere woman's simple question. Clearly, your reputation for scholarship is vastly overstated. Is there such an island or not?"

"Aye, there is," he said testily. "Braellafgwen." He pointed to the spot at one of the crooks of the Thames on Edlington's map. "The name is a compound of several old Welsh words. *Brae* meaning hill, *llafn* blade and *gweiniau* sheath. Literally, 'hill of the blade and sheath.' Do not trifle with me over scholarship, Miss Drake. If you presume to try, I warn you, you will be irretrievably out of your depth."

"Braellafgwen," she repeated as she leaned forward and narrowed her eyes at the map, clearly marking the island's location in her mind. "I stand corrected, Sir Alistair. It appears your reputation as a repository of arcane information is well deserved, after all."

Alistair could have kicked himself. If he hadn't responded to her goading, he might have been in sole possession of the name of the island she sought. He'd miscalculated the Drake chit's cleverness.

As she thanked him and took her leave, he made a mental note not to underestimate her again.

"No one faults a general for preparing his battle plans. Why shouldn't a woman strategize the course of her love tryst? At least, until passion mocks reason into oblivion."
—the journal of Blanche La Tour

Chapter Thirty-one

It was still fairly early, not yet ten by the chimes of Westminster. Most members of the aristocracy rarely rose before noon, but Daisy's country upbringing in Cornwall never allowed that sort of indolence. Now she was glad for the lethargic habits of her peers. It meant she could gad about London without fear of being seen. Besides, she'd never understood wasting the best part of the day lolling in bed.

"Unless, of course, Lucian were lolling with me," she murmured to herself as her chair was borne in a bouncing trot through the narrow streets. That delightful thought faded as the enclosed compartment combined with the unpredictable motion of the chair made her stomach roll uncertainly. She parted the curtain to peer out for a whiff of fresh air.

And recognized a milliner's shop.

"Stop, please," she called, and the chair came to a chugging halt.

She'd almost forgotten the little hat she'd dropped off there at Mrs. Hepplewhite's millinery to be refitted. It was the one she'd smashed hopelessly on Lucian's square chin that day she ran into him at the Society of Antiquaries. The milliner had made *tsk*ing sounds when Daisy brought the ruined fontange in for her to examine, but the excellent craftswoman had promised to try to repair it.

In years to come, that cunning bit of feather-and-lace frippery might serve as a sweet reminder of her reunion with Lucian. Even though Miss Daisy Drake was supposed to be in Cornwall and therefore should *not* be seen larking about London, she had to retrieve that hat.

Daisy had managed to get in and out of the Society of Antiquaries without any problem. One more stop wouldn't hurt. She glanced up and down the street from behind the safety of her chair's curtain. She recognized no one, so she told her bearers she would be back in an instant and scurried into Mrs. Hepplewhite's tidy establishment.

One other patron was in the shop, counting out coins into Mrs. Hepplewhite's open palm, and Daisy stopped dead for a moment. The woman's striped skirt was fashioned from sturdy, practical fabric, not some exotic silk, and the heels of her sensible shoes bespoke someone who was on her feet most of the day, not lounging on a fainting couch. She was someone's lady's maid, out and about on an errand for her mistress, and not one of Daisy's many acquaintances. She breathed a sigh of relief.

Until the woman turned around to leave.

"Mam'selle!" Nanette said, her eyes wide. "*Quelle surprise!* We thought you had left the city."

"I did."

"But you missed the hustle and bustle of London there in the country, no?"

"No, I mean, yes," Daisy stammered. *Why, by all that's holy, did I not stay in the covered chair?*

"Madame will be overjoyed to see you again," Nanette gushed. "She was very sad for you to leave. But now you have returned. Wait until I tell her—"

Daisy stopped her with a hand to her forearm and drew her away from Mrs. Hepplewhite. The only thing that worthy merchant was more famous for than her clever hat designs was her unending font of gossip about those who wore them.

"Nanette, I must ask a favor of you."

"Anything, mam'selle. You have only to name it and I will give. You know that."

"Good," Daisy said. "I must have your solemn promise that you will not tell a living soul you have seen me in London."

"What?"

"I don't intend to return to my great-aunt's home just yet," she said, turning her gaze in the shopkeeper's direction.

Mrs. Hepplewhite was doing her level best to seem intent on deciding which satin trim to attach to the rim of a straw bonnet, but her ears were certainly perked to their conversation.

Daisy lowered her voice to a whisper. "I'm not in town as myself, you see."

Nanette's lips formed an *ooh* of understanding. "Mlle La Tour, I presume."

"Naturally . . . I mean, *naturelement*," she said, switching to French. With any luck at all, Mrs. Hepplewhite didn't speak the language. "I've leased a house on Singletary Street so I can continue my work with Lord Rutland—"

"Please, mam'selle, tell me you do not regard making the love as work!" Her delicate sniff proclaimed that Nanette's Gallic soul was insulted by the very idea.

Daisy's cheeks burned. Nanette didn't need to know everything.

"I'm speaking of his Roman treasure," she said, willing her cheeks to stop betraying her. "We've discovered where to look for it. So you see why it is imperative that you tell no one you saw me here. We don't want anyone else to know how close Lord Rutland and I are. To discovering the treasure, I mean."

Was carnal experience something that others could sense?

Was the loss of her maidenhead somehow stamped on her features, invisible yet clearly discernible to one who took the time to look closely?

As Nanette was doing now . . . ?

She cocked her head at Daisy and narrowed her gaze. "And when shall you be telling madame you are not in Cornwall, as she supposes?"

"As soon as we've found the treasure, Nanette, I promise."

"Very well, *cherie*." Nanette smiled at her. "But only because I see that you are happy with your young man. A handsome devil, that one."

Now Daisy smiled. Nanette didn't know the half of it. "A handsome devil, indeed." Then her brow furrowed. "I have your promise?"

"*Oui*, mam'selle, I promise. I will tell no living soul I have seen you." Nanette winked. "Your heart may rest easy. After working for madame for all these years, I have great experience in the keeping of the secrets. Yours, she is safe with me."

Daisy wondered, as she returned later to her chair with her refurbished hat neatly boxed, if Nanette would have given her promise so willingly if she'd known what Daisy was planning.

Night settled over London like a heavy black shawl. One by one, the thousands of small lanterns required to be lit by householders began to wink on around Lucian, bathing the soot-choked city in a kindly, hazy light.

Lucian bounded up the steps to Daisy's new residence, taking them two at a time. The day seemed long without her, but he suspected wanting only increased his joy in having. Not only was he looking forward to discovering new delights with her, but the old Oxford don he met with at

White's had not disappointed him. Lucian now had the name of the island on the Thames where he fully expected to find Caius Meritus's Roman cache.

Braellafgwen. The name sang in his ears and sent his blood surging hotly through his veins. He couldn't wait to see the look on Daisy's face when he told her.

He hammered the knocker on the bright red door and smiled warmly at the dour butler who admitted him.

Must be Witherspoon, he decided. The man was just as briny as Daisy had described him when she told Lucian of her newly established household in London. Witherspoon might be sour-looking, she'd said, but he was the very devil for efficiency and, more important, discretion. In light of Lucian's fortuitous news, his heart was brimming with goodwill, even for an old pickle like Witherspoon.

"You would be Lord Rutland, I presume. Mlle La Tour is expecting you," the sticklike man said, his face a bland mask. "Allow me to escort you to her chamber."

Lucian was glad Daisy had been forward-thinking enough to lease the house and hire the servants in the guise of Blanche. That way, there was no need to hide their libertine activities from the servants. They already expected the worst from their employer. And if they spread tales, the fact that Daisy's true identity was safe from evil gossip was icing on the cake.

There was no reason to hide his own identity. In certain circles, a man's reputation was enhanced, not diminished, by association with a notorious woman of pleasure. An inequity, doubtless, but true all the same.

"No need, Witherspoon," Lucian said as he mounted the wide stairs. "I can find my way."

"Very good, milord. Second door on the left."

Lucian smiled. Witherspoon was an unlikely prophet who had no idea he'd just announced the way to paradise.

Lucian climbed the stairs, his body thrumming with anticipation. Would she be wearing that naughty nipple-displaying red gown again, or maybe the elegant corselet with all those lovely lace ties? Perhaps this time he'd manage not to befoul the ribbons as he undid her.

But when he rapped sharply on her door and heard her call out, in French for the servants' benefit, for him to enter, he discovered she was wearing neither of those delightful confections.

She was naked as a newborn babe.

"*Bonsoir,* Lucian," she said from the burnished copper hip bath in the center of the room.

She'd dispensed with Blanche's mask and wig, her own blond curls piled on top of her head, just a couple of wayward locks teasing her slender neck. Her breasts were wreathed in bubbles on the surface of the bath. Where the froth of soap parted, the water was like molten gold in the glow of the candles.

He knew his mouth was opening and shutting, but no sound would come from his lips.

She laughed softly. "You might close the door behind you. The hall is drafty, you know."

She leaned back and propped one foot on the end of the tub, water and soap bubbles slithering from her ankle, past her shapely calf and back into the bath. She sank into the tub up to her shoulders.

"I so enjoy a good soak, don't you?"

"From this vantage point especially," he finally managed to say as the latch clicked behind him. A bath had never seemed like anything other than a method for getting clean. Daisy Drake festooned with soap bubbles was as far removed from something next to godliness as anything he could imagine.

He wasn't conscious of ordering his feet to move, but he found himself standing over her. The mysteries of her delectable flesh were hidden in the water's shadows. His groin clenched anyway.

"A few more candles would not come amiss," he said.

She laughed again, and this time, he thought he detected a little nervousness in the sound. He was a bit relieved by it. He knew she'd been a virgin when they made love in the Duke of Lammermoor's library. But she played the wanton with such devastating conviction; he wondered where she'd learned the courtesan's arts. True, her great-aunt was a famed paramour, but surely she wouldn't initiate her innocent niece into those mysteries.

"No more candles." She wagged a wet finger at him. "Blanche always says, 'A man's imagination is a woman's best asset.' It's true, don't you think?"

"Your assets need no enhancement." He dropped to one knee beside the tub, letting a hand trail in the water. It was quite hot. No wonder her exposed skin was so flushed. "Blanche says? Then there really is a Blanche La Tour?"

"Indeed."

Before he reached the soapy knee that was his goal, she found his fingers with hers and set his hand firmly back on the side of the tub. Evidently in this new game he was allowed to look, but not touch.

"I've never met her in person, of course," Daisy said, lifting her arms in a languid stretch. Her breasts rose almost, but not quite from the water, their rosy tips visible for a blink before disappearing beneath the suds once again. Lucian's breeches were becoming unbearably tight. "But I've read most of her memoirs, and believe me, she has plenty to remember. Blanche La Tour is a font of information."

That explained much. "Ah! Bookishness has its reward."

"Is that how I seem to you?" She sent a teasing splash his way. He recognized Daisy in the gesture instead of the courtesan and didn't care that she was water-spotting his best and only remaining frock coat. "Bookish?"

"No. You seem . . ." He had no words to describe her. She was so much of everything—vixen and virgin, siren and saint, Eve and Jezebel at once. Dark and bright, she was a contradiction with feet. Lovely, soapy feet with delicately arched insteps. Lucian finally settled on ". . . womanly."

She smiled, a satisfied feline smile, and he knew he was lost.

And didn't care one whit.

He fought to maintain eye contact with her, but it was a losing proposition. Her skin gleamed wetly, and where the bubbles parted on the surface of the bath, he was treated to tantalizing glimpses in the shimmering depths below. A curved waist here, a dimpled knee there, a quick peek at her belly with the tiny indentation of her navel winking at him—it was all he could do not to hoist her from the bath, throw her over his shoulder and carry her off to the waiting bed in the corner. The little minx was treasure begging to be discovered.

Lucian suddenly remembered the news he had for her. "Oh! I found the name of the island where—"

She put a wet finger to his mouth. "Later. Now we search for other riches." She drew her thumb across his lower lip, then raised herself to her knees, her upper body rising from the bath like Venus rising from the waves.

She leaned to kiss him and her breasts fell forward into his waiting palms. Soft, full, just the right size for his hands. They were a perfect fit. Her nipples hardened against his palms.

Her skin was slick and smooth. As their kiss deepened, he slid his hands down her ribs, into the water to cup her sex. She was even softer there, and when he slipped a fingertip in the small crevice, she moaned into his mouth. Her legs parted in invitation.

She was wet, more than wet from the bath. Her intimate folds were heavy with the dew that meant she wanted him as much as he did her. He slid a finger into her opening, caressing and seeking.

She pulled away from their kiss. "Not yet," she said breathily. "You haven't had *your* bath, sir."

"A man must hear a few nos in order to fully appreciate a yes."

—*the journal of Blanche La Tour*

Chapter Thirty-two

"My bath?" Lucian said with a hard blink.

"Of course, you need a bath, too," she purred. "Those are fresh linens on the bed. Don't you think fresh, clean bodies should romp on them?"

Romp? God, yes.

He stood with alacrity and peeled out of his frock coat. He was already fumbling with his waistcoat buttons when Daisy's laughter stopped him.

"In good time, milord," she said. "This tub is only big enough for one."

He eyed it in randy speculation. "I can think of at least three ways we could both fit. I'm certain more will come to me if I put my mind to it."

She grinned wickedly. "Later, perhaps," she promised. "For now, I simply want you to relax and enjoy your bath. Would you please bring me that towel over there?"

Relaxing and enjoyment didn't seem to go together in his mind at present, but he did as she bade. The Turkish cloth, with its tiny little loops and silk-embroidered hems, was draped over her vanity chair. As Lucian went to fetch it, he heard her rise from the bath behind him, the water tinkling merrily as it sloughed off her body.

Daisy, naked and aroused and dripping wet. This was more than enjoyment. This was the stuff of his dreams.

He turned and found her standing beside the tub with

her back to him. He was disappointed for only a moment before he began admiring the slope of her shoulders, the delicate indentation of her spine, and the curve of her bottom. His mouth went dry.

He imagined her in one of the poses from the Roman mosaic, bent double, grasping her own ankles, all her vulnerable parts open to him.

Spread for him.

He swallowed hard. Was it possible for a man to die of an erection?

She lifted her arms and peered over her shoulder at him with an impish grin. "Are you coming, or do you intend for me to drip dry?"

Reluctantly, he brought the cloth.

"This is a great deal too much fabric for the subject at hand," he said as he wrapped it around her form.

She tucked a corner over her bosom and turned to him. The soft cloth covered her from breast to knee, but the sight of her bare calves and naked feet was still almost unbearably erotic.

"You look like some exotic princess escaping from a Turkish bath, all flushed and rosy," he said.

"If I were, no doubt I'd have a band of frantic eunuchs at my heels," she said with a laugh.

He smiled. "And the pasha would be after you, too, if you tried to get away." Lucian pulled her close, all traces of merriment suddenly gone. "I certainly would if you thought to elude me."

"No danger of that, my sultan." She eased herself away from him. "Now, sir, if you'll stand perfectly still," she said as she started to unbutton his waistcoat, "I will try my hand at undressing a man."

Her hands trembled a bit on the last button. He caught them and brought them to his lips for a quick kiss.

"Don't worry," he said. "There's no way you can make a mistake."

"On the contrary, society would say we are making a huge mistake. Or it would say I am, at least." She gently pulled her hands away from his and eased his dimity waistcoat off his shoulders. "I've a feeling this would be much easier if I were still playing at being Blanche."

"But it wouldn't be real," Lucian said.

"And you want it to be real?"

"Yes, Daisy." He kissed her softly, then rested his cheek against hers and inhaled the fresh, clean scent of her skin. "What we're doing is as real as it gets between a man and a woman. And I want you. Not Blanche."

Her lips turned up in a slow smile. "That doesn't mean I can't put what I've learned from Mlle La Tour into practice, does it?"

"Not if you care for me in the slightest," he said fervently.

She stood on tiptoe to kiss him and gave him a quick nip on his lower lip. "I assure you, sir, there is nothing the least slight in the way I care for you."

Ever since Daisy caught her first glimpse of Lucian with his shirt off at his excavation site, she'd longed to run her fingertips across his broad shoulders. She'd ached to trace the indentations of his ribs and circle his brown nipples with her thumbs. To place a reverent kiss on his belly button and maybe dart her tongue into the space to see what he'd do.

Turned out, he was the one who groaned with need.

But he stood perfectly still, just as she'd asked him to. Tease the Statue was one of Blanche's games, and like all her naughty suggestions, this new diversion was delivering plenty of titillation.

And Daisy hadn't even gotten to the good parts yet.

She took her time, walking around him, trailing her fingertips along his narrow waist.

My, his fine bottom fills out those breeches.

She ran her hand down the indentation between the firm globes of his buttocks, teasing him through the threadbare Manchester velvet of his breeches.

A sharp intake of breath hissed over his teeth.

When she completed her circuit, the front of his breeches was so strained she feared she'd have difficulty with the buttons. She brushed her palm across his erection, caressing him mercilessly through the fabric.

"Have a care," he said through clenched teeth. "You may push me beyond what I can bear."

"Then it must be time for your bath," she said as she undid first one, then the other button on his drop-front breeches. "Before the water gets too cold."

"At this point, I view that as a mercy."

"Never fear. I have a kettle on the hearth. We can warm the water a bit."

She knelt to tug the breeches over his hips and down his muscular thighs. His erection sprang free and took aim at her, point-blank, like a loaded pistol at a burglar.

She swallowed her giggle at that thought. She suspected Lucian wouldn't find anything funny about that part of his anatomy.

Besides, she was quickly overcome with wonder at its thickness and length and the engorged vein that snaked along its left side. His scrotum was drawn tight, the dark skin dusted with darker hair. The sight of him made her belly clench, and a spurt of moist warmth gushed between her legs.

"You were right," she said.

"About?" The tension in that one word told her he couldn't venture more for fear of losing his control.

"That lewd little lamp wasn't anywhere near life-size."

Laughter made his balls shake.

She made a mental promise to return to the region for further study while she bathed him. She considered kissing him, pressing her lips to the flesh so aching for release, but she thought better of it. For now.

After all, he'd already complained that she was teasing him beyond what he could endure. Daisy continued to pull down his breeches.

"Can I move yet?"

"Not quite." She stared at his ankles in consternation. His breeches were hopelessly hung up on his pewter-buckled boots. "I guess I should have taken off your shoes first."

He grinned down at her, past his waving cock. "And I thought that when it came to undressing a man, there was no way to make a mistake."

"It appears I've discovered one," she said with a wry grimace. "Perhaps I should grant you permission to move before you topple over like a felled pine."

He didn't need further encouragement. He was toeing off his shoes and peeling off his breeches and stockings before she could utter another word. In an instant, he swept her into his arms and kissed her.

They were pressed together, chest to breast, belly to belly. She could feel his hardness, his need. Only her towel separated them. When he released her mouth to kiss her cheeks, her closed eyelids, the sweet spot of her temple, she pushed against his chest.

"Lucian."

"Hmm?" His kisses headed south now, leaving her jaw and traveling down her throat to the tops of her breasts.

"Your bath," she reminded him gently.

He released her with a hint of a scowl and stomped to the tub. As she suspected, his derriere was glorious, the tight musculature bunching and flexing beneath his smooth skin as he moved. Lucian Beaumont, clad in only the skin God gave him, was, without doubt, the finest thing Daisy had ever seen.

He stepped into the tub and lowered himself with no concern about the water surging over the sides. Daisy shrugged. Mr. Witherspoon could worry about the water stain on the carpet later.

"It's barely warm," Lucian said, his knees rising like mountainous isles from the surface of a soapy sea.

"That's something I can remedy." She skittered to the fire and brought back the steaming kettle. "Tell me when."

She tipped the spout and, taking care to aim at a place on the surface where there was nothing of Lucian poking out, she let the steamy water flow. As the heat spread throughout the tub, Daisy could see his muscles unclenching in the growing warmth. She emptied the entire kettle.

"Better?"

"The water's warmer, if that's what you mean." He laced his fingers behind his head and leaned against the raised back of the tub. "My definition of *better* would be for you to lose that towel."

"That can be arranged." She tugged at the corner of the fabric she'd tucked over her left breast and drew the towel off slowly, basking in the complete approval she saw in Lucian's dark eyes. "And now for your bath."

She knelt beside him and felt for the soap and washcloth along the bottom of the brass tub. She brushed his skin in several sensitive places before she came up with the items she sought.

"Not that I'm complaining, but what are you doing?"

"Wouldn't the harem girl bathe her prince?"

"I'd rather find out if Daisy will bathe Lucian," he said. "Remember, whatever games we may play, this is still real."

"All right, Lucian. Real it is."

She lathered up the cloth and took one of his hands, soaping and caressing. She moved up his arm, then across his chest to his other arm. She took her time, committing him to memory, every pore, every inch of skin.

She met his gaze when her hand slipped beneath the water to wash his belly and to dip lower. She held him, rubbed the nubby cloth along the length of him. She handled his balls, lifting and kneading gently.

A fire blazed behind his eyes, but he remained still, except for one hand. He found her breast and teased her nipple with his fingertips while she continued to wash him.

He made her ache something fierce.

She stroked his inner thighs, down to his knees and calves. Finally she lifted his foot from the water and soaped it, massaging the ball and instep with her thumbs.

"That feels wonderful," he said. "But you've had your hand on the tiller of this little adventure long enough. It's time for a change of command."

He drew his foot away and crooked his finger at her.

"Come here."

"Lucian, the tub—"

"Let me worry about how we'll fit." He sat up straight and caught both her wrists. "Just step in. Here and here."

He pointed to either side of his hips.

If she did as he asked, she'd be astraddle him, totally open to his gaze and whatever else he might have planned. "But that will have me . . ."

His smile grew wicked. "Yes, it will. Soon I'll know all your secrets. All you have to do is trust me, Daisy."

Trust him. It was either that or stop breathing. She didn't think she could live in a world where she couldn't trust Lucian.

She stepped into the soapy water.

"The thing to remember about adult games is that unlike in whist or hazard, the rules are not hard-and-fast. Laws governing adult play are not to be regarded as permanent. They shift like smoke or disappear entirely in the blazing inferno of molten passion."

—the journal of Blanche La Tour

Chapter Thirty-three

Blanche's words tumbled through Daisy's head while Lucian slid his hands up her legs. The teeniest bit of fear tingled alongside his fingers. She couldn't remember any reference to this sort of game in Blanche's exhaustive tome, never a mention of letting a man view and handle a woman from Lucian's unique perspective.

Soon I'll know all your secrets, he'd said. He'd know more about her body than she. Daisy had no idea what she looked like from that angle. And there was no way to bring her legs together with one foot on each side of his hips.

Courtesans must be careful always to present themselves to their patrons in the most favorable light, according to Blanche.

Would he find this view "favorable"?

He reached the tender skin of her inner thigh and teased around each leg, front to back. So far, he certainly approved. Heaviness settled in her groin, making her swollen and prickling with sensitivity.

"So soft," he murmured.

Then he caressed her intimate folds, his fingers sliding easily in her slick wetness. He avoided her "spot," and she forced herself not to move so his touch would ease the familiar ache. But she clenched her teeth with effort.

"No hair, though," he said. "That surprises me. Are you always thus?"

"No," she admitted. "It's a courtesan's trick. I kept having the hair removed so I could play Blanche more convincingly. Do you . . . do you like me like this?"

"Daisy, I would adore this part of you regardless," he said as he touched her gently. "Even if you were hairy as a bushman."

"A bushman!" She smacked the top of his head. "I rather think I'm not as bad as that."

"Hold a moment," he said. "I thought we were still playing Tease the Statue. Since when are statues allowed to move?"

"When the one doing the teasing does so with his mouth instead of his hands," she said, glaring down at him.

"With his mouth. What a capital idea!"

Lucian sat straighter and grasped her bottom, pulling her close. "Now, stand still, Daisy." He glanced up at her, smiling wickedly. "If you can."

His breath was hot on her, and when he covered her naked sex with kisses, her knees quivered. When his tongue invaded her, they nearly buckled. The world went suddenly liquid, and Daisy's only goal was remaining upright. If she went down, it meant he would stop.

And she thought she might die if he did.

He'd avoided her special place before. He did not avoid it now. He twirled his tongue around her seat of pleasure, flicking it with quick strokes. He suckled. He tormented. He danced her to the edge of completion and pulled back in maddening retreat. The empty ache threatened to split her open.

She moaned his name. She pleaded. He would give no terms. She could only surrender and hope for mercy.

"Bend your knees," he finally ordered. She sank down

into the cooling water with him. As she settled on him, the tip of him slid into her with the rightness, the naturalness of two halves coming together to make a whole.

"Oh, Lucian." She sighed.

He filled her completely in one sure stroke. The emptiness was gone, but the ache remained. She rocked her pelvis and he moved beneath her, hands on her hips, meeting her with strong thrusts. They started a tidal wave in the small tub, the water surging over the sides in cascading waves.

Daisy arched her back, presenting her breasts to Lucian's mouth. He took her nipple between his lips and sucked in rhythm with their long strokes. Daisy felt the coil tighten inside her.

"Bite me," she urged, and immediately felt his teeth on her hard nipple. The pinch of pain cut all her bonds, and she unraveled completely, pulsing around his hot shaft in strong contractions.

Lucian groaned. He pulled her down hard against him, and she felt his release as hers subsided. When the last throb faded, she collapsed on him, breathing hard.

His heart pounded beneath her. Hers was beating in time. There was no need for words. Their bodies had said it all. No need to do anything. For the moment, just breathing, just pushing the blood through their veins, just *being* was enough. So long as they were *being* together.

"I can ring for supper if you like," Daisy said much later. They'd moved to her large featherbed and discovered that lovemaking on a mattress had every bit as much to commend it as dallying on a duke's desk. Or coupling in a copper bath. At this rate, Daisy was sure Lucian and she could manage to unite their bodies almost anyplace and find the experience transcendent. She molded herself to his long frame, laying her head in the crook of his shoulder, totally at peace with the world. "Are you hungry?"

"Famished," he admitted, "but too sated with love to care for my belly just now. Besides, ringing for your servants would mean getting dressed, and I find you delectable just as you are."

He kissed her forehead and ran his hand over her crown.

Sated with love. He'd done it again: he implied that he loved her without actually saying it. He was the one who insisted that what they were doing must be real. How hard could it be for him to put the words together?

The real ones.

Her peace frayed a little at the edges. With a sigh, she hooked her ankle over his calf. How good, how right this could all be if—

"Oh!" He sat bolt upright, making the bed bounce Daisy into a trough in the soft mattress. "I almost forgot. The professor I met with gave me the name of the island we're looking for. It's—"

"Braellafgwen," she said along with him, then added, "Hill of the blade and sheath."

He leaned on his elbow and looked down at her. "How did you know that?"

"Because you're not the only one who can discover things, Lucian," she said, tracing a circle around his brown nipple. "I understand why you didn't want to go to the Society of Antiquaries, but I had no trouble there at all."

"After I told you not to—" He caught her hand and held it still. Anger sizzled in his tone. "Whom did you speak with?"

"Sir Alistair Fitzhugh," she said. His grip tightened so she almost cried out. Then he released her hand, his brows lowering like thunderclouds. "He was most helpful and—"

"What did you tell him? No, never mind. It doesn't matter now." He threw his legs over the edge of the bed and climbed out. "You gave him enough, and now he knows where to look for the treasure as well."

He stalked back to his discarded clothing, picked through the pile and pulled on his stockings, smallclothes and breeches. His silence bristled with fury.

"Give me a little credit." Daisy pulled the sheet up and tucked it under her armpits to shield herself from his gaze. Of course, he'd have to deign to look at her in order to feel the slight. "I gave him nothing at all, and I certainly didn't tell him we're seeking Roman treasure."

"You didn't have to." Lucian shrugged his shirt on and tucked the hem into his breeches. "He already knows."

"After your presentation at the Society, he knows *you're* looking for it. I'd wager half of London knows you are, but he couldn't possibly connect me with your Roman treasure," Daisy said, puzzled by his irritation. "I gave him a perfectly plausible tale about my ladies' sewing circle being interested in druid sites on the Thames."

"You gave him everything he needs," Lucian accused. "I told you not to go to the Society."

"You categorically did not. You merely said you couldn't go. That didn't mean I shouldn't, and I don't know why you think you can order me about." She glared at him. "It's not as though we're married."

"You'd never be a biddable wife, at any rate," he growled.

"Probably not. In fact, it would be my duty to be as unbiddable as possible so long as you insist on being so mulish," she agreed, her own anger rising to meet his. "But I am not your wife. Neither am I in your employ."

"But Mr. Peabody thinks you are my assistant, and he's been spying for Fitzhugh since he started working at the site. So Fitzhugh saw through that flimsy tale you told him like—Oh, blast and damn! He may be halfway to the island already."

"Peabody was spying?" She climbed out of bed with the

sheet wrapped toga-style about her. "Why didn't you give him the sack?"

"I wanted to know what he was up to." Lucian put on his waistcoat and began buttoning the long line of pewter marching down his chest.

"Why didn't you tell me about Mr. Peabody?"

"Because I didn't want you to know my—" He stopped himself. He'd nearly said it aloud. *My father may be involved in a plot to overthrow the king.* Just thinking it was terrible. Speaking it was more than he could bear. He straightened and looked her in the eye. "My business. I didn't want you to know my business."

She flinched as though he'd slapped her.

"Your business," she repeated woodenly.

"Yes, my business."

"You come here and make love to me and tell me you want things real and demand to know all my secrets." Her voice started softly, but now was building toward shrill. "And you don't want me to know your *business?*"

Better to have her angry with him than delving for the unspeakable truth.

"What an astute mind you have." He shoved an arm into the sleeve of his frock coat. "You've managed to grasp my point very quickly . . . for a woman."

He probably should have expected the kettle to come flying, but Daisy was so quick, he barely had time to duck. It sailed within a finger's width of his head and crashed into the wall behind him. A spiderweb of cracks rippled the plaster.

"Careful! That might have been me!"

"That *should* have been you," she said, green eyes blazing. Her hair was wondrously tousled, and the sheet drooped low on her breasts. "Stand still next time."

Lord, she was magnificent. Part of him wanted nothing

more than to heft her over his shoulder, carry her back to bed and swive the living lights out of her.

Another part warned that it would be more than his life was worth to try.

Besides, if Fitzhugh was already in possession of the name of the island, he had no time to lose.

"Where are you going?" she asked.

"To Braellafgwen." He bent to buckle his shoes, careful to keep his eyes on her in case she should rearm herself.

"And how do you intend to get there? Swim?"

"No, I'll hire a boat."

"With what as payment?" She laughed mirthlessly. "Your skills as a gigolo?"

"Why? Are you offering to write a letter of recommendation?"

He wasn't quite quick enough to dodge the cake of soap that zipped across the room. It was hard and Castilian and beaned him squarely on the bridge of his nose. Stars danced across his vision.

He probably deserved that.

"Now that I have your attention, it occurs to me as your *business* partner"—she spat the words at him—"that between the two of us, I am the only one with sufficient funds to make a journey to Braellafgwen. Therefore, *I* shall see to the arrangements."

Before he could object, she tugged the bellpull and Witherspoon appeared at her door. If the man was shocked by the soggy carpet around the tub, the disheveled bed or his mistress's state of undress, he gave no indication. His expression was locked in perpetual neutrality with a hint of boredom.

"How soon can you arrange to hire a boat and crew capable of taking Lord Rutland and me upriver to an island called Braellafgwen?" she asked. "No, wait, better just say an unnamed destination until we settle on our arrangements. We need to travel with all speed and extreme discretion."

Witherspoon cast his eyes heavenward, as if he might receive a sign from above. Then, satisfied he'd made the correct calculations, he lowered his gaze. "I shall make a few inquiries among my connections, but I believe you may rely upon a dawn departure," Witherspoon said.

"Very well. Meet me on the wharf at dawn, Lord Rutland, or I shall go alone."

Her bearing was so regal, Lucian figured she'd completely forgotten she was clad in nothing but a rumpled sheet.

"Witherspoon, please see this . . ." She glared at him as if he were a particularly repugnant sort of vermin. "Show this *gentleman* out."

"'The course of true love never did run smooth,' or so said the Bard. Wouldn't it be boring if he were wrong?"
                     —the journal of Blanche La Tour

Chapter Thirty-four

The six-oared shallop Mr. Witherspoon engaged was perfect for their needs. It was captained by a Mr. Crossly, who, despite his dour name, had a pleasant way about him. Daisy found his aromatic pipe comforting as he deftly managed the tiller one-handed and kept up a running conversation punctuated by frequent gestures with the other. The oars were manned by his six strapping sons.

"Wanted to go for an eight-oar tilt boat meself, but the missus drew the line at birthing six boys and started poppin' out daughters instead," he explained with a laugh.

The merry little craft was graced with a small tilt, a cloth-covered, open-sided cabin, where Daisy could shelter from the sun. The day had dawned cloudless, the water a rare blue, the breeze fresh and frequent. They were making remarkable speed, thanks to the surging tide in addition to the strong backs of Mr. Crossly's sons.

All things considered, Daisy should have been pleased. The shallop was an exceedingly comfortable mode of travel, much nicer than a dusty coach on a rutted road. It only reinforced her faith that she and Lucian had correctly deciphered Caius Meritus's poem. The current was strong; she could easily imagine the ancient thief making his way up the Thames, even in a single-occupant craft. Mr. Crossly estimated that they'd travel the thirty miles or so of river to Braellafgwen in about six hours.

Daisy was finally having an adventure. She should have been outrageously happy.

And would have been, except for the other passenger with whom she shared the tilt.

Lucian sat with his arms folded over his chest in taciturn surliness. He propped his tricorne over his face and lounged with his long legs outstretched. The rapier he'd worn as part of the highwayman costume turned out not to be ornamental. It was strapped to his left hip, and the angle of the sheath kept Daisy from sitting too close to him.

Not that she wanted to. He hadn't apologized yet, and she had no need to, thank you very much! Lucian deserved everything she gave him.

Including that faint purple bruise on the bridge of his nose.

So they spoke to each other only when absolutely necessary, and even then with cold civility. Now that he seemed intent on a nap, they glided along in stony silence.

Daisy leaned her cheek on her palm and sighed. Even though they were making good time, this was going to be a very long trip.

"I still don't see why we had to wait to follow them to the treasure when we might have stolen the march by leaving yesterday and beaten them to it," Lord Brumley complained.

"Because we may not be privy to all Rutland and the Drake chit knows," Sir Alistair explained. "There may yet be pieces to this puzzle we couldn't begin to guess."

He raised a hand to shield his eyes from the glare on the water and squinted at the other tilt boat in the distance. The viscount and Miss Drake were making excellent progress, but Fitzhugh's vessel managed to keep them in sight.

"We might spend weeks stumbling about on Braellafgwen looking for the treasure and still come away with nothing. Following them to it is a much simpler matter," Alistair concluded.

He didn't feel the need to add that neither he nor Brumley could afford to hire the little shallop they now rode in, so he had to skulk about in the shadows waiting until Rutland left his home slightly before dawn. Only then could he approach Lord Montford to demand the earl step in and aid the true king's cause.

He'd sworn to, after all.

At first, his lordship was furious at being rousted out of bed so early, but once Alistair mentioned the name of Rutland's traveling companion, Lord Montford had been eager to join them. Alistair had the distinct impression the earl was not at all happy his son had taken to cavorting with Miss Daisy Drake. Whatever his motivations, it was gratifying to have another peer of the realm on board, on the theory that nobility further ennobled the cause.

Even so, Lord Montford was reduced to handing over some silver serving spoons, all black with tarnish, as payment for their passage. Yet another example of a land-rich, cash-poor peer groaning under the German usurper's hand. Time was, the mere dropping of a man's title was enough to earn him credit at the finest establishments throughout the land. Now, not even the river rats rowing this excuse for a boat would board a noble passenger without collecting the fare up front.

"But if he finds the treasure first," Brumley said, "Rutland's not likely to give it up without a fuss, is he?"

"Let me worry about my son, Brumley," Lord Montford said, joining in the conversation for the first time since they boarded the shallop. "I can vouch for his cooperation. I need only give the word."

Brumley frowned with concern. "But that woman, that Drake girl, she's not the sort to go quietly, if you know what I mean. How many times have you tossed her from the

Society's meetings, eh, Fitzhugh? And yet she keeps turning back up like a bad penny."

"Lucian thought himself so clever when he hid these, but Avery still takes his orders from me, not my son," Lord Montford said, patting the handle of the pistol shoved into his waistband. It was part of a matched set of dueling pieces. He'd given the twin to Alistair. "Do not trouble yourself over Miss Drake. She's the reason I made certain we are armed."

The scrape of booted feet and the rumble of masculine voices sounded in the hall. Isabella looked up from the lavender-scented writing paper on her escritoire and saw her brawny son-in-law standing at the parlor door with his scruffy friend at his side.

"Gabriel, how lovely to see you," she said, extending a hand to him. The former pirate captain who'd married Isabella's only daughter bent over her fingertips as smoothly as any dandy. Of course, Gabriel Drake was considered a baron or some such, but in Cornwall, of all rustic places, so Isabella never put too much stock in his title. She was far more impressed by the man himself.

"You grow more beautiful each time I see you," Gabriel said with a wink. "Luckily for me, Jacquelyn favors her mother." He straightened and turned to nod at Geoffrey, who'd been reading when he came. "Wexford. I don't think you've met my friend, Joseph Meriwether, Baron—"

"Aw, belay that baron stuff," the squint-eyed old mariner said. Isabella knew Mr. Meriwether had been awarded the small barony north of Gabriel's estate for service to the Crown. "Just call me Meri."

The fellow pumped Geoff's hand vigorously.

Isabella rang for tea. "What brings you to London?"

"My old ship is due in port with a consignment of cotton," Gabriel said. Carding and spinning the cotton into thread provided piecework for his tenants through the winter and a chance to earn some ready coin without leaving their homes. "Besides, I'm hoping to catch up with my old shipmates."

"And see if they're managing to sail as honest mariners yet, without being bored into excessive drink or an early grave," Meri said.

"An early grave, in any case," Gabriel said with a grin. "Excessive drink is a foregone conclusion."

"The day's a bit young for strong spirits yet, but we can certainly accommodate you after supper. Say you'll stay." Isabella shepherded her guests to the comfortable chairs across from the settee, where she sat. Her young husband hooked a thigh over the arm of the settee next to her, leaning toward her, the picture of the doting swain.

Isabella sighed. *Say what one will of Geoff, he has a knack for appearances.* "Geoffrey just discovered a remarkable case of port. He thinks it's the best he's ever had, but he's dying to have another man's opinion."

Meri clapped his hands together and rubbed his palms with enthusiasm. "I'll drink to that. When it comes to port, everyone's entitled to my opinion."

"And here's our tea," Isabella said amid the laughter as Nanette brought the silver tray in and placed it on the low table. Isabella waved her away. She liked to pour out herself, but Nanette knew enough to hover nearby in case something else was needed. "Why didn't Jacquelyn come with you?"

"She said Charlotte was too young to enjoy London yet, and dragging the boys about town would make her feel too old," Gabriel said. Their daughter, Charlotte, was nearly eleven, and the twin boys were eight.

"Those two would outdevil Old Patch himself," Isabella said, remembering how she'd had to hide every bit of her delicate breakables the last time they came to visit. "Well,

Jacquelyn must enjoy having Daisy back home to help corral those two little imps."

Nanette erupted in a fit of coughing.

Gabriel cocked his head at Isabella. "Daisy is here. With you."

"No, she left for home, oh, it must have been over a fortnight ago." Panic bubbled in Isabella's chest. "We expect to hear from her any day, saying that she arrived safely."

"Well, she never did." Gabriel turned an evil glare on Lord Wexford. "She was in your care. Why didn't you escort her home properly?"

"I offered, but she wouldn't hear of it." Geoff rose from his perch on the settee arm. "So I arranged for her to travel with a widow and her daughter who were going to Bath. I put her on the coach myself."

Gabriel Drake and his friend began talking at once, and Geoff's voice chimed in, his tone harsher by the minute. Isabella was trying to think how to soothe all the ruffled masculine feathers in the room. She had to shut them up long enough so they would realize that angry talk would solve nothing. Then they might actually come to a decision about what must be *done* about this calamity.

But then she noticed Nanette sending her furious, silent signals and decided the men would have to shift for themselves. When her maid slipped into the hall, Isabella rose quietly and followed her. She hoped the discussion would not come to blows before she returned. Geoff was an amateur pugilist, and acquitted himself admirably in arranged matches, but Gabriel Drake had been a fighting man all his adult life and no doubt held little truck with sporting rules.

Nanette was wringing her apron in her hands when Isabella joined her.

"Nanette, is there something you wish to add to the discussion?"

"*Oui*, madame, most desperately I wish it, but I cannot."

"And why is that?" Isabella asked, trying to sound calmer than she felt.

"Because I swore I would not," Nanette said with anguish. "And you know, madame—who knows better than you?—that I am a trustworthy keeper of the secrets."

"Yes, Nanette." Isabella nodded. "I've always appreciated your discretion."

"Then you know I cannot go back on my oath, not even if it means . . ." She dissolved into tears. "Even if I knew a street name, a place where one might find . . ."

"There, there." Isabella patted her servant on the shoulder. So Nanette knew where Daisy was staying in London. "Perhaps it's not as hopeless as that. What *precisely* did you swear to?"

"I swore not to tell a living soul."

Isabella smiled. "Then your dilemma is solved. You can't tell me, even though I know you want to."

"But, madame—"

"I'm not finished, Nanette." Isabella picked up a figurine from the foyer table.

It was the naughty little statue of Pan that Daisy had left in her room. It was just risqué enough for Isabella to need to display it in her foyer, where her visitors could be either shocked or amused by it, as they chose.

"You swore, and I would not have you break your oath for worlds," Isabella said. "Therefore you must not tell a living soul."

Nanette erupted in fresh sobs.

"However, you can tell Pan here." She waggled the statuette between her two fingers. "He is not a living soul, but he's an extremely good listener. Unburden yourself to him, my dear, and if I should happen to overhear your counsel"—Isabella shrugged expressively—"it will not be your fault."

"Say, I pray thee, thou art my sister."

—*Genesis 12:13*

Chapter Thirty-Five

Daisy pleaded with Mr. Crossly, but he was adamant.

"I'm sorry as I can be, miss, but it don't change the particulars," he said, scratching his freckled, balding pate. "We rowed all the way around the blasted place. That island yonder has no proper dock, no way for me to know where's a safe place to pull me shallop along. Not a curl of smoke to be seen. That tells me no one lives there. And if no one lives there, it stands to reason there's cause for it. Most likely, no decent place to make landfall."

"But—"

"If I was to tear the bottom out of the boat on some rocks under the surface, well, how would I feed me family, I asks ye? Besides, if I was to lose me livelihood, Mrs. Crossly would tan me hide and pin it up on her kitchen wall."

"But our agreement was for you to take us to Braellafgwen." Daisy glared first at Mr. Crossly, then at Lucian, who stared disinterestedly into the distance, refusing to take part in the discussion.

He might at least make himself useful instead of merely ornamental, she thought with vehemence.

"No, I agreed to take ye upriver to an unnamed location. If ever a spot looked as if it were lacking a name, it's that little hamlet there just between them trees." Mr. Crossly swung the tiller around. "I can set ye alight at this village dock and ye can see if there's a ferryman what can take ye the rest of the way, or ye can ride back to London town with us now and call this a pleasure cruise."

"Mr. Crossly, this is wholly unaccept—"

"That'll do, Mr. Crossly," Lucian finally spoke up. "Leave us here for now, but we'll need you to fetch us back to town later."

"You want me to come for ye tomorrow, then?"

"No." Lucian eyed the island that divided the river into equal channels. "Better give us two days."

The river man nodded and deposited them on the dock.

Daisy watched the tilt boat head back downstream with a sinking feeling in her gut. They were so close. She could see the island, its outline hazy through the mist that rose around it. But if they couldn't find a way over to it, they might as well have stayed in London. Of course, if they had to find a ferryman, so would Fitzhugh. Perhaps the other treasure seekers hadn't gotten too far ahead.

"Now what?" she asked.

"Were you speaking to me?" Lucian said as he started up the goat track toward the village.

"I don't see anyone else here," she answered testily. "How do you propose to proceed?"

"So I'm allowed a say in my own expedition now? I thought you were making all the travel arrangements," he said, not slowing his stride.

"So I did."

"And look how well that turned out."

"I got us this far." She scrambled up the slope after him. "We'll just have to find someone to take us to Braellaf-gwen."

He stopped and extended a hand to help her over the crest of the rise. The tiny hamlet spread out before them, a collection of ramshackle huts around a little stone church. Besides the church, one other structure looked as though it might have been erected after the Norman conquest. A shingle with a picture of a boar on it twisted in the breeze over the only proper door in the village.

"A public house?" Lucian wondered.

"Or, please God, an inn," Daisy suggested hopefully. "Thanks to you, we'll be here two days."

"And nights," he muttered under his breath.

"Don't presume to think about it." She wasn't ready to forgive him yet, certainly not enough to allow him to share her bed.

"Think about what?" He raised a questioning brow, but the smolder behind his eyes told her exactly what was on his mind. For a moment, the memory of heat, the wickedness of his mouth on her surged back over her in palpable waves. Her belly clenched.

She almost slapped him for resurrecting that memory, but he offered her his arm in the nick of time.

"Well, my Lady Clavenhook, adventure calls among the rustics. Shall we sally forth?"

"Let's. But tread warily, Sir Knight," she warned. "Or Lady Rowena of the Deadly Pike will be forced to rise again."

Sir Alistair consulted his map once more. They'd met the other tilt boat heading back downriver, without its passengers, but the bends in the Thames prevented them from seeing where Viscount Rutland and Miss Drake were put ashore. An island rose ahead of them, mist-wreathed and ethereal even in the early afternoon.

"There," he said, pointing toward it. "That's Braellafgwen."

"It may be, but the party you're followin' didn't put in there," the boat's captain said. "An ill-omened sort of place, that island be. I've heard tales. Reckon the folk you're after have gone to that village over there. Fine little dock they have, to be sure."

"Nevertheless, that island is our destination." Alistair rolled up the small map he'd torn from the pages of Edlington's *Age of Magic* and stuffed it into the turned-back cuff of his jacket.

"That's as may be, gov, but lookit how steep the land lies. No proper beachhead, not according to the charts. Without no dock, we got no place to put ye ashore."

"Just get us close enough," Alistair said. "We're not afraid of wet feet."

"It's not yer feet I'm frettin' over. It's the bottom of me boat. This water's so silty ye can't see a foot down. I'll not ruin me boat for a single fare."

"Perhaps you'll like me to alter our arrangement." Alistair pulled Lord Montford's pistol from his pocket and pointed the business end toward the man at the tiller. "Now, order your men to row and take us to the island with all speed."

The tilt-boat captain barked an order and they crept toward Braellafgwen. One of the rowers knelt in the prow, trying to judge the draft beneath the craft with his oar. As they neared the island, the current quickened and they had to row faster to maintain even their slow pace.

"Bottom's coming up fast, Cap'n," the crewman shouted when they were still ten feet from the steep banks of the isle. "There's naught but two feet under the keel. Maybe less."

The captain called a halt and the rowers shipped their oars. One of the crewmen dropped the anchor over the side to hold their position in the current.

"Shoot if ye must. I'll not risk the boat or the crew another moment in this madness," the captain said. "A mist like this on a cloudless day ain't natural. This is an evil place. Don't ye feel it?"

"What are we to do now?" Brumley whined.

"We leave ignorance and superstition behind." Alistair

threw a leg over the side and stepped down into the dark water. It rose to midthigh. Lord Montford followed suit.

"But I can't swim," Brumley whimpered.

"You don't have to swim. You can walk, fool. Now come," he ordered. When Brumley still hesitated, he added, "Or crawl back to your well-placed wife with your manhood tucked between your cowardly legs."

The moment Brumley lowered himself over the side, the tilt-boat crew hauled anchor and rowed away, pulling for all they were worth.

"Come along, Brumley." Alistair sloshed toward the island. He heard a yelp behind him and turned to see Brumley step into a hole and sink from sight, his white wig bobbing in the current. Alistair scrambled back to the spot, felt under the water and grasped a handful of his hair. He jerked him to the surface. Brumley came up sputtering and gasping and trying to climb up Alistair's arm.

"Good thing you're not bald or you'd be a dead man," Alistair said. He kept hold of Brumley's collar as he waded back toward the island.

Ahead of them, Lord Montford plowed through the water steadily, but was not making much progress. He held his pistol over his head to keep his powder dry. Alistair would have to reload his later. For just a blink, it seemed as if the island retreated from them with every step, but Alistair dismissed that notion as fanciful in the extreme.

"Evil place, my aunt Fannie's arse," he said with derision when he finally reached the steep shoulder of the island. He'd never admit it to a living soul, but for a few heartbeats, he'd been beginning to believe the island might indeed be "ill omened."

The men scrambled up the fifteen feet of nearly vertical face before the slope relaxed and the island spread out, a tree-covered oval with a high point in the center.

"Let's get a fire going so we can dry our clothes," Brumley said.

"We can't have a fire." Alistair wished he'd never brought Brumley into this venture if the man was going to be so dense. "Someone might see the smoke."

"So we're stuck here like this. Wet and miserable and . . . I'll bet neither of you thought to bring any food." Lord Brumley plopped down on the decaying trunk of a fallen ash. "Why didn't we go to the village, like Rutland and the Drake girl?"

"Because two strangers are enough for one small hamlet to absorb," Lord Montford said. "Three more would be impossible to conceal without the first two becoming aware of them." He tossed Brumley a withering glance. "Since we have arrived on Braellafgwen ahead of my son and . . . that other person, we will be able to easily shadow them once they arrive. Our presence here must remain a secret until the opportune moment."

"Quite," Alistair concurred. "To that end, let us find a spot to conceal ourselves and take turns watching for boat traffic from the mainland. If we miss them, we might lose the trail."

Permanently, he added in silence. Besides, they'd need whatever craft Daisy Drake and Lucian Beaumont traveled in to carry them away from this cursed rock.

"Braellafgwen?" the innkeeper, whom they discovered was called Mr. Dedham, asked. "Why ever would ye be wanting to go there? No one goes there. Haunted, it is. And the woods—all full of eyes, they says." The innkeeper's surprise reassured them that no other party had asked about Braellafgwen recently. Perhaps Fitzhugh wasn't dogging them, after all.

"Nevertheless, my sister and I wish to visit the island," Lucian said.

Mr. Dedham slanted a knowing glance at Daisy. Evidently, more than one young man had traveled this way with his "sister" before.

"We're very keen on old druid sites and heard the island has a connection to that defunct religion," she said.

"Don't know as I'd call it defunct. Not very loudly, at any rate," the man said. "Don't do to upset the spirits, they says."

"But there is a way to travel to the island?" Daisy said.

"Oh, yes, there's a way. Peter Tinklingham has a shallow drafting punt what can make the trip."

"Excellent," Daisy said. "And where will we find Mr. Tinklingham?"

"You won't. Leastways not till tomorrow morning," the innkeeper said. "He took the doctor upriver to see about Mrs. Bossy. She's carrying twins, ye ken."

"Well, I hope all goes well for her," Daisy said. Childbed was no light matter. Graveyards were littered with the final resting places of young mothers who met their untimely ends trying to bring a babe into the world.

"Aye, so do we all. Mrs. Bossy is the best milker in the shire. And since Will Tweazle filed off her horns, she's of a much sweeter disposition to boot."

"So, Mrs. Bossy is . . . a cow?" Lucian asked.

Mr. Dedham regarded Lucian with raised brows, as if he thought the young man were a bit softheaded. Daisy was beginning to remember why she wasn't sorry not to be living in the country any longer.

"If all goes well, Tinklingham should be back by tomorrow morning," the innkeeper said.

"Very well." Daisy pulled her coin purse from her reticule. "We require lodging then. Two rooms, if you please."

"I'd be happy to oblige ye, but the Wounded Boar has only one room left. Tomorrow's the day the skiff comes up from London with a load of goods. Folk come to town to trade and they want to have first pick, ye see, so we're a mite more crowded than usual." He tossed Lucian a wink. "The room's got a fair-size bed. Ye and your 'sister' may find it a tight fit, but I reckon ye'll do."

"My sister will take the available chamber, sir," Lucian said. "I'll make do in the common room, if you don't mind."

If Lucian had wanted to flash his title about, Daisy knew he could demand one of the other rooms from the commoners. He was likely the first viscount the sad little Wounded Boar Inn had seen in centuries.

Of course, Lucian wasn't dressed like a lord, so Mr. Dedham might not have believed him. His dark ensemble was serviceable, but worn. The only bit of wealth about Lucian was the lethal-looking rapier at his hip, but the hilt was so plain, so utilitarian, it was obviously not the ornamental small sword of a gentleman. It was a serious weapon for an uncertain world.

So Lucian would bed down before the common-room hearth. Of course, Daisy was in perfect accord about not sharing a room with him.

But it rankled her soul not to have been able to refuse him first.

"A man and woman may strip naked and couple in every conceivable manner, but there is still no true intimacy until they bare their hearts."

—from the journal of Blanche La Tour

Chapter Thirty-six

Daisy and Lucian spent the rest of the afternoon wandering the village and picking their way through the small churchyard. They read the headstones that were still legible and wondered at the ones whose inscriptions time had reduced to mere dimples in the rock. The vicar turned out to be a genial man who was willing to discuss the island with them.

"Time out of mind, Braellafgwen has been a . . . a sacred place, if you will," the vicar had said. "Some may name it pagan, but there's no denying there's an unusual power, a strange sense about the place."

"You've visited the island?" Lucian asked.

"Only once," he admitted with a sheepish half smile. "It's difficult to describe what it's like."

"Please try," Daisy said.

"Well, the nearest I can come is this," the vicar said. "I used to live in London when I was a lad, and sometimes, I'm ashamed to confess, I used to creep out at night to explore. Once in a while, I'd wander down a dark lane where I didn't belong and all the hairs would stand up on the back of my neck. It's like that on Braellafgwen. The island doesn't want me there. If a place has no use for you, it's best not to tarry."

As they strolled back to the inn, the vicar's words rolled around in Daisy's mind. The innkeeper claimed Braellafgwen was haunted, and Mr. Crossly certainly hadn't wanted to put in there. Now the vicar had added his testimony to the growing mound of evidence for the strangeness of the place.

"Braellafgwen sounds a bit daunting, doesn't it?"

"If you don't want to go, you can wait for me here," Lucian said.

"I didn't say that," Daisy said, clasping his arm a bit tighter than necessary. "It's just . . . I hadn't thought of it before, but the Roman treasure's been lost for centuries. Perhaps with good reason. Do you suppose there are some things that aren't meant to be found?"

"Rubbish. I think rumors of hauntings were started by the druids to keep the uninitiated from stumbling on their rites," Lucian said. "No doubt Meritus saw the tales about the place as a way of keeping the treasure safe, even if someone managed to get this far." Grim determination settled on his features. "I'm not about to let fairy tales or a nervous vicar's talk of a prickly scalp stop me."

His straightforwardness should have calmed her. When Daisy had found the hidden gold beneath the castle of Dragon Caern, she'd been a child, afraid of the boom and hiss of surf she mistook for a real dragon. Back then, she enlisted the help of an old pirate, her friend Mr. Meriwether, for the final exploration.

Now the little pixies of fear were dancing once again on her spine. But this time, she was no child.

"No, you won't be rid of me so easily." Daisy wanted an adventure. She wouldn't let jitters rob her of one. "I'm going with you tomorrow."

He smiled at her for the first time since their kettle-hurling argument. "I'd be hugely disappointed if you didn't."

They strolled back to the inn in companionable silence, willing to declare a cessation of hostilities, if not a formal truce.

The innkeeper served up a hearty supper of thick stew in

the black-timbered common room. The rowdy patrons who'd booked up the other bedchambers crowded around the long trestle table, sopping up their stew with chunks of barley bread and telling randy stories, each more ribald than the last.

Daisy and Lucian kept to themselves till one of the men at the far end of the room wondered loudly "if a lady's tits are softer than a barmaid's."

Lucian slammed his fist on the table. "I'd mind my tongue, if I were you." He didn't raise his voice, but the menace in his tone traveled the length of the room quite effectively.

"And who's going to make me, gov?" the man said. "I got me three friends here, and looks to me as if you and the lady are traveling alone."

Quick as a blink, Lucian was on his feet, the blade at his hip out and poised to strike like an adder. "We may be alone but we are not entirely without resources."

Surprise coursed through Daisy. She'd observed Lucian without his shirt and knew he was well muscled, but she'd come to think of him as more the scholarly type. She'd never seen him move with such lethal grace.

The men pushed back from the table, swiping their mouths with their sleeves and brandishing long dirks. Now panic followed surprise through Daisy's limbs.

"Lucian—"

"Daisy, go upstairs and lock yourself in the room."

It wasn't a request. It was a command, spoken with such ringing authority, it didn't occur to her to disobey. Besides, she reasoned correctly that her presence would only be a hindrance and a distraction to him.

She scurried up the rickety staircase, but couldn't bring herself to full obedience. She stopped halfway and sank onto the steps, pressing her face between the spindles on the barrister. If she could find something to hurl from this height, perhaps she could dispatch one of his attackers, but there were no friendly potted plants available.

Where on earth had that blasted innkeeper gotten off to?

Her heart pounded with fear.

The men circled, looking for an opening. Lucian turned with them, feinting with his length of steel like a great cat lashing out with its claws to keep the hunting dogs at bay. Daisy shoved a knuckle into her mouth to keep from crying out.

Then it began. One of the men lunged, and Lucian's blade flashed. Muscle and sinew, intelligence and instinct, everything came together in perfect concert as Lucian danced with the rustics' dirks. Daisy was both terrified and awestruck at the nimble, masculine beauty of his sword-work. He fought to disarm, not to kill. One by one, they yelped and swore and finally dropped their weapons, unwilling to step within the reach of Lucian's longer blade.

All but the first man.

"Bloody cowards," he said when his friends withdrew.

Throwing a knife was a final recourse in a brawl. If the aim was true, the gamble paid off. If not, the fighter found himself disarmed and at his opponent's mercy. The man must have liked his chances. He flipped his dirk around, grasped it by the blade and launched it at Lucian.

Lucian tried to dodge clear, but the blade caught his sword arm just south of his shoulder. Daisy screamed. Lucian yanked the dirk out with his left hand and brandished both blades at his attacker, bellowing with pain and bloodlust.

"What's going on out here?" The innkeeper finally reappeared through the door that led out to the summer kitchen, bearing an old but serious-looking blunderbuss. "You're getting blood all over the floor, ye heathens. Get ye to yer beds, and I mean now or out ye all go."

"I have no bed," Lucian reminded him.

"Get ye upstairs with that 'sister' of yers then, before I throw the pair of ye out." He cast a murderous glance around the room. "And if I hear anything louder than a mouse's fart out of any of ye, ye'll be sleepin' with the pigs and payin' me double for the privilege of finer bed companions than ye deserve. Now go!"

"I can climb the stairs by myself," Lucian complained. Daisy fluttered about him, lifting his good arm over her shoulders as if she could actually bear his weight. "Stop. What are you—I don't need your help. You're more likely to send us tail-over-teakettle than anything."

"It would serve you right," she said as she kicked the bedchamber door open for them. "I mean, honestly! Taking on four simpletons with knives."

"That's just it. I was never in any real danger." He removed his sword belt and draped it over the back of the only chair in the spartan room. "You said it yourself: they were simpletons."

She snorted and slammed the door shut, throwing the bolt for good measure. "They weren't the only ones."

He yanked off his jacket and shirt. The wound was shallow, but he needed to stop the bleeding. Daisy was two steps ahead of him. She'd already ripped the flounce from the bottom of one of her petticoats and was dabbing at his biceps with part of it.

"We need some spirits. Mr. Dedham is probably still in the common room." She pressed the wad of cloth to his wound and moved his left hand to cover it. "Hold it there. I'll be right back."

"No, Daisy—"

The door slammed behind him and he sighed. For a moment, he had a dizzying glimpse at the rest of his life if Daisy Drake swirled at the center of it. No matter what he said, this woman was always going to do exactly as she pleased. Surprisingly enough, that didn't bother him as much as it should have. He sank onto the chair and waited.

She bustled back in with an armful of fresh muslin, already torn into strips. Apparently, knife fights weren't all that uncommon at the Wounded Boar, so the innkeeper was well prepared. Lucian noted with pleasure that she brought up a small jug of spirits, as she'd intended.

"I don't mind if I do." He reached for the jug. She hugged it to her breasts, twisting to hold it beyond his grasp.

"Not yet. Only if there's any left after," she informed him. All business, she scrubbed his arm, first with soap and water from her washstand, then with the raw spirits.

"Yow!" he yelped when she dribbled a little on the gap in his flesh. It burned like the fires of hell.

"Careful," she said. "That was definitely louder than a mouse fart, and I don't think you particularly want to sleep with the pigs."

"Aside from inflicting the most possible pain, why did you do that?"

"I was raised by pirates, remember. Mr. Meriwether said his mates who sloshed a bit of rum on themselves while the ship's surgeon stitched them up seemed to fare better than those who only drank the spirits." Twin slashes of concentration formed between her brows. "Now you may have a drink."

He tipped the jug and watched her as she wound the muslin around his arm. She turned her lips inward and sighed as she worked.

"Where did you learn to fight like that?" she asked.

"There was a girl once who bested me with a pike," he said with a grin. "I promised myself that would never happen again, so I took my fencing lessons seriously from that day forward."

"Then it seems you owe that *girl* a debt of gratitude instead of constant recriminations for something that you know beyond doubt was an accident. There." She tied off the bandage and fisted her hands at her waist. "I suppose we must be grateful the wound wasn't worse."

"Well, my arm isn't the only casualty." He picked up his frock coat and examined it. Blood stained the sleeve to the elbow, and the knife hole was too jagged to patch without being noticeable. "That settles it. My association with you has officially ruined my entire wardrobe."

"Would you have preferred I bared my breasts so they could satisfy their curiosity about their relative softness?" she said.

He caught her by the waist and pulled her between his spread knees. "I'm thinking to reserve that privilege for myself."

He reached a hand behind her neck and brought her down for a kiss. Her lips trembled, then stilled beneath his as he slanted his mouth over hers. She was so sweet, so tender. He didn't push when she failed to open to him, though it pained him to hold back. The rush of excitement from his fight coupled with her nearness had given him an aching cockstand.

She pulled away from him. "No, Lucian."

"No?" he repeated with incredulity. He'd just faced down four armed men for her. What more did the woman want?

"We've behaved . . . *I've* behaved rashly in the past," she amended. "It is an error I do not intend to repeat."

"An error. You believe what we've shared, what we've been to each other is wrong?"

"As the world counts sins, definitely," she said with a sad little smile. "As for myself, I would have said no until very recently. But I've come to realize it was all a game with you."

"That's not true."

"How can it not be?" she said, stepping back from him

another pace. "You don't trust me. Not enough. It was wrong of me to become . . . intimate with someone who cares so little for me that he doesn't wish me to know his *business*."

"Oh, Lord, we're back to that."

"If two people don't share something as ordinary and mundane as the business aspects of their lives, how can they hope to achieve a deeper bond?" Her face threatened to crumple. "I know things have been difficult for you, Lucian, but believe me, money is not everything. I certainly don't think any less of you for your financial situation."

If only it were that simple . . .

"I've never met a man who worked harder than you," she went on. "Society may frown on your efforts, but I admire you for them—"

"Daisy, stop." He held up his hand. "This has nothing to do with money. Once we find the treasure, my concerns on that front are over, in any case."

"Then why didn't you tell me Mr. Peabody was spying on your progress and working in concert with Sir Alistair?"

"Because of why they want to find the treasure. Fitzhugh intends to use it to fund another Scottish uprising to put James Stuart on the throne," he said.

"But that's treason," she said, aghast. "If you didn't want to tell me, why didn't you go to the authorities and have them arrested?"

If he said the words, if he admitted his fears aloud, it would remove all doubt and make them real. But nothing was more real than his feelings for Daisy. And sharing this horrible truth was one way to show her how he trusted her. Needed her. His shoulders slumped. "Because I fear my father may be in league with the traitors."

> "And the Lord God said, 'It is not good that the man should be alone.' Perhaps it has escaped His notice, but it's no treat for the woman either."
>
> —*the journal of Blanche La Tour*

Chapter Thirty-seven

Lucian dragged a hand over his face. "And it's not just that."

"Not just that? Not *just* treason, you mean?" Daisy's eyes widened with surprise.

"I fear my father's losing his mind," Lucian said.

"Well, I knew he had an unreasonable hatred of my family, but plenty of people hold grudges, whether they have cause or not," Daisy said softly. "It may mean they're cantankerous, but it doesn't mean they are mad."

"No, this is more than a grudge," Lucian said. "He means your family, your uncle in particular, grave harm. I came across his journal lying open in the study. . . ."

He hadn't meant to pry, but the volume was spread on his desk, as if his father had been called away suddenly and hadn't taken the time to sand the page and close it. His father's normally spidery script was ballooned all out of proportion, almost a childish scrawl. The page was pocked with inkblots, and passages describing the earl's most fervent ill wishes were virulently underlined. Some was pure gibberish. And the rest was deeply troubling. The venom in his father's pen chilled Lucian's heart with foreboding. No one should have that much hate boiling inside them.

No sane person did.

He looked up at Daisy's clear-eyed face and couldn't

repeat what he'd read. "There's more than that. He talks to himself. Late at night, far gone in drink."

"If I could count the number of nights I heard my uncle's friend Mr. Meriwether stumbling about Dragon Caern singing to himself, I could count the stars," Daisy said.

"Yes, but did Mr. Meriwether sing of dismembering someone?"

Daisy sank onto the edge of the sagging bed. "Pirate songs are not noted for delicacy, but no, there was nothing like that."

"The earl hides it well, but there's something wrong behind his eyes. With each day, it's more pronounced." Being able to finally voice his concern flooded Lucian with relief. The problem wasn't resolved, but he was exorcizing the demon a bit. "It's as if little parts of him, all the good and decent parts I remember from my childhood, are going to sleep and something much darker is waking to take their place."

"And you fear he's involved with Sir Alistair's plot?"

Lucian nodded.

"I wonder if someone else doesn't suspect it as well," Daisy said, knitting her fingers together. "When Lord Wexford forbade me to see you again, he didn't come right out and say so, but he hinted that he knew something about your family, something scandalous. 'Something dangerous' were his exact words. He didn't wish to see me or, by association, himself and my great-aunt caught up in it." She studied her tangled fingers. "I thought it must be some silly society debacle, but now, I wonder if he meant this Jacobite scheme."

Lucian's lips flattened into a grim line and he stared down at the braided rug between his feet, a miasma of faded colors with no discernible pattern. It looked as hopeless as he felt.

"Wexford must have caught wind of the plot," Lucian said. "He doesn't strike me as the sort who suffers society's foolishness gladly."

A man who'd married a former courtesan, and one who couldn't give him an heir to boot, effectively thumbed his nose at convention. Clearly the Earl of Wexford didn't court public opinion that fastidiously. But treason would give any man pause.

"Each time my father tried and failed to reverse the family fortunes, he slipped a little farther into the abyss," Lucian said. "His latest ploy was to see me well married."

"To Clarinda Brumley."

Lucian nodded. "Maybe it's my fault he's become desperate enough to be taken in by the Jacobites. I told him in no uncertain terms that I would not wed Miss Brumley, not even if her chastity belt were cast from solid gold."

Daisy's tinkling laugh lifted his spirits a few finger widths.

"I'm glad you refused Clarinda."

"Not even the fealty a son owes his father could compel me to that," he said, grinding a fist into his other palm. He was still staring at that miserable rug to avoid her direct gaze. Would she see his father's desperation in his eyes as well? "That's why we have to find the Roman treasure, Daisy. We just have to. If I can restore Montford, maybe . . ."

"Maybe your father will be restored as well?"

The bed creaked, and Lucian heard the soft swish of Daisy's slippers on the worm-eaten wood floor. Her hand came to rest on the crown of his head, the fingers kneading and caressing. Tension drained out of him at her touch.

"Oh, Lucian," she whispered. "You've borne this load alone for so long."

She stepped closer and brought his cheek to the sweet

trough between her breasts, still stroking him, still threading her fingers through his hair. Lucian closed his eyes. He wrapped his arms around her waist and inhaled her sweet scent, content just to hold her.

She was warmth and light and all good things. And he'd wandered too long in threadbare darkness, not allowing himself to feel his need of anyone.

But he needed Daisy. Needed her like he needed meat and drink, light and air. Like he needed his next heartbeat.

Her lips were on his brow, his closed eyelids, his cheeks. Her touch swept across his bare shoulders, a feather's wisp, healing and accepting. She seemed to want him to stand, so he did.

He'd do anything she wanted.

Her lips found his. His hands moved of their own accord. On the periphery of his mind he was vaguely aware of lacings being loosened and buttons undone and fabric sliding over silken limbs. But he was lost in the wonder of her mouth as they shed their clothing.

Her skin, cool and delicious on his. Smooth and soft. The crook of her elbow, the dip of her waist, the flare of her hips. Her giggle was music when he brushed the ticklish spot behind her knees. He wanted to touch every part of her.

Especially the hot, slippery parts.

Helpless little gasps and pleading. The sounds she made went straight from his ears to his cock.

I don't sing, she'd told him once.

He'd never tire of this song.

She was in his embrace; then she was sprawled on the quilted coverlet, eyes heavy-lidded with desire. She lifted her arms to him, not in supplication or surrender, but in welcome.

And he came home.

Home to her warmth. Home to her softness. Home to her accepting heart.

I love you, his body sang. As spasms of release racked his frame, his lips repeated the refrain.

"I love you, Daisy Drake."

"The only true magic in this world is love."
—the journal of Blanche La Tour

Chapter Thirty-eight

Sunlight shafted through the shuttered window, striping the soft, worn quilt with light. Daisy lifted a hand to shield her eyes, which seemed to be caught midstripe.

She was lying on her side, with Lucian spooned around her, his long arm draped over her, his hand splayed possessively on her breast. Her nipple tightened at his finger's nearness, and the skin on the nape of her neck prickled at his warm breath. Something hard and blessedly now very familiar pressed against her bottom.

The slow expansion and contraction of his ribs against her spine told her he still slept. She sighed, perfectly content for the first time in her entire life. An angel in heaven couldn't have been happier. If she and Lucian never left this plain little room, it would be fine with her.

He loves me.

She drew the sheet up to her chin. He'd wrapped her in his love, safe and secure. Last night, she wasn't pretending to be someone else. There was no libidinous lesson being taught. They were no longer grown children playing naughty games.

They were lovers in the truest sense of the word, souls bared, hearts open. The pleasure given and received was a rending fire, stripping away all essence of self and merging them into a new entity, a shared spirit.

Now in the quiet aftermath of passion, Daisy tested the

ink that had been forged and found it still sound. Love
ound them together.

*In the days to come, he may yet try to shut me out and deal with
is troubles alone, and I will probably still vex him beyond bearing.
But love unites us.*

Lucian stirred and Daisy turned to face him, ready to of-
er her body and her heart to him once more. He responded
n half a heartbeat, accepting all of her with joy.

The plain little room faded around them.

An hour later, they were standing on the village dock with
Peter Tinklingham, deliverer of cattle midwives and proud
owner of a slatternly-looking watercraft.

"You're in luck, gov. I usually don't punt out to Brael-
afgwen this time of year." Mr. Tinklingham seemed to-
ally unconcerned about the inch of standing water in the
null of his shallow-draft boat. "But the tide's with us and
he mist is a mite thinner than usual today. Besides, I knows
a trick or two about putting in there."

"So you've been to the island often?" Lucian handed
Daisy into the punt and hopped in after her. The bow
hreatened to dip below the surface, but the vessel righted
tself quickly.

"Not more often than I can help, ye understand." Mr.
Tinklingham took his station at the stern, laying a sly finger
alongside his crooked nose. "There be a few about who still
nold to the old feast days. Every Samhain and Beltane, I
nake a good bit o' coin ferrying odd folk to the island.
Don't know what they do there. Don't want to know.
'Tain't none o' my business, long as they pays their fare."
He cocked his head at his new passengers. "You don't have
he look of them folk."

"Our interest in Braellafgwen is . . . scientific, not reli-
gious," Lucian assured him.

"If you say so," Mr. Tinklingham said as he poled into the broad channel. "Science or Satan worship. Expect folk could go even odds on them two."

The river was a dark ribbon of silty water, sparkling silver-brown in the sun as they eased around to the far side of the island. True to his word, Mr. Tinklingham brought them in close. Behind a partially submerged, moss-covered boulder, a hidden set of stairs was carved into the rock, leading up to the tabletop of the island. Lucian asked their guide to return to this spot an hour before sundown. Then he and Daisy disembarked and ascended the mist-slick stairs. At the top, they turned to look back down. Mr. Tinklingham had already poled away from the island. His boat faded into the mist and disappeared from sight.

"A person could sail past that spot every day for years without realizing what's behind that rock," Daisy said.

Lucian nodded. "Inaccessible. All the more reason to suspect we'll find what we seek."

"Not many folk come here, and those who do don't have Roman treasure on their mind. Caius Meritus was a genius to choose this island," Daisy agreed.

Leaves rustled in the wood nearby. Daisy turned sharply toward the sound.

"What was that?"

"Some animal." Lucian grasped her elbow to lead her up the game trail. "Just because no people live here doesn't mean there aren't a few beasts about."

"Beasts?"

"Small ones, I'm sure. The perfectly harmless sort," he said. "Squirrels and rabbits, a deer or two."

When they broke free of the trees into a central clearing, Daisy drew a sigh of relief. The woods seemed oppressive in their tangled wildness and, as Mr. Dedham had said, full of eyes.

A sharp prickle tingled her nape. A vestige from a more

primitive time, Uncle Gabriel had explained once, when knowing one was being watched might be the difference between taking to one's heels for safety or the sudden death that stalked the unwary. It didn't do to ignore a prickly scalp.

The vicar would have agreed, she remembered. *If a place has no use for you, it's best not to tarry.*

No one out of the ordinary had come to the Wounded Boar but she and Lucian. And Mr. Tinklingham was the only ferryman who regularly plied these waters, so she was fairly certain Fitzhugh and his Jacobites were far off their trail. But she couldn't shake the feeling that *something* watched them. She glanced at Lucian to see if he felt the chill of unseen malice too, but his eyes were alight with discovery.

"Would you look at that? Pagan blade and goddess heath," he whispered.

Though the perimeter of the island was still murky with mist, the sun shone brightly on the center. In the middle of the clearing, there were two standing stones of dark gray granite, glittering with embedded mica.

One was a six-foot obelisk, an ancient phallic symbol pointing skyward. Formed from one stone, the four-sided monolith had been shaped by man, the tool marks leaving fading grooves in the granite. The other stone was carved in a large circle with the center chiseled out, an obvious reference to the goddess.

"There are plenty of exposed boulders on this island, but the stone is much lighter in color than these." Lucian approached the goddess stone and ran his hand over the inner curve. "Have you seen this granite nearby?"

"No," she said softly. To speak louder would have felt like sacrilege.

There was a strange emptiness in the place. Barring that first rustle she'd heard in the woods and the occasional soughing of the breeze through the treetops, there was no sound. No drowsy hum of insects, no birdcalls, just a . . . silent expectancy, as if someone were waiting.

If she listened hard enough, would she hear the stones themselves speak in slow, measured syllables? She gave herself a little shake to ward off the odd notion. Her imagination had always been keen. She usually considered it a blessing. Now she wondered if it might not be a dual-edged sword.

"The stones were quarried elsewhere," she said, relieved to focus on something as mundane as geology. "Brought here for a purpose."

"And long before the Romans, from the look of them," Lucian surmised. He turned in a slow circle, taking the measure of the place. "But how do they help us find the treasure?"

"'Where pagan blade points to goddess sheath,'" Daisy quoted. "That's just the trouble. The monolith is not pointing at the circle. It's pointing straight up. Do you suppose we've got the wrong island?"

"No," Lucian said quickly. "This is the place. We're close, very close. Don't you feel it?"

She felt something. All her senses were on heightened alert. They were definitely being watched, but she couldn't voice her apprehension. Lucian would dismiss it as fancies, or worse, vaporish womanly weakness for listening too attentively to the wild talk of the locals about Braellafgwen. He might even laugh at her.

So she held her tongue as they walked in circles around the great stones, measuring the distance in Lucian's long strides.

"Might Caius have buried the treasure between the stones in the center of the clearing?" he asked. "That would be using them as markers of sorts."

"If adherents of the old religion are still using the island even now, it stands to reason that Braellafgwen has never been without occasional visitors."

"A disturbance of the ground would have been noticed and investigated," he said, following her logic.

They made another slow circuit, wending their way in a figure eight this time.

"Perhaps that's what happened," Lucian finally said with a frown. "The Romans didn't find the treasure, but do you suppose the Celts did?"

Disappointment draped over him like a cloud casting its long gray shadow over the land.

"Shadow!" Daisy said more loudly than she intended. "That's how the blade points to the sheath. Look!"

The monolith threw a long, dark shadow on the grass, knife-sharp and creeping inexorably toward the stone circle. They watched, spellbound, hardly daring to breathe. As the sun reached its zenith, the shadow struck the center of the circle squarely and spilled past the opening toward the vine-covered rise beyond.

"'Where pagan blade points to goddess sheath, there shall my love be pleased.' It's definitely pointing." Lucian hugged Daisy and pressed a quick kiss to her temple. "You are brilliant. Come. Let's see where it leads."

He grabbed her hand and they ran together like children escaping a tutor's heavy-handed class, laughing and talking at once. The laughter stopped when they reached the raised ground, which seemed to be a rock outcropping obscured by dense overgrowth.

"Another dead end," Daisy said with a sigh.

Lucian scoured the area with his gaze, standing stock-still. "I feel something," he said after a moment. "A draft. There's a void behind this greenery."

He began shoving the tangled vines aside, ripping them

when he had to and slashing with his penknife when they would give no other way. The fragrance of fresh-cut clippings filled the air, along with an older, darker smell.

"There," he said, stepping back to let Daisy survey his handiwork.

Behind the hacked greenery, a black space yawned, a toothless maw in the rock face. Lucian stepped forward.

"Are you coming?" he asked, when she didn't immediately follow. "If you'd rather not, you can wait for me here."

"And miss the adventure?" she said, more lightly than she felt. "Surely you jest."

She turned sideways to slide through the narrow opening and followed him into the mouth of the hidden cave.

"Did you see that?" Lord Brumley said from his place of concealment behind the broad trunk of an old beech. His hand tremored against the smooth gray bark. "They just . . . disappeared."

"Brumley, you idiot," Sir Alistair said. "They've found an opening in the rock behind the vines. A cave of some sort. We could have searched the island for months without stumbling across it."

"Stay here for months? I should say not," Brumley mumbled. "Not without even packing so much as a food hamper."

"What I mean is, they obviously have information to which we are not privy," Sir Alistair continued. "We were wise to arrive soon enough to observe them undetected."

Lord Montford grunted noncommittally. The three had spent a miserable night on the island. The strange mist that surrounded Braellafgwen not only spawned fairy stories, it was an ideal breeding ground for mosquitoes. When the sun sank beneath the horizon, the woods came alive with their whining hum, and the voracious little demons feasted on the blue blood of two English lords and a knight of the realm without discrimination.

"I could have sworn that Drake girl saw us," Brumley said. "She looked this way. Several times."

Alistair raised a brow at Brumley. If the man could only see himself—wig gone, hair askew and filthy, cuts and welts from the predation of insects all over his grimy face, his ensemble ripped and muddied. If Daisy Drake had seen him, she'd have thought him a wild man in the woods. As it was, his miserable turnout probably concealed him better than a hunting blind.

"Now we follow them. Right?" Brumley asked.

"No," Lord Montford said before Alistair could. "Now we wait to see if they find something. One does not follow a bear into its den."

Alistair looked sharply at Lord Montford. They weren't stalking a wild beast. They were tracking the man's own son and a slip of a girl who would be no trouble at all. He narrowed his eyes at the earl in uneasy speculation. Of his two confederates, now he wasn't sure which of them troubled him more.

Lord Montford pulled back the firing pin and checked his pistol. Apparently satisfied, he shoved it back into the waist of his breeches. "At least, not until one is sure the bear is thoroughly distracted by something else."

"A hint of danger, the threat of harm, makes a body so quiveringly alive it's a wonder more don't meet their fate courting death."

—the journal of Blanche La Tour

Chapter Thirty-nine

Sunlight fought to enter the opening Lucian cut through the vines, but once they stepped into the cave, darkness pressed around them. He found a row of old torches jammed in a fissure in the wall and pulled his tinderbox out to set one ablaze.

"There we are," he said as he lifted the smoky torch. "Seems someone used this cave at one time and expected to return. Kind of them to leave us a light."

"Caius?"

"Or, before him, the druids."

The reek of pitch stung Daisy's nostrils, but she and Lucian were bathed in a wavering circle of light that shot through the dark, throwing macabre shadows against the uneven walls and rock-strewn floor. The cave receded past the reach of the torchlight in a long, narrow tunnel, just wide enough for them to walk abreast as it angled down. The air that feathered her cheek felt dry and cool and smelled musty enough to suggest that no one had disturbed this chamber for a very long time.

Daisy slipped her hand into Lucian's. She was brave enough to want an adventure, but sensible enough to have a healthy fear of the unknown.

"Don't worry," he said as he helped her over a small outcropping of rock. "I've a feeling the worst we might encounter here is a bat or two."

"That gives me small comfort," she said dryly, wishing she'd thought to wrap a fichu about her neck. She'd never much cared for rodents in the first place. Adding wings did not improve them, in her estimation. She strode forward, keeping pace with Lucian, trailing her fingers along the rock wall at her side to keep her bearings. Then she brushed against something that was decidedly not mineral.

"Jupiter!" Daisy grasped Lucian's hand with both of hers.

Lying in a carved niche in the wall of the tunnel was a body. Or rather, what was left of one. The flesh was long gone and the cloth shroud had rotted into tatters, exposing chalk-colored bone. A small oval of gold glinted on the sunken ribs. Delicate. Dainty. A woman's necklace.

"That is not a bat," Daisy said.

"No, it seems to be a lady who's been dead for a very, very long time."

"Do you suppose . . . Could this be . . . Deirdre?" Daisy asked.

" 'There shall my love be pleased,' " Lucian quoted. "If we're right about this place, she might be Deirdre. Perhaps Caius thought she'd rest easy here."

"All his treasure in one place," Daisy said thoughtfully. Traveling up the Thames with the body of his lover would be a sad, lonely journey indeed, even if Caius bore the wealth of Rome as well.

Carefully, they stepped past the skeleton, leaving her undisturbed. They pressed forward, feeling their way, climbing over and around the rocks that obstructed their path. Their voices echoed in retreating sibilance. The scuff of a boot on stone was amplified several times over. Occasionally Daisy imagined some of the echoes were a bit long in coming and wondered if they were being followed, but when she turned to look back up the tunnel, she saw no silhouette against the distant opening of light. After a few moments, they reached a place where they could go no farther.

A gaping abyss yawned at their feet. It was a little more than ten feet across. The lip on the other side was narrow, no more than a foot or so, before rising in a solid wall marred by one long, sloping crack. Even with a running jump, a body couldn't be sure of being able to leap across. Lucian raised the torch higher. The ledge that ran along the left wall provided a precarious way to cross over, but it was even narrower.

"It looks like we've reached the end," she whispered.

"No," Lucian said, waving the torch before him as if he could will the light to reach farther. "We haven't found the treasure yet, and it has to be here. I know it looks like the cave ends, but remember the hidden staircase. Would you have ever guessed there was a way up that steep slope that didn't involve a rough scramble and a stout rope? This island takes pains to keep its secrets. There must be a way through that wall as well. It's just not evident from this vantage point."

"I don't know," Daisy said. "There doesn't seem to be a way across. I mean, if Caius Meritus were hauling in the treasure, he certainly couldn't have crept around on that narrow ledge with a load in his arms."

"Perhaps the chasm wasn't here back then. Or if it was, he might have built a little bridge of sorts. It wouldn't have taken much, and there's plenty of wood here on Braellafgwen. Then when he was done, he could have pushed it off down there." He squatted to peer into the void. The light of the torch didn't reveal the bottom. Lucian picked up a small rock and dropped it over the edge.

Daisy counted silently to ten and still didn't hear the rock hit.

"I have to cross it," Lucian said.

"No, don't," she pleaded. "It's not worth it, Lucian. Honestly, it's not. If you were to slip—"

"Miss Drake," a voice came from the darkness, "I wouldn't try so hard to dissuade him if I were you."

Daisy nearly jumped out of her skin. She turned to see two faces rise from behind a large boulder.

"Sir Alistair Fitzhugh and Lord Brumley, fancy meeting you here." She lowered her voice and hissed to Lucian, "So much for only encountering bats."

"Well, gentlemen," Lucian said. "As you can see, we have reached an impasse. The trail has gone cold, and Miss Drake and I are leaving."

"I think not." Sir Alistair raised a pistol and brandished it toward them as Brumley fumbled with his tinderbox to light a second torch. "As you rightly pointed out, this island has ways of keeping its secrets. I believe you are correct, Rutland. There may indeed be a false wall on the other side of yon abyss, and you, Miss Drake, are going to investigate that notion for us."

"Me?"

"Yes, indeed," he said. "You're the smallest here. You'll fit most easily along that ledge."

"Leave her out of this, Fitzhugh." A muscle ticked along Lucian's jaw. "I'll go."

"Oh, you'll get your chance," Sir Alister said. "If something unfortunate happens to Miss Drake, you'll try next. Now go, girl, before I decide it's necessary to put a shot through the viscount's knee in order to properly motivate you."

"No, don't. I'm going," Daisy said as she started toward the ledge.

"Oh, no, you're not." Lucian grabbed her forearm to stop her.

"You, sir, are neither my husband nor my keeper. You have no right to tell me what to do."

"Spare us your lovers' spat and get going," Sir Alistair said. "I grow weary of holding back my trigger finger."

Daisy pulled free of Lucian and kept moving.

"He's bluffing," Lucian whispered as he followed close behind.

"Stand still, Rutland," Sir Alistair ordered.

"Don't be an ass. I'm going to light her way with the torch. You don't expect her to do it blind, do you?" Lucian said over his shoulder, not slowing his pace. His voice dropped again. "Besides, he's only got one shot. I'll draw his fire. When he shoots, I want you to run toward the light."

Daisy looked up the long, dark incline. A hint of daylight beckoned in the distance. Then she looked back at Lucian.

"Brumley may have a pistol as well. Besides, if you think I'll abandon you, you don't know me at all," she hissed, then raised her voice. "Hold the torch higher so I can see what I'm about, then."

Facing the wall would be easiest. She could see to clutch at handholds on the rocky face. Even more important, she wouldn't be able to look into the hypnotic pull of the darkness yawning behind her.

"Just a moment," she said. "I have to remove my hoops."

She reached under her voluminous skirt and untied the wire-and-wicker contraption that expanded the width of her hips by a foot on each side. Then she reached between her knees, grasped the back of her skirt and hauled it between her legs, tucking the long end into her bodice. The effect was something between a harem girl's scandalous silk pants and a baby's nappies. She was back to being, as Lucian once named her, a tomboy, but at least her legs were free and she wouldn't be hampered by the underpinnings of her garments. She'd be able to hug the rock face as if it were her dearest love.

Her dearest love.

She looked up at Lucian. His face was drawn with concern. If Sir Alistair hadn't been sporting a firearm, Lucian would have fought. Even though he'd faced down those ruffians with knives, a pistol had a much longer reach than his sword.

She flashed him a quick grin, determined to put a bold face on things. "If ever I express the need to have an adventure again, you have my permission to paddle me."

He snorted. "I'll hold you to that."

She edged her way onto the narrow space, clinging to a jutting rock with one hand and a stout root with the other. "But you have to swear not to enjoy it."

"I make no promises." He lifted the torch higher. "There's a fissure about a foot from your right hand. You should be able to shove your fingers into it and use it to steady yourself."

"I see it," she said through clenched teeth. She shuffled her feet sideways on the narrow lip of rock, trying not to think about the sheer drop inches behind her. "And what about you? When may I paddle you with impunity?"

"If ever I forget our anniversary, you may paddle my arse till it bleeds," he said.

Her foot slipped and she felt nothing but empty space beneath her sole for a moment. Then her toes found the ledge once again. She stood still, glancing right and then back to her left. Lucian drew a relieved breath and cast her a lopsided grin.

"If that was a proposal of marriage, it was singularly lacking in elegance," she said, moving along the ledge once again. She knew he didn't mean anything by it, but their ridiculous talk of paddling and matrimony kept her fear at bay.

"Lacking in elegance, was it? I find that observation difficult to take seriously from a woman whose skirt is tucked between her legs," he said. "But if elegance comes at the expense of covering those ankles of yours, it is a highly overrated commodity. There, you made it."

Daisy heaved a sigh. She was across the chasm.

"Now, if you're finished treating us all to your unmaidenly banter," Sir Alistair said, "see what you can discover about that rock face."

The ledge widened to only about a foot, but it seemed luxurious after the narrow lip she'd just traversed. Daisy looked down the ledge and was surprised to find that there was an opening. From across the chasm, it appeared as a long crack in a single wall of rock, but now she could see it was two rocks of identical color and texture. One of them was behind the other, leaving a gap of eight or ten inches. If she turned sideways, she might squeeze through.

"There's a way through," she called over her shoulder. "Very narrow and dark. I can't go without a light."

"Now's your opportunity, Rutland." Sir Alistair leveled his pistol on his forearm and aimed the barrel squarely at Lucian. "Take the lady a torch."

"He's going to do it one-handed?" Brumley asked, contributing to the conversation for the first time.

"Unless you'd like to go in his stead," Sir Alistair snapped, then turned back to scowl at Lucian. "Get moving."

Daisy shuffled back to the narrow ledge she'd just traveled. "Don't look down, Lucian. Just a few steps and you can hand me the torch."

She leaned out as far as she dared and extended her arm to him.

"Stay back," he ordered sharply; then he softened his tone. "I can't concentrate if you're hanging off the edge like that."

She nodded and straightened, sidestepping to make room for him once he made it across. She had to remind herself to breathe as he eased his large frame over the limited space, holding the torch in his left hand and leading with his right.

He made sure his feet were solidly planted before he advanced his hand, skimming the surface of the rock, seeking a fingerhold. He swung at one point, hanging on to a root and lifting both his feet in the center.

Daisy thought she'd aged a decade by the time he joined her on the far ledge. He pulled her close and gave her a quick kiss.

"You haven't answered my inelegant proposal yet."

"And I won't until we're clear of this and in daylight again," she said.

"Tease."

"'Pleasure deferred is pleasure enhanced,'" she said, quoting Blanche.

"Then let's see about that treasure," he said, his dark eyes glinting with excitement. A pistol was trained on them, but Lucian was still on the trail of a dream.

"Wait," Sir Alistair called across to them. "Brumley, get over there with them."

"Me? Why?"

"If there's a way through the rock, there may also be a way out, you idiot. They could collect the treasure and slip out the back door while we're standing around in the dark holding our own cocks." He strode over and took Brumley's torch from him. "Get going."

Lord Brumley looked as if he'd just swallowed a bite of herring that had turned, but he did as he was bidden.

"All right, Fitzhugh," he said. "But when this is all over, King James is going to hear about your high-handedness. That's all I've got to say."

"Squawk all ye like then. At least we'll have a sovereign who speaks our language. Now move."

Brumley scuttled to the ledge with a whimper.

Lucian held his torch higher, so Lord Brumley could see the space he was about to travel.

"Take it slowly," Lucian said. "There's a soft spot about

halfway across. You'll feel it give a bit, but keep a good hold on that root and bear your weight up."

Now Daisy could see why her foot had slipped. The dirt beneath her had given way. Lucian had avoided the spot by swinging himself over it.

"I don't think this is a good idea," Brumley said.

"I didn't sign ye on to do any thinking," Alistair said. "Get on wi' ye!"

Lord Brumley started along the ledge, his breathing noisy and labored. When he reached the center of the span, the dirt beneath his feet crumbled. He screamed like a woman, clinging one-handed to the root, feet scrabbling to gain purchase on the sheer face of the remaining rock.

"Swing your legs up, man," Lucian said as he handed the torch to Daisy and took a step back out onto the narrow lip. He curled the fingers of his right hand over a protruding rock and extended his left to the flailing Lord Brumley. "Give me your other hand."

Brumley tried, twisting and wailing, his legs bucking wildly. Then, with a sickening crunch, the root cracked and ripped from the rock. Lord Brumley plummeted downward, his screams reverberating. Then the horrible sound stopped suddenly, his long wail a thread snipped off by a giant's scissors.

"Wanting is ever so much more pleasurable than having. It is the difference between fancy and cold truth. As long as I desire, I may indulge my whimsy. Having crushes all hope of imagination."

—the journal of Blanche La Tour

Chapter Forty

Daisy bit her lip to keep from crying out. Lord Brumley may have wished them ill, but he was obviously a coward at heart. She shoved aside the image of his horror-stricken face. In the years to come, it would probably haunt her nightmares, but she couldn't dwell on it now.

The tiniest candle of sympathy glowed in her heart. No one deserved to die so horribly, alone in the dark.

"Well, don't just stand there," Sir Alistair barked at them. "See what's beyond yon rock."

"Let me go first," Lucian said.

"No, it's too narrow here to switch places. Just raise the torch a bit so I can see."

Daisy turned and eased herself through the stone crevice as Lucian followed close behind. After a couple feet, the space opened into a large chamber.

When Daisy had found the pirate's gold, she'd stumbled upon a partially submerged sea cave. A smuggler's hole, Mr. Meriwether named it. There, she'd discovered several large chests deposited haphazardly, with golden doubloons spilling onto the dirt, winking like fallen stars.

Now Lucian's torchlight illuminated dozens and dozens of small crates stacked in ranks, all very methodical and organized.

The difference between a steward of Rome and a crew of pirates, she thought with a smile.

Lucian stood transfixed. Only his torch moved, lighting the chamber from one end to the other. The entire space was crammed with crates.

"Oh, Lucian," Daisy said, clasping his free hand. "We've found it."

"Now let's see if we can discover a way to keep it," he said grimly.

Daisy dropped to her knees before the first chest, so giddy with excitement she'd almost forgotten Sir Alistair and his pistol. "One thing at a time. Don't you want to see it?"

He chuckled. "I've seen it in my mind so often, I almost don't need to, but since you insist."

He knelt beside her and used his knife to pry open the crate. The wood was so rotted with age, it fairly crumbled under the pressure. He lifted the lid and the contents glinted whitely in the torchlight.

"What's this?" He reached in and grabbed a handful, crushing it in his grip. The tiny grains trickled between his fingers and drained back into the crate, like sand in an hourglass.

"Oh." A downward spiral in Daisy's belly made her feel sick. "I'd forgotten. But it makes perfect sense. Of course."

Lucian tried another crate. The same crystalline whiteness leered up at him. By the time they'd opened a sixth chest with the same result, tears trembled on Daisy's lashes. She felt Lucian's despair, sharp as a blade to her heart.

He drew a deep breath and picked up one of the open chests. "Let's show Sir Alistair his treasure. By God, he can have it, and welcome."

Daisy led the way again, carrying the torch this time, while Lucian lifted the open crate over his head to squeeze through the crevice.

"You found it?" Alistair called across to them.

"Here it is," Lucian said. "Choke on it."

He dumped the entire contents into the abyss.

"Are you mad?" Sir Alistair exclaimed. "What are you doing?"

"It's salt," Daisy explained. "In our excitement over a treasure, we all forgot that in ancient times, the Roman legionnaires, especially those at the far reaches of the empire, were sometimes paid in salt."

"Salarium," Sir Alistair said woodenly.

"Exactly. Hence the expression 'worth his salt,'" she babbled, taking comfort in academia. "Difficult to come by. Easy to trade with the locals. I'm surprised that, as head of the Society of Antiquaries, you neglected to consider this possibility."

"No!" Sir Alistair shouted. "There must be something else. Go back and search again."

A clatter and scuffle erupted behind him, and Sir Alistair turned to see who was making his way down the passage. Whoever it was had taken a tumble in the dark and ruined any hope of stealth.

Daisy peered into the blackness, trying to make out the identity of the man silhouetted against the distant opening. He was picking himself up from a rather nasty fall, dusting off his clothing and mumbling curses.

"It's my father," Lucian said softly. Then he raised his voice. "Take care, sir. Fitzhugh is armed."

"I know." Lucian's father stepped into the torchlight. His frock coat was torn and covered in dirt. A bloody brown patch was spreading on one knee of his breeches. "I armed him myself." He nodded to Fitzhugh. "I couldn't wait outside a moment longer. There's no one following, so I had to come in and see how things are progressing here." Then he turned back to Lucian. "Now be a good lad and do as Sir Alistair asks. Go look again or I might just have to shoot our lovely assistant. Miss Clavenhook, is it?"

"Bah! She's no Clavenhook," Sir Alistair said. "Remember, I told you—she's Daisy Drake. But if there's any shooting to be done, it's Rutland who deserves a dose of lead for dragging us all on this wild-goose chase."

Fitzhugh raised his pistol to menace them once more.

"That's my son!" Lord Montford shouted, and lunged at Sir Alistair, who dropped his torch, but not his weapon.

The sharp report of a pistol echoed, beating a furious tattoo throughout the cave. The ball ricocheted off the rock face next to Daisy's head. She would have crouched, but there was so little room. The acrid stench of powder filled the cavern.

"I didn't mean to fire. I wasn't going to—Stop, I say! No!" The earl and the knight wrestled with each other near the edge of the pit. Another long wail pierced the dark as Sir Alistair Fitzhugh fell headlong into the chasm.

Daisy feared she might be sick, but this was no time to indulge her belly. Lucian didn't need her to have an attack of the vapors. He needed her to be strong.

Lord Montford stared down into the deep hole, as if puzzled by what had just happened. Then his face contorted in a mask of rage and he glared at Daisy.

"Just look what you made me do. A curse on all Drakes," he yelled, and raised his pistol.

"No!" Lucian bellowed, and shoved Daisy so hard against the rock face she saw stars over his shoulder. He covered her with his body, his back to his father.

A strange sound, like a small explosion, pierced their ears. They flinched in unison. And waited. There was a soft gurgle and a thud. Then silence reigned for the space of several heartbeats.

Daisy shifted to peek under Lucian's outstretched arm. Lord Montford's form lay in a disordered heap, still as stone, on the far side of the pit. A shiny bit of metal protruded from one eye, and a dark stain spread under his head.

"Oh, Lucian. Your father . . ."

Lucian eased himself off her and peered across the precipice. "The barrel exploded," he said softly. "The pistol must have become plugged with dirt when he fell on the way into the cave."

She wanted to say something, to tell him how she ached for him, but no words would form in her mouth. She couldn't even touch him. Lucian's father was dead because of her. How could he ever bear to look at her again?

And even worse, how were they to escape their little oubliette now that the Jacobites and Lucian's father were all dead? There was no way to scuttle around the narrow path, since Lord Brumley had taken such a large section down with him.

But before she could find a way to express her sorrow and voice her concern, she saw another wavering torch. Two figures were creeping toward them in the dark, one tall and well made and the other squat and tottering.

"Who goes there?" Lucian shouted.

"Who's asking?" came the sharp reply.

"It's Mr. Meriwether," Daisy said to Lucian before raising her voice to ask, "Is Uncle Gabriel with you?"

"Aye, lass." The sound of the rumbling baritone of the man who'd guarded her childhood sent relief flooding her veins. The pair came into the range of her torch, and she saw them clearly. Concern, relief and anger were etched on their dear, familiar faces.

Gabriel glared at Lucian. It was the look that had sent the fear of God into pirates and honest seamen alike when Daisy's uncle had sailed the Spanish Main as the Cornish Dragon. To his credit, Lucian didn't flinch. He returned Gabriel Drake's intense gaze, and for a moment, Daisy feared they'd burn holes in each other.

"You've put my niece in harm's way," Uncle Gabriel said.

"She came willingly," Lucian returned.

Why didn't he tell her uncle how he'd sheltered her with his own body when his father intended to put a pistol ball through her? How he'd protected her at every turn?

How he loved her?

"Did ye find another treasure, Miss Daisy?" Meriwether asked in an attempt to lighten the mood.

"No, Meri. Not this time," she said with a sigh. "And I'm sorry to say several men are dead because of this mythical treasure. Lord Brumley, Sir Alistair Fitzhugh and . . . Lord Montford."

"We'll sort that out later," Uncle Gabriel said gruffly as he slid a loop of rope from his shoulder. "Right now, I'm taking you home."

"To love is to risk all. Yet we do it without a second's thought because the heart knows no other course."
    —the journal of Blanche La Tour

Chapter Forty-one

Daisy picked up the queen's rook and considered a sweeping move across the chessboard. Then she thought better of it and replaced the piece in the same square. Isabella was a serious chess player. No doubt the rook was what she was expecting, given Daisy's usual reckless performance.

No more impulsive chances for her. It was time to play it safe. Daisy moved one of her pawns instead.

"And so," she said, finishing up the narrative of her experience on Braellafgwen, "I've come to the firm belief that adventures are highly overrated."

"You didn't used to think so." Isabella knocked Daisy's unprotected knight from the board.

She hardly noticed. She was running the events of the last fortnight through her mind. "I didn't know then what I know now."

Uncle Gabriel and Meriwether had freed her and Lucian from their little prison. They offered to help Lucian remove his father's body from the cave, but he declined. Gabriel Drake was taking care of his family. Lucian would care for his. Mr. Tinklingham would return at sundown. Lucian planned to hire him to help bear Lord Montford's body off the island, and then Lucian would wait for Mr. Crossly and his sons to return with their tilt boat the next day.

Besides, it might look better for all concerned if Lucian didn't return to London in their company.

Daisy had been relieved to see her uncle and Meri, but couldn't imagine how they'd trailed her to the island. She learned they'd paid a quick visit to her residence on Singletary Street after gleaning her whereabouts from the usually closemouthed Nanette. Mr. Witherspoon might be an efficient butler with connections on the wharf, but she evidently hadn't paid him enough to ensure his silence when faced with the likes of Gabriel Drake and his first mate.

After they knew their destination, Gabriel and Meri hadn't bothered with a tilt boat. Being master mariners, they sailed up the Thames in a little skiff, using the tide and bending the wind to their will. That meant there were no rowers for whose ears they must have a care on the little craft. Daisy was grilled like a goose on a spit all the way back to London.

She told her uncle everything about Lucian's excavation and following the clues to the location of the Roman payroll. She told of the Jacobite plot and Lord Montford's unfortunate involvement, while touting Lucian's innocence in that part of the scheme. She even admitted to masquerading as Blanche La Tour.

"Did that bastard take your maidenhead?" her uncle demanded.

"Lucian is no bastard," she returned smoothly. "And the answer is no."

It was even the truth. He hadn't *taken* her maidenhead. She'd given it to him freely.

Along with her heart.

When she saw Lucian last, he was standing alone on the island at the foot of the hidden stone steps. As the skiff pulled away from Braellafgwen, he was swallowed in mist as completely as if the fairies had stolen him away to their hollow hills.

And she hadn't seen him since.

Daisy convinced her uncle to allow her to remain with

Isabella instead of being dragged back to Cornwall. Of course, she had to promise she'd have no more adventures disguised as a courtesan. Isabella and her husband vowed to hold Daisy to it.

They needn't have worried. She had no desire to play Blanche with anyone but Lucian, and he was nowhere to be found.

He said he loved me.

Evidently love wasn't enough to erase the pain of his father's ugly death.

A voice told Daisy it was her turn. She moved one of her chess pieces mechanically, not caring one way or another what befell it.

"Checkmate!" Isabella sang out. "Oh, my dear heart, I fear you are not attending to the game."

"I'm weary of games," Daisy said, not meaning chess.

Nanette appeared at the parlor door. "*Pardonez-moi,* there is a gentleman caller who wishes to see Mlle La Tour."

"Who is it?" Daisy asked, hope making her body thrum like a plucked string.

Nanette squinted at his calling card before handing it over. "Do you know the Marquess of Chadwycke?"

Isabella raised a silver brow at Daisy.

She frowned in disappointment. "I have no idea who he is. Tell Lord Chadwycke that Blanche has gone to France and never intends to set foot on the British isle again."

"If that is the case, then he instructed me to request a moment with Miss Drake," Nanette said.

"Persistent, I'll give him that." Isabella leaned back from the playing table. "Aren't you the least bit curious?"

Daisy snorted. "He's just someone who either wants to tumble a French courtesan or court a fortune, and doesn't much care which," Daisy said. "I don't know any Marquess of Chadwycke, Nanette. I have a new rule on adventures, you know. The answer is still no."

"My dear," Isabella said after Nanette scurried to do her bidding. "I wish you wouldn't shun all adventures. It's not your nature. Take this new lord, for example. You haven't even given him a chance."

"And why should I when all I really want is—Lucian, what are you doing here?"

He filled the doorway, resplendent in dark blue velvet. The frogs and epaulettes on his frock coat sparkled in silver, and his tricorne sported a jaunty white plume.

"Lady Wexford, Miss Drake." Lucian made an elegant leg to them. "I hope you'll forgive my intrusion, but sometimes a man can't hear 'no' unless it comes from the lady's own lips."

"Of course, my dear Lord . . . Chadwycke, is it?" Isabella purred as she stood and crossed to him, hand extended for his gentlemanly kiss. "From viscount to marquess. That is a tale I'd love to hear, but I believe there is only one set of ears you need to share it with just now. If you two will excuse me, I'll see to some refreshments." She glided past him with a wink. "And . . . it may take some time for me to return, so please make yourself at home."

Once Isabella left the room, Lucian set his hat on the side table. Daisy rose to her feet slowly. She'd dreamed so often of him coming for her just like this, she couldn't be sure she wasn't asleep.

"Is the answer still no, Daisy?" he finally said.

"No! I mean no, the answer is yes!" she cried, and ran to him. He caught her up in his arms and swung her around. His lips settled over hers in a warm, wet kiss, tasting, questing and then pouring his love into her.

They finally came to a halt on the third circle.

"Better sit down before we fall down." Daisy led him to the settee. "Tell me, Lucian, what's happened?"

"Many things." He clasped her hand between his. "I'll start at the beginning. After you left Braellafgwen, I returned to the cave and covered my father's body with my frock coat, since I had nothing else to do until Mr. Tinklingham came later with his punt."

The thought of him alone in the dark with his sorrow made her heart ache.

"Then I realized we hadn't really done an exhaustive search of the Roman hoard, so I rigged up a little bridge of sorts, using an old log, and went back to investigate."

"Oh, Lucian." He might have plunged to his death and she would never have known what happened to him.

"You were right," he admitted. "The Roman army was paid in salt." A grin spread over his face. "But the proconsul was paid in silver. Lots and lots of silver."

He pulled a coin from his cuff and put it in her palm. The hapless Emperor Honorius glinted up at her from the coin's face.

"Oh, I'm so happy for you," she said. "But now you're Marquess of Chadwycke. How did that happen?"

"For that, I must thank your uncle," he said. "It seems he went to the king with word of the Jacobite plot and embellished out of all knowing my hand in foiling it. Your uncle even told His Majesty that my father had died trying to stop Sir Alistair's plans. So, in gratitude, the king awarded my father the marquessate posthumously." Lucian sighed. "And it devolved immediately to me."

"Uncle Gabriel was never your father's enemy, you know."

"He certainly proved it by protecting his memory," Lucian said. "My father wasn't always as you saw him last."

"I know. Hold on to the good in him," she said, giving his hand a squeeze.

He nodded. Then a smile stole over his face and he slipped off the settee to drop to one knee. "Someone told me once that my proposal of marriage was 'singularly lacking in elegance.' I thought I'd try to rectify matters."

"Oh, I don't know," she said impishly. "Now that I think

on it, there was something in the previous proposal about paddling your arse, which I'll admit does hold a certain appeal."

He choked out a laugh. "Daisy Drake, you are without doubt the most trying woman in the world, but I love you with all my heart. And if you think you're done vexing a viscount, I wonder if you'd consider marrying a marquess?"

"Hmm. Viscount Rutland, Earl of Montford and Marquess of Chadwycke," she said as she palmed his cheek, kissing him once for each of his titles. "I've vexed the viscount and I'll marry the marquess, but perhaps you'll allow Blanche to return on occasion so she can finish the education of the earl!"

He swallowed her laughter in a kiss that quickly lost all trace of hilarity and left them both breathless. When he finally released her, his hot gaze seared her.

"Blanche may return whenever she likes, so long as she knows it's Daisy I love."

"Then maybe she'll stay in France," Daisy said, "and you and I can educate each other. After all, I intend to learn you by heart. And won't that be the grandest adventure of all?"

Epilogue

And so I end this account. Of my life, I will say that I have known joy and sorrow, passion and loneliness, love and hate. Even though I have lived as a woman of pleasure, I can count on the fingers of one hand the number of men I have actually taken to my bed. I loved them all. In my way.

And now in my advancing years, I am the wife of a husband who cannot love me except in his way. The irony is fitting. Is that heaven I hear laughing?

So at last, I lay aside my nom de plume. Blanche La Tour has written her final scandalous entry. I now sign my true name.

Her boudoir door opened a crack and Isabella laid aside her quill. "Geoffrey, what are you doing here? It's not Thursday."

"No, Bella. It's not Thursday," he said sheepishly, stepping in and closing the door softly behind him. "But you asked me to stay one night, and I've been thinking and . . . well, you know nothing can . . . We started as friends, Bella, and by God, if I don't think we like each other better than some who actually . . . What I mean is—"

"Geoff, please come to the point."

"If it would be all right with you, I would like . . . to just hold you." He shrugged. "May I stay?"

Nothing had changed. There would never be passion between them, but perhaps the warmth of their friendship was a treasure itself. Isabella smiled.

"Of course, Geoffrey. Please stay."

Author's Note

Even in a work of fiction such as *Vexing the Viscount*, there is always some basis in fact. The Society of Antiquaries met regularly in 1731, and the association still exists today for the express purpose of "the encouragement, advancement and furtherance of the study and knowledge of the antiquities and history of this and other countries" (Royal Charter, 1751). The earliest recorded minutes of the group are dated December 5, 1707. But instead of having their own edifice, complete with lecture hall, as described in this novel, the Society was obliged to meet in various taverns until 1780, when George III granted them use of Somerset House. I hope readers will forgive my slight shuffling of the facts to serve my story.

My description of the disastrous South Sea Bubble, which so devastated my hero's father, recounts a historically accurate stock swindle. The debacle has been dubbed "the Enron of England." Shares in the South Sea Company soared to such ridiculous heights in the summer of 1720, it inspired shysters everywhere to urge investment in *their* schemes. One newly formed enterprise advertised itself as "a company for carrying out an undertaking of great advantage, but nobody to know what it is." When the South Sea Company defaulted, the entire market crashed with it. However, since the principal cargo the company intended to market to the New World was slaves from Africa, I can't help but feel the cosmic justice of total financial ruin was fitting.

Rome controlled portions of Britain for four hundred years. The time referenced in *Vexing the Viscount* (A.D. 405) was near the end of that occupation. Rome was imploding. By A.D. 410, the Emperor Honorius advised Romans in

Britain to defend themselves, for he would send no more troops from the south. My freedman, Caius Meritus, is fictional, but he would have been pleased by their fate, had he lived long enough to see it.

The druid isle of Braellafgwen is purely the product of my imagination, but barrows and standing stones dot the U.K., enigmatic glimpses into what was. You can't walk the land without sensing the magic of the past. My heroine, Daisy, is right: sometimes, the rocks do cry out with words only the heart hears.

I hope you enjoyed *Vexing the Viscount*! I had a wonderful time writing it. If you'd like to know what's coming next, please visit me at www.emilybryan.com.

Wishing you the best of everything,

Emily

EMILY BRYAN

"An author to watch."
—Michelle Buonfiglio, LifetimeTV.com

BURIED TREASURE

All it took was a flick of the wrist. A deft touch of his sword point and Drake the Dragon bared her bound breasts. Then with the heat of his hands along her skin, he bared her soul. All the wantonness Jacquelyn had denied herself as a famous courtesan's daughter, all the desire she'd held in her heart while running Lord Gabriel Drake's estate flooded through her at his touch. Not that she could let a bloody pirate know it.

Gabriel may have left his seafaring days behind, but his urge to plunder was stronger than ever. Especially if it involved full, ripe lips and a warm, soft body. Unfortunately, he needed Jacquelyn's help, not her maidenhead, to learn how to behave properly toward a lady so he could marry and produce an heir. Yet Mistress Jack was the only woman he wanted, no matter what her heritage. And everyone knows what a pirate wants, a pirate takes....

Pleasuring the Pirate

ISBN 13: 978-0-8439-6133-1

To order a book or to request a catalog call:
1-800-481-9191
This book is also available at your local bookstore, or you can check out our Web site **www.dorchesterpub.com** where you can look up your favorite authors, read excerpts, or glance at our discussion forum to see what people have to say about your favorite books.

USA Today Bestselling Author
RITA Award Winner

JENNIFER ASHLEY

"Readers who relish deliciously tortured heroes and spirited heroines who can give as good as they get will find much to savor...from the consistently satisfying Ashley."
—John Charles, *Booklist*

It was whispered all through London Society that he was a murderer, that he'd spent his youth in an asylum and was not to be trusted—especially with a lady. Any woman caught in his presence was immediately ruined. Yet Beth found herself inexorably drawn to the Scottish lord whose hint of a brogue wrapped around her like silk and whose touch could draw her into a world of ecstasy. Despite his decadence and intimidating intelligence, she could see he needed help. Her help. Because suddenly the only thing that made sense to her was...

The Madness of Lord Ian Mackenzie

"Jennifer Ashley fills the pages with sensuality."
—Romance Junkies

ISBN 13: 978-0-8439-6043-3

"Mega fun, fast-paced and with a sexy to-die-for hero—
my favorite kind of historical romance."
—Lori Foster

LISA COOKE

Texas Hold Him

As if losing the war to the Yankees hadn't been bad enough, Lottie Mason now needed $15,000 to keep her ailing father out of prison. The only place she could think of to get that kind of money was a riverboat poker tournament. Problem was, she didn't know a thing about playing cards.

Dyer Straights may have been the best cardsharp in New Orleans, but the true goal of this hardened gunslinger was vengeance, not profit. He didn't have time for a beautiful belle who wouldn't take no for an answer. So to scare her off, he upped the ante with a proposition: He'd give her the lessons she was so desperate for. And if she won the jackpot, she'd owe him one naked night in his bed. He didn't realize she couldn't afford to refuse.

As the cards are dealt and the seduction deepens, the two find they're taking a gamble on a lot more than a good hand and a one-night stand—they're betting on a lifetime of love.

ISBN 13: 978-0-8439-6254-3

Bonnie Vanak

NOBLE IN ALL BUT NAME

Anne Mitchell, born illegitimate and raised in a workhouse, sold by her mother and packed off by her father to the East, had every reason to lose faith. But in Egypt she found identity with the Khamsin, a tribe of Bedouin warriors. Greater even than the secret they entrusted to her was her newfound honor, and for that she would give all.

NOBLE IN ALL BUT ACTION

Nigel Wallenford was an earl. He was also a thief, a liar and a libertine. Regaining his birthright of Claradon had been a start. Next he required wealth, and he knew of just the fabled treasure...and its key's guardian was a ripe fig waiting to be plucked. Never before had he scrupled to cheat, steal or even murder. One displaced Englishwoman, no matter how fair, would hardly be his match.

The Lady & the Libertine

ISBN 13: 978-0-8439-5976-5

❑ YES!

Sign me up for the Historical Romance Book Club and send my FREE BOOKS! If I choose to stay in the club, I will pay only $8.50* each month, a savings of $6.48!

NAME: _____

ADDRESS: _____

TELEPHONE: _____

MAIL: _____

❑ I want to pay by credit card.

❑ VISA   ❑ MasterCard   ❑ DISCOVER

ACCOUNT #: _____

EXPIRATION DATE: _____

SIGNATURE: _____

Mail this page along with $2.00 shipping and handling to:
Historical Romance Book Club
PO Box 6640
Wayne, PA 19087
Or fax (must include credit card information) to:
610-995-9274
You can also sign up online at **www.dorchesterpub.com**.
*Plus $2.00 for shipping. Offer open to residents of the U.S. and Canada only.
Canadian residents please call 1-800-481-9191 for pricing information.
under 18, a parent or guardian must sign. Terms, prices and conditions subject to
ange. Subscription subject to acceptance. Dorchester Publishing reserves the right
to reject any order or cancel any subscription.